BAD APPLE

SELENA

Bad Apple

Willow Heights Preparatory Academy: The Exile

Book One

selena

Bad Apple

Unabridged First Edition

Published in the United States by Selena and Speak Now.

ISBN-13: 978-1-945780-56-1

Man is not made for defeat. A man can be destroyed but not defeated.

—Ernest Hemingway

Trigger Warning: The world of Faulkner is dark, gritty, and at times fucked up. The books set here may contain any of the following: dub-con, non-con, abuse, assault, coercion, sharing, suicide, unapologetic feminism, neglect, adults using children for their own gains, rich kids with no consequences, poor kids with nothing to lose, and people living in abject poverty, doing things to survive and escape that might make sensitive readers uncomfortable.

If you don't like the thought of teenagers participating in questionable acts such as unprotected sex, violence, sexual violence, drugs, pornography, gambling, bullying, and other acts of debauchery and desperation, this series is not for you. Also, if you're offended by people taking the Lord's name in vain or the word *cunt,* please return this book for a refund. This author is probably not for you.

prologue

Royal Dolce

"Are you ready, son?" Dad asks, clapping me on the shoulder like he's oh-so-proud of me, the way he does whenever I show myself capable of doing his fucked up bidding. He might not give a fuck about me most of the time, but when he needs to get shit done, it's all pride and flattery.

I don't need his flattery, don't want it.

I grip the knife, staring down at the pathetic excuse for a human being who once tortured me. "I was born ready," I say, stepping forward.

That's a lie. I wasn't born for this. I was *reborn* for it. I lived sixteen years as one person, and then this asshole and his family kidnapped me. I went into that basement thinking I was a bigshot, that no one could touch me. I came out a different man.

Mr. Darling hiccups out a high-pitched sob, his eyes all bloodshot terror. I stare into them, frustration gripping me in its teeth like an inescapable vice. Each time, each revenge, should make me feel better, but it doesn't. I want him to hurt like he hurt me, to make him see what it did to me. But he can't. None of them can. No one in this whole fucking world will ever understand.

"I have a wife and kids," Mr. Darling babbles. "Please don't kill me."

"Oh, I'm not going to kill you," I say. "Death would be too kind for a monster like you."

Like all the best monsters, this one cannot be killed. Even after he took his last breath, he would live forever inside me, destroying me every day of my life.

"What are you going to do?" he asks, his voice high and trembling with fear.

He's been tied up for only twenty-four hours, and he's already begging like a little bitch. I was at his mercy for seven days.

Seven. Fucking. Days.

I'll show him as much mercy as he showed me.

"Go on, son," Dad says.

I bend and slide my knife through the piss-stained fabric of his pants. He flails and screams, but the ropes hold him fast. It's just me and Dad today. He would have brought the twins, but I didn't want my little brothers to see this. My oldest brother used to protect us, but he's gone, moved on with his life. His parting words when he left this shithole town still haunt me.

"Take care of our brothers."

It's a heavy burden. I didn't know how much it would take, what King endured for us all those years as the oldest, shielding us from evils I didn't know. But he's working for the mob now, and I'm here in Arkansas.

It should have been the other way around. Even before the week that changed me, I was the fighter. King is the protector.

"Please," Mr. Darling sobs, rolling onto his back. "Don't do this. You don't have to do this."

"And you didn't have to do what you did," I say. "But here we are. Monsters create monsters create monsters. And here I am. Your demon, here to collect his pound of flesh."

"Don't worry," Dad says with a sadistic grin. "It'll be less than a pound."

Mr. Darling hyperventilates through a sob, rolling onto his belly.

"Unlike you, when you tortured a little sixteen-year-old boy who'd never done shit to you, I've got a conscience," I say. "So I'm giving you a choice. You can lay face down and get the knife in your ass, or turn over, and I'll take your dick off."

"No," Mr. Darling chokes out, writhing as best he can against the ropes. "Please, no."

"One way you live, one way you die," I say. "Your choice."

He takes a shuddering breath, a strangled cry escaping as he rolls over onto his back.

"Go on," Dad says, nudging me forward.

I crouch and grab Mr. Darling's shriveled old dick in one hand and the knife in the other. He screams so loud my ears ring, but I don't hear him. Even through gloves, the squirmy sensation of his dick in my hand makes me retch. It's so limp and impotent. One slice and the thing comes away in my hand. I stand and shove it at Dad.

"There's your fucking souvenir," I say.

If I could put him on the floor next to the asshole I cut, I'd do it. It makes no difference to me. He's every bit as responsible.

"You did good, son," Dad says.

Even though I know that revenge won't make the nightmares go away, at least I know justice has been served. At least to one generation of Darlings.

Mr. Darling is still screaming, and blood is pooling around him. I crouch and cut through the ropes. He'll have to drive himself to the hospital. He won't die. I didn't even make him suffer. I did it quick, with one cut.

Like I said, I have a conscience.

Dad claps me on the back again. "He's the last one. It's over."

It's not over.

But for him it is, and that's all he thinks about. We've avenged ourselves to his enemies, the Darling parents who shunned him twenty years ago. But I know the truth. There are more Darlings in this town, hiding like cockroaches, not bearing the name.

His war is over. Mine is just beginning.

one

Harper Apple

I have to find a way out of this fucking town. It's slowly wearing away my soul, grinding it down to dust that will hang in the air like the stink from the papermill on a sweltering summer afternoon. As Mr. Behr drones on, I scrunch down in my seat, resting my feet on the rack under the desk in front of me. If only I had a teacher interesting enough to make me learn something, I might have a chance. But the teachers at Faulkner High are as trapped and hopeless as the students. Maybe more so. They've had longer to realize they're never getting out, that their whole lives will be spent in this sweaty armpit of a town.

I sigh and let my mind wander as I stare out the narrow window at the balding lawn, patches of dust showing through the dead spots. The good teachers go across town to the private school where the air conditioning always works, the building doesn't get mistaken for a prison when out-of-towners drive by, and the powerful people's kids supposedly have as much passion as money.

I wonder what that's like. Power. Passion. Money.

"Harper, would you care to answer this one?"

Even delivered in Mr. Behr's monotone, my own name cuts through my zoned-out haze.

"Can you repeat the question?" I ask as a couple kids snicker. There's only one place I'm special, and it's sure as fuck not in the halls of Faulkner High. Here, I'm bottom of the pack all the way. Fine by me. It's easy to avoid attention in a big school with too many drama queens.

"Why don't we let Chase get this one," Mr. Behr says, turning away.

I shrug and slouch down in my seat again.

"Oh, and please see me after class, Miss Apple."

Damn it. Premature relaxation.

"Whatever," I mutter, turning to stare out the window again.

Two years to go. I feel like I've already done my time, though, including summer school after Mom didn't bother making me go to school most of freshman year. At the time, I thought I had it made. I mean, who the fuck wants to go to school? And it's not like anyone expected me to think ahead, to consider the consequences.

Now I know what a dumbass I was to skip basically an entire year. I'm in a bunch of classes with sophomores, and I fell out with the friends I had before that. Not that they were real friends. Just more people with the same hobbies as anyone in a small, pointless town. Fucking, fighting, and going fast in their shitty cars.

At least having a deadbeat mom and no dad doesn't make me special at Faulkner. Lots of kids have more fucked up lives than I do. There are girls who get Slut Club invitations dropped on their desks and realize their reputations are toast, and boys who get busted up on the football field and whose glory days will always be high school even when they're bitter, middle-aged alcoholics. Foster kids and those who live with various uncles and grandmas because their parents are in jail. Kids who smell like cat piss and chemicals because they live in meth labs. Kids who get shot or have to shoot other people for their gangs.

Fuck all that. I need a ticket out.

I just haven't figured out how to get one.

The lecture ends, and I look down at the screen of the donor laptop for the day's assignment. Most of the people in my flunkie classes aren't here for learning, and they start goofing off, throwing spitballs and pencils at the ceiling, listening to music or getting on their phones. A few of us know that's not the way out, and we open the homework, ready to get a jump on things.

A message pops up on my screen, some kind of messenger app I didn't even know was on the school computers. It's an old-school one called *OnlyWords* that's supposed to look retro, a little box with square green letters blinking at me with a message.

MrD: Hello Darling.

The school really should invest in a better firewall to keep the creepers out. I'm about to X out of the little box when a second message pops up after the first.

MrD: I have a proposal for you.

I roll my eyes to myself and decide to engage. There are only 5 minutes left in class, anyway. I won't even be able to finish a single problem of the homework. I don't bother making a messenger handle, just type in the box to reply. I may not be getting a scholarship to Yale anytime soon, but I'm smart enough to know not to trust men on the internet. Doesn't mean it's not fun to fuck with them.

Faulkner189: Mr. D? Really? That's original.

MrD: You could call me Big D if you'd rather.

Barf. Just like I thought, some creeper hacking into the school computers to harass girls. Just about sums up the Faulkner High experience.

Faulkner189: Rnt u going to ask if I like older men?

MrD: Do you?

Faulkner189: Or if I'm a virgin?

Mr. D: Are you?

Faulkner189: In case u couldn't tell, Im on a school computer. UR prolly going to get arrested

MrD: I don't think so.

Faulkner189: I seriously doubt ur as smart as u think u r

MrD: That's where you're wrong.

Faulkner189: Well, aren't we full of ourselves

MrD: Just honest.

Faulkner189: U missed the chance to say I could be full of u 2

MrD: I think you're the one flirting.

Faulkner189: been there, done that, can predict the lines

MrD: You've flirted with older men online?

Faulkner189: ur all the same

MrD: You didn't answer your questions.

Faulkner189: U 1st

MrD: Don't like older men, not a virgin.

Faulkner189: Ditto. The real question is, Y R U propositioning underage girls?

MrD: I wasn't aware that I was.

Faulkner189: U just happened to break into a school computer account to message me & u didn't know I'd be in school???

I wish this app had emojis so I could add an eye roll, but I can only make faces out of symbols on the keyboard, so I leave it off.

MrD: Who said I was propositioning you?

Faulkner189: You legit started out with 'I have a proposition'

MrD: I said "proposal."

Faulkner189: Sure sure

MrD: It would be easier to talk in person. Things get mixed up online like this.

Faulkner189: Bahahaha!!!

Faulkner189: Nice try.

Faulkner189: gg. Try not to harass any more little girls.

MrD: Very funny. Talk soon.

Faulkner189: dont think so

MrD: Oh, we will.

The bell rings, and I scramble to log off and return the laptop, glancing around like I was doing something bad. I guess I was. Sort of.

No one notices, though. The other kids jerk upright from their naps, gather their books, and slog out of the room. Mr. Behr has a planning hour next, so he doesn't have to worry about keeping me into his next class. He erases the board while the kids file out. I return the laptop to the cart and sit back in my desk to wait for Mr. Behr to do his thing.

Maybe Mom is right. I think of all the times she's said things to me, warned me about creepers online and elsewhere.

All men like younger women. It's in their biology. So stay in your room tonight, Harper. I'm having Jerry over.

Or was it Jim, or Gordon, or D'Aron? I lost track of them over the years.

When the last students file out, Mr. Behr comes around his desk and sits on the front of it. "Everything okay, Harper?"

"Yep."

"How are things at home?"

"Picture perfect." I give him my fakest smile.

Mr. Behr smooths his short-sleeved button-up shirt over his belly. He licks his lips and glances at the door, then pushes off his desk and creeps toward me. "It's been a while since we've seen each other."

"You see me every day in class."

He fidgets, but I pin him with a glare. The high of having power over him wore off a long time ago. Now he disgusts me.

If we didn't have laws, they'd all take girls so young they couldn't get them pregnant, so they didn't have to worry about birth control. Not that they care once they do. Just look at your dad…

Not that I have that option. I've never met the guy. Mom has plenty to say about what a good-for-nothing loser he was, but I doubt she even knows who knocked her up.

"Let's meet today after school," Mr. Behr says, his voice an urgent whisper. "Our usual spot. I'll drive you home afterwards."

"I didn't know we had a usual spot."

"Are you feeling neglected?" I think he's trying to tease, but he just sounds whiny.

"What if I have plans?"

"Oh, Harper," he says, straightening. "You don't have plans. Plans require friends."

"I might have family plans."

"You know, Harper, you're such a smart young lady," Mr. Behr says. "One day, I'm sure you'll get into a great college if you study hard and keep your grades up."

"I got an A in your class last year," I point out. I've never thought of him as threatening, but then, he probably made me feel like I had control on purpose. What power does a sixteen-year-old have over a grown man?

I know what Mom would say. She'd say plenty. She'd cluck her tongue in disgust and say, *Girls your age, Harper. Walking around looking like they belong on a street corner. And then they pretend to be the victim when they get what they were asking for all along.*

"Yes, you did get an A," Mr. Behr muses. "You were such a good student, too. So willing to learn and follow instruction. I'd hate to see you have to repeat geometry next year. But then, I could request to have you in my class again…"

I push up out of my desk, pick up my books, and head for the door, pausing just long enough to call back over my shoulder, "I'll be there."

A Father's Love

If he knew
I wrote this shit

He'd say
I was less of a man.

If he knew
What happened in the missing days

He'd say
I wasn't a man at all.

If he knew
There was no hate left inside me

He'd say
I've grown.

If he knew
The cold thirst for vengeance where a heart should beat

He'd say
I was justified.

If he knew
It could never be sated

He'd say
"Now there's a real man."

So I don't say anything
at all.

two

Harper Apple

At home, I peel off my damp T-shirt and pull on a tank, dragging my dark hair out the back of it and twisting it up. Then I tape up my hands and head to the basement to punch the bag that hangs from the ceiling in the corner. One of Mom's boyfriends got it for himself one year, vowing to get in shape, but he's long gone like the rest of them. I don't blame them. Nothing good lasts around here.

I'm lucky Mom keeps a job and brings home enough money to keep us in this roach-infested trap. The paycheck lasts just long enough to cover the bills and Mom's increasing need to buy shit to impress her men that has me wondering if one day she'll disappear with one of them and stop coming home at all. At least she's stuck around up until now, I have to give her that. It could be worse. I could get shipped off to foster care, and who's going to take a surly teenager with an attitude problem?

Hell, even moving back to the trailer park where I grew up would be worse than a house. This isn't so bad. Mom scrapes together rent just in time to keep us from being evicted each month, and even though our house is a shit hole in Faulkner's version of gangland, it's not a trailer.

I slam my fist into the bag, dancing back when it swings toward me. Then I deliver a flurry of punches.

That one's for Mom and her preference for men and their drugs over groceries and running water.

The next one's for my dad, whoever the fuck he is.

There's a one-two combination for Colin, whose leather jacket and foreign accent seduced me out of my virginity under a bridge when I was thirteen.

There's a right hook for the cop who chased me away when I tried to make some beautiful art on the wall under said bridge. I just wanted to give other girls something prettier than a bleak cement wall to bear witness to their shame when a guy pulled out, dropped the bloody condom on the ground, and tossed them a cigarette before bailing.

I save my most vicious blows for Mr. Behr, though. I curse the administrator who put me back in his class this year. It's been two weeks since school started, and I actually let myself hope he wouldn't talk to me again. That he moved on and found some other sad sap with no hope, so he could pretend to be sympathetic while he lured her into the back seat of his car.

After an hour, I'm spent, not to mention drenched in sweat. I jog upstairs, chug some water from the tap, and head for the shower. When I get there, I falter. Why am I getting myself all clean for nasty old Behr? I peel off my tank, pull on a clean tee, and because I haven't completely abandoned all human decency, I throw on another coat of deodorant. A pair of jeans and a belt prevent hands from wandering, and tennis shoes will save my feet on the mile walk to the place I don't even want to go.

But what choice do I have?

I glance over at my books. I get good grades without having to suck off any of the other teachers. Since the infamous freshman year off, I've busted my ass to make it happen. I decided that year of summer school that no matter what, I was getting out of this place before it sucked me down like quicksand, the way it has so many others.

Instead of rushing off to meet Behr, I power on the old desktop computer we still have—mostly because it's so slow that even a pawn shop won't buy it—and open the homework. Maybe if I keep records of everything, prove I turned it in, he can't fail me.

I'm halfway through when OnlyWords message box pops up.

MrD: We meet again.

I jerk my hands off the keyboard like it's turned to lava and glance around nervously.

I don't know shit about technology, but what the actual fuck? Who is this guy and how does he know it's me? How did he get from a school laptop to my ancient desktop at home?

I take a breath and wipe my palms on my jeans before carefully placing my hands back on the keyboard.

The app prompts me to create a username, so I type one in and then sit there, trying to think of what to say. Most of me wants to close the messenger box and block the app, but something stops me. My skin crawls, the hair on the back of my neck standing up like I'm being watched. How did he find me? I have to know.

BadApple: Have we met?

MrD: Oh, we're playing that game?

BadApple: No games.

MrD: Agreed.

BadApple: So how did you find me?

MrD: I have my ways.

BadApple: Thot u said no games

MrD: That's not a game, it's a secret. Magician never reveals and all that.

BadApple: Now ur a magician? Explains the creepiness.

MrD: You wouldn't think I was creepy if you met me.

BadApple: I bet $ ur wrong

MrD: Okay. Let's meet.

BadApple: lol

MrD: How much are we betting?

BadApple: not happening

MrD: 10k

I stare at the computer screen, my mind unable to comprehend the number he put in. I mean, even if the dude's a total perv… Ten thousand dollars is a lot of money to get in my pants. If I thought he'd actually pay that, I'd be on my way in a second.

Does that make me a whore? Sure, maybe. But I really don't care what anyone thinks. It's my body. Why shouldn't I get to set the price? I'm trailer trash with nothing going for her, as my mother likes to remind me. I've done worse than sell sex.

Hell, if we're talking prices, all I got for my virginity was a cigarette and a pair of bloody underwear.

The most I've ever gotten out of sex is some cool tats. Mav was a friend, he needed a canvas to practice on, and I was bored. Between the two of us, apparently we couldn't resist the skin and the pain, and next thing you know, we were in bed together. That arrangement lasted about as long as it took him to finish inking my thigh and hip. We really had no interest in each other after that, but at least I had something to show for it. Where else would a girl like me get the money for tats?

MrD: Not interested?

I shake my head, coming back to the present. This guy obviously wants more than to get laid. Even a gross uggo like Mr. Behr can find someone to fuck if he tries hard enough. Which means this guy is after something else. If I meet him, he's either going to sell me to get his money back or harvest my organs. And that's if he actually has the money, which I one hundred percent guarantee he doesn't.

BadApple: nope

MrD: I know a girl like you could use it.

I shiver again, but I'm not going to let him get to me. Of course I could use the money. I'm not the only poor girl in town. Pretty much everyone at FHS who has tats got them from Maverick.

BadApple: What does a girl like me need $ for? I got it all

MrD: College. Travel. A car. A better school. A better house.

My fingers still on the keyboard, that uneasy feeling crawling up my back again.

BadApple: IDT 10k covers a house, not even this one

MrD: It covers the rent on one.

My heart is pounding now. I have to remind myself he doesn't know where I live, that we rent. He assumes I live in a shitty house because I go to Faulkner High. That's it.

BadApple: How do u know I need any of that?

MrD: I've been watching you, Harper.

My whole body freezes.

Harper.

He knows my name. He knows who I am. And if he knows that, he probably knows where I live. I force myself not to glance around, not to peer out through gaps in the dusty slats of the blinds.

No, I tell myself. He doesn't know who I am. He got it off the school computer I'd logged into. He doesn't know where I live, he doesn't have ten thousand dollars, and he's not watching me. And if he tries to snatch me off the street… Well, he can fucking try. He'll see how well that goes. I may have zero prospects in life, nothing in life to call my own but the body I was born with, but that taught me a thing or two. I know how to use my body for more than sex.

BadApple: U like watching?

MrD: I love it.

BadApple: then watch this

I yank the computer cord out of the wall without waiting to log out. Then I stand, check the time on my third-hand phone, and head out, glad to leave the eerie sensation behind. I can't believe I let that creeper get to me. But as unsettling as that was, and as alluring as the daydream of more money than we've ever had in my whole life is, that's not real.

Mr. Behr is real.

For a girl like me, this is the only way out. The price you pay for a dream. You blow your teachers to get good grades, and maybe get a scholarship to a state college, where you probably have to blow your professors. Eventually, you get off the casting couch and walk on your own two feet.

At first, I left Mom notes when I went to meet Mr. Behr, always halfway terrified and halfway hoping she'd ask me where I went. But Mom stopped seeing me as her daughter and started seeing me as competition around my twelfth year, when boyfriend number ninety turned out to be a dick like the first eighty-nine she dragged through the house in my lifetime. Except this one proved to be a dick of the sort who wanted in her daughter's pants instead of hers. From then on, she was glad to have me out of the house. After a few months of blowing Mr. Behr, I walked out while she was right there in front of the TV. She didn't even look my way.

The younger the better, if it's up to them. That's why you'd better cover yourself up when this one's coming over, Harper. I'm not about to lose a man to some kid who doesn't know her ass from her elbow.

When I step from the dim interior into the blinding late afternoon sun, I have to stop and let my eyes adjust. Between our decrepit brick house and the next, Blue's crouched over a kiddie pool half filled with sand, picking through it with an old plastic ladle. Beside her, Olive sits in a folding beach chair made of cracked plastic with aluminum legs that's probably been around since her mom was a teenager. She runs a toy car up and down the metal bars of the chair, waiting for her big sister to clean her sandbox.

Normally, I'd say hi. We're not exactly friends, but proximity and age make Blue about as close as I come to friends. Between the two of us, we have too many walls. One of us would have to want to break them down to become friends, and we're both too guarded. She has her sister, and I have my fists, and we're both respectful of the fact that those things matter most to the other.

"Fucking cats," Blue swears, hurling a scoop of shit out of her yard and into the road. "Does this look like a litter box?"

"Probably to them," Olive says. "It's not their fault. Everybody shits somewhere."

Blue sighs and tosses a cigarette butt out of the sand before standing.

"Okay, you can play," she says, and the sisters change places. She waves when she sees me, blowing her lank blue hair out of her eyes and pulling out a pack of cigarettes. She holds it out to me as I step over the sunken spot in our broken walkway, rubbing my arms to get rid of the chill I got from the conversation with Mr. D.

"Thanks," I say, stepping across the dirt patch between our walkways to grab a smoke. "I'll get you back."

"Cool," Blue says, lighting up and handing me the lighter. I'm just stalling, putting off the inevitable, but it doesn't stop me. Mr. Behr can wait—and he will. In truth, he's not the only one who gets something out of it, though. I like watching people, studying them, seeing what makes them tick and what they'll do. I know the lure of my teenage flesh is too strong for weak Mr. Behr to resist. He won't even dare scold me for being late. I'm taking pity on a lonely old fat guy who can't get it any other way, and we both know it, just as well as we know he'll fail me in math if I don't show up at all.

"You going out?" Blue asks, watching Olive drive her little car through the sand and leap it over a cigarette butt she's unearthed.

"Yeah."

We aren't close enough for her to ask where I'm going, or for me to tell her. Olive, like most six-year-olds, has no such reservations.

"You going to work?" she asks, squinting up at me from the sand.

"Just an errand," I say, crouching so she doesn't have to stare into the brutal sun.

"What's an erin?"

"An errand is like a chore," I explain.

"Oh," she says, digging a finger into the sand and pulling up another toy car. She holds it out to me. "Wanna play?"

"She doesn't want to play with you, Olive," Blue says, dragging on her cigarette.

"I would, but I better go," I say.

"Okay," Olive says, sounding wholly unconcerned as she goes back to making a road in the sand.

I stand and wave goodbye, stepping into the pothole ridden road.

"I'll play," I hear Blue say as I walk away. I glance over my shoulder to see her perched on the edge of the plastic tub, toy car in hand. I turn away and face forward, trying to get in the right headspace for doing what the next hour requires.

Today's the first time I'll meet Mr. Behr since the end of last school year, but my feet follow the familiar path. At first, it was electrifying, if a little terrifying. Mom always talks about this kind of thing as if it's inevitable, and maybe it is. At least it was for me. Maybe I was always expecting it. Knowing I could intoxicate a grown man made me feel powerful.

But it didn't take me long to figure out that I only had power because Mr. Behr let me. It was all an act—how he couldn't live without me, couldn't think, couldn't teach. That's how bad he needed to have his dick in my mouth.

I jump a ditch filled with dried mud and dirty beer bottles to walk along the railroad tracks for a few minutes until I come to a large parking lot beside the tracks. Mr. Behr's car is parked there, almost hidden behind a couple graffiti-covered cars in the railyard. My gorge rises, as if I can already taste his sweaty little limp dick in my mouth.

I think about turning around, going back home to the empty house, waiting for Mom to stomp in from work and yell at me for ruining her life by being born a girl. I think about climbing on one of the trains the way I did with Blue when we first moved out of the trailer park the summer after eighth grade, and I learned I had a neighbor my age. I thought we might be friends then, so I joined her when she walked down here to smoke a cigarette she stole from her mom. And then we saw the train leaving.

I fell off the side of the train onto gravel and cut myself up so bad I still have scars. Blue made it all the way to Ridgedale.

I start across the lot toward Behr's car.

I think about a suitcase full of money, stacks and stacks of crisp bills like you see in movies. Then I shake the thoughts away. I'm getting out of this town one way or another, and if sucking off Mr. Behr gets me the grade I need to do it, it's a small price to pay. I swallow the bile in my throat as I stride toward his car.

Ten thousand dollars. What would I even do with that?

I picture myself lying on a bed making snow angels in money.

Being rescued by some rich guy is a fantasy so far from reality I've never even entertained it. There are no shortcuts in life, as Mom likes to remind me. When you come from a trailer park, you don't get out like that. You get out like this, crouched in the back of a teacher's Corolla, your feet going numb, your eyes squeezed closed, wishing you could close your nostrils to shut out the putrid smell of his sweaty pubes.

Fifteen minutes later, Mr. Behr's clammy hand paws helplessly at me as he grunts and hunches, trying to keep it up long enough to get off. I wish he was faster. I can feel him grabbing the headrest, going at it with renewed vigor. When I get home, I definitely need a long shower, mouthwash, and probably to puke.

Then I'll scavenge for dinner, though I don't know what we have in the cabinets. Mom never does the shopping unless she has a guy coming over. Then she might pick up a few things. I'm in charge of shopping and cooking, but lately, there hasn't been any money left by the time Mom finishes partying with whatever his name is. Pretty sure they've been snorting crystal judging by how little money is left. Which means I've been dipping into the meager savings I have stashed under the carpet in the back of my closet just to eat. Every time I have to take money out, I see the horizon receding, the dream of leaving Faulkner drawing further away.

Mom never asks where the food came from. Maybe I should stop, so she won't think she's been giving me money when she's blacked out. Knowing her, though, she hasn't even noticed, and she sure as shit doesn't care if I'm fed. If she knew I had that money, she'd crawl back in my closet and take every cent of it, use it for a weekend binge with her man. Hell, she'd be pissed as fuck if she even knew it was there. According to her, I owe her everything in life because she gave me that life.

My stomach growls, and I press my fist into it, cursing Mr. Behr's slowness. Maybe he'll take me through a Mickey D's drive-through for a burger.

Fat fucking chance. Of course he won't do that. We might be seen. This is a small town, and people talk.

Maybe there's an expired box of mac and cheese at the back of a cabinet.

More likely, I'll have to peel another twenty off my roll.

A noise jerks me out of my thoughts, something so foreign to these encounters that for a second, I can't identify it. It's not the grunting, panting, desperate mumbling of a middle-aged man trying to hold onto his youth by blackmailing his student into letting him violate her mouth every few weeks. It's a deep, choking sort of… Giggling.

three

Harper Apple

I lift my head from Mr. Behr's dick and find myself staring straight into the back of a cellphone.

Fuck!

Mr. Behr is doggedly hunching away, trying to shove my head back down, but I'm frozen in shock. My forehead collides with his dick, and the three guys outside honk with laughter.

At last, I manage to twist out of Mr. Behr's grip. He catches a glimpse of the guys outside the car, and his face goes white. He looks like he's about to have a stroke.

"Let's get out of here," I say through gritted teeth. Thank all the demons in hell I'm fully clothed. When we first started, Behr would bring me cheap wine and try to undress me, though he said he didn't want more, that what we did wasn't wrong because it wasn't sex. I always knew in the back of my mind he was full of shit, even when I let him convince me how badly he needed me.

Now, he doesn't even pretend, and I just want to get it over with as quickly as possible. No conversation and drinks, no touching or kissing, no need for clothing removal. We both know what we're getting out of it, and we don't pretend otherwise.

Instead of running off, the guys stand outside the car, laughing like idiots. Thank the devil in hell I don't recognize them. They must be the Willow Heights version of delinquents, out getting their kicks by stirring up the kind of trouble their rich daddies can bail them out of.

I slide onto the seat, turning my back toward them, my mind racing. Maybe they didn't get a clear shot of my face. At least they aren't going to see me around school and make my life a living hell. Still, there are way too many kids from Faulkner who could get their hands on that pic if it gets out. Kids who have cousins at Willow Heights, party with the rich kids, or go to their church. It's just across town from Faulkner High.

If Mr. Behr was my size, he'd scramble through the front seats and take off. But he's not, and he can't get into the driver's seat without climbing out of the car. I sit there with my head down, my hair hiding my face, silently cursing the assholes who witnessed my humiliating, shameful act—and captured evidence.

"You kids need to get out of here," Behr says, adopting his teacher voice as he addresses the boys over the roof of the car. He reaches for the door handle, at least, ready to get in the driver's seat.

Just go! I silently scream at him. *Don't make it worse.*

"Or what?" one of the boys says, his voice tinged with laughter and an accent that doesn't belong in Arkansas.

Just get in the car, just get in the car…

"This is totally inappropriate," Mr. Behr says. "You could be arrested if you show that to anyone."

"You could get arrested for face-raping your underage girlfriend in the parking lot," the guy shoots back. "We're the one with the blackmail material here. You don't got shit."

"She's not underage," Mr. Behr protests, throwing open his door. "Seventeen is legal!"

One of the guys fakes a lunge forward, that thing bullies do to make their victims cower while they laugh, and Mr. Behr dives into the front seat while the guys crack up outside.

"That's it?" I ask in disbelief. This guy is such a pathetic excuse for a human I can't believe he ever coerced me into a car with him.

He collapses into the front seat and drops his head into his hands. "My career," he says, sounding shell-shocked and hollow. "My marriage. My family."

"You're fucking married?" I ask. "You said you were so lonely since your wife *died*, that only I could make you feel alive again. You're the fucking iceberg lettuce of the world. No, you're the slimy brown stuff the lettuce turns into while it sits in the bottom drawer of the fridge because even starving people won't eat it."

"Harper—"

"Don't call me that," I snap. "You don't deserve to use my name. In fact, don't ever speak to me again. The only thing you have to say to me is the big fat A-plus on the top of my final. Now drag your limp dick home to your wife and hope to god that even assholes like this are better human beings than you are."

With that, I get out of the car and slam the door. I don't get out on the far side like he did. I don't talk shit, either. I don't even look at the smart-mouthed kid. I step right up to the guy in the middle, the one holding the evidence. "Give me the phone."

Even if I were tall, my head would only come up to his shoulder. As it is, my eyes are about level with his pecs. He towers over me, a smirk on his lips, his dark eyes unreadable in the lingering evening. Orangey security lights bathe the parking lot, casting the boys in stark shadows, almost silhouettes against the pale glow.

The tall guy searches my face for a long minute, like he's looking for something. The rumble of the train in the distance catches his attention before he finds it, and he jerks his chin toward the Range Rover parked fifty feet away, a gesture meant for his two buddies. "Let's go."

Without thinking, I grab his arm. "Fuck no," I say. "You're not leaving until you erase that picture."

He gives a little snort of disbelief and jerks his arm easily from my grip, then turns and walks away.

There's no way I'm letting a bunch of spoiled, rich punks drive off with a picture of me with a dick in my mouth. I jump in front of the guy, my fists raised out of habit.

He pauses, quirking a brow. "What, you think you're going to hit me?"

The train whistles as it approaches, the sound interrupting our confrontation.

"You can't actually be interested in that picture," I say when the sound quiets. "It's probably not even a clear shot."

"Sure," he says, his asshole smirk making me want to punch him just for the fun of it.

"What do you need it for?" I challenge. "If you want to jerk off, look at porn on your phone like everyone else."

His dark eyes skate over my body, and he gives a little scoff. "Don't flatter yourself."

"Fine, then what do you need it for?" I challenge.

One of his friends comes up, another guy with the same dark hair, though his is shorter on top and shaved close on the sides. A lollipop hangs from the corner of his mouth as he grins at me, but I can't see his eyes past the reflection of the lights on his glasses. "If you don't want people taking pictures of you in compromising positions, don't be in them in a public place," he says, slinging an arm around the taller guy, the cameraman. His accent tells me they're more than friends—they're brothers.

I've never had a brother or anyone else to back me up. But that's okay. I learned not to need anyone. I look out for myself. That's the way it works on my side of the tracks. You get smart or you get dead. I've made it this far on my own, and I sure as fuck don't need someone telling me what to do, nagging me not to sleep with teachers or play chicken with the trains. I glance at the tracks just fifty feet off, so close I can feel the ground tremble underfoot as the train roars our way.

"Look, you could only want that picture for two reasons," I say. "Either to ruin lives, which you probably do for kicks, or as blackmail, like you said. If you want money, you're gonna need to pick on someone closer to your own size in the wallet department because trust me, I have nothing you'd want."

If anyone's going to make money off my body, whether it's a picture of it or the real thing, it'll be me, not these assholes.

And I walked away from that offer earlier today. Even trailer trash has standards.

"I don't know if I'd say you have *nothing* we want," says the third guy, the loudmouthed one who talked to Mr. Behr. One look at him, and it's easy to see these assholes all descended from the same genes. They've got the whole tall, dark, and handsome thing pegged.

Loudmouth looks me over with more interest than his brothers, his eyes lingering on my tits like they're a hell of a lot more impressive than they are. I was not blessed—or cursed, depending on your perspective—in the chest department, and I couldn't care less. Tits have one purpose, and that's to attract male attention, which I have no use for.

"You think I'm going to fuck you to get the picture back?" I ask.

All the guys at my school are equally predictable when pussy is introduced to the equation. Apparently, rich guys are no different.

"Are you?" asks the one with glasses, cocking his head.

"No," I say. "So just delete it, and we'll leave you alone, and you can laugh about it to all the other entitled pricks at your school."

"You said there was another reason we'd want it," says the big guy in the middle, his phone held casually in his hand, as if he's just dangling it there to tempt me.

I snort at that. "If you want to ruin lives, you're going to be in for a serious disappointment with me. My life is already ruined. Hell, I was born ruined. Your worst day would be a fucking stroll in the park for me."

Cameraman just smirks at me, that infuriating look that makes my fingers curl into a fist. "You think we can't ruin you. That's cute."

"Do you even know who we are?" the other brother asks.

"Some sick bastards from the right side of the tracks who want to come gape at the rest of us like we're zoo exhibits before you go home to sleep on your pillows made of money," I say, raising my voice to speak over the din on the tracks. "Am I supposed to know your names? Y'all all look the same to me."

"Aw, she thinks money solves all problems," Glasses Guy says. "It's so quaint. I didn't know people so naïve still existed, even in Arkansas."

"I think there's nothing you could dream up in your fancy mansion with a pool that would be worse than the shit a Faulkner High kid survives on a daily basis."

Cameraman's eyes glint with malicious intent. "I wouldn't be so sure."

I've spent my life clawing my way out of the trash heap of an existence I was born into, and I'm sure as fuck not going to let that picture wind up on the internet and kill whatever slim chance I have of getting a scholarship out of this place. I have one shot. I need to get that phone, and reasoning is obviously not going to work with this asshole. So, I use a language his primitive brain can understand. I kick him in the nuts.

He lets out a rough exclamation, doubling over in pain.

I snatch for the phone, wrenching it out of his hand before wheeling around and sprinting across the lot.

Mr. Behr's car is gone. He must have snuck off while I was busy saving both our asses. I'm exactly zero percent surprised, but it still pisses me off that he ditched me to deal with three huge men while he slunk off to safety, using the noise of the train to cover his retreat. Whatever. It's every man for himself in this world.

One of the guys shouts behind me, but I don't turn back. I run straight for the train as it barrels down the tracks, the beam of its light transforming the rails ahead into gleaming silver streams. The glow only barely illuminates the lot, but I know my way. I run for the bright parallel lines, glancing at the looming dark shape behind the light, knowing that timing is literally everything in this game of life and death. One second separates one from the other. One second.

I think I have it. I'm never sure—that's the thrill of playing chicken. My feet slam the pavement harder with each step as I curl into myself, my muscles tensed to spring. The horn screams above me, the scent of hot creosote and exhaust filling my nose, my lungs. I jump. The light blinds me.

I hear a shout of warning. Alarm. Panic.

But it's too late. I'm suspended in the light like the particles of dust caught in the beam.

For a second, I'm weightless. I'm free. Life and death are the same. There's nothing but sheer, raw existence. I am both infinite and utterly insignificant at once; the infinity between stars and the pause between heartbeats.

I am—

I am—

I am.

I hit the ground hard, my senses coming back to me after the moment of magic, the one where I leave my body for a second, where I'm not Harper Apple, the girl from the trailer park who ruined her mother's life by being born, the girl who skipped freshman year, the girl who's blowing her math teacher. Returning is harsh. My breath is ripped from my lungs, the asphalt burning into my face. My body is so heavy that I don't realize it's not only my weight for a second. The stink of the train, the tracks, the ground, all invade me as I feel the crush of his body on top of mine.

He flips me over, crushing his forearm down on my throat, cutting me off from drawing in the air he knocked out of me. The train is so loud, the thwack and clank of it rushing over the tracks so close I can feel the heat blasting from it, the air a hot rush over my burned skin. It pulses louder and quieter as he holds me pinned, red spots throbbing across my vision.

I open my mouth, wanting to scream at this psycho, demand to know if he's fucking crazy or just has a death wish, but I try not to ask obvious questions even when I have all the air in the world. And right now, I don't have any. I buck my hips, trying to throw his weight off, but he's lying on me, between my thighs, his body too tight to mine to throw off our center of gravity.

His face hovers over mine, his eyes twin pits filled with darkness that threatens to swallow me whole.

"I could kill you right now." His eyes hold mine, and I feel myself sinking into that darkness, feel it calling to mine, sucking me in like a black hole. "No one would even care."

I know he's right, that it would barely make the news, a little paragraph in the paper, "Body Found Near Tracks." I'm nothing, just another casualty of poverty, chalk it up to gang violence like every other death that gets a mention on *Local News with Jackie* before she cuts back to the anchorman.

I struggle, but the lack of oxygen makes my muscles burn, weakening already. I try to get in a right hook, but he snatches my wrist and pins it to the ground. I use my left hand, but he barely flinches when it connects with his cheek. He watches me for a second, his eyes dark and hollow. They're not the eyes of someone pissed that I kicked him in the nuts and stole his phone or punched him in the face. No rage burns in his gaze as he weighs whether he wants to watch my life blink out in his hands. His eyes are empty.

I can see what it is now, how he could risk the train the second after me, the second that he should have died.

He doesn't have a death wish. He's already dead.

My vision blinks out, and then the pressure is gone from my neck. I suck in a loud, hideous sounding breath, rolling onto my side, choking on air. He's already standing, but he bends to swipe his phone from the ground where it fell. The end of the train shoots by, the lights from the lot beyond suddenly casting him in silhouette.

The two other guys are there in seconds, grabbing him, yelling at him.

"What the fuck?" the loud one yells, punching him and hugging him at once.

"Get off me," he says, shrugging the guy away and glowering at him.

"What are we going to do with her?" asks the one with glasses, bending down to inspect me like I'm an ant he might burn to a crisp under a microscope as a diversion on a summer's afternoon. He rolls the sucker from one side of his mouth to the other with his tongue as he watches me.

"Leave her," says the guy with the dead eyes. Then he turns and walks away, his brothers following him across the tracks. A minute later, I hear the Range Rover roar to life, and I scrape my ass up off the ground so they don't get any ideas about jumping the tracks in their fancy SUV and running me down. I jog across a stretch of pavement and jump the ditch growing more empty chip bags and used condoms than grass. Sparing a glance over my shoulder, I see the car speeding off as I reach the boarded-up storefront of an old Fred's store.

I step around the side of the building and crouch between an old Dumpster and a wall tagged up in Zeph's signature style. My head feels like it's being squeezed in a vice after hitting the asphalt so hard, and my face is burning from its encounter with the pavement. Gingerly, I reach up to touch my cheek. My fingers come away bloody in the worst places, but it's mostly just scraped. I pick a few pieces of small gravel out of my palms and flex my hands to make sure they're okay. My jeans are torn on both knees from where the asshole slammed me to the ground, but nothing's broken.

I know it could have been worse. I shiver when I remember that huge guy's body between my thighs, crushing me into the ground. I remember his brother checking me out before that. Wouldn't be the first time a girl was gang raped and left for dead on this side of town. On this side of town, if you can walk away from a fight with nothing but a few bruises and a wounded ego, you call yourself fucking lucky.

Small Town

Young blood
Young thugs
Have some respect
Says the old man
With his cock in a young mouth.
New blood
Young punks
What's happened to this town?
Say the old men
With our money clutched in their fists.
New money
Fresh meat
Up to no good again, I see
Say the housewives who undress us
With their lonely, hungry eyes.
Fresh perspective
Sweetheart:
Maybe bad feels better than good
(Just ask your husband
When he gets home from the tracks).
Blood money
New reign
We *happened to this town*
So have some respect,
Say the boys
With the crowns on their heads.

four

Harper Apple

Almost a week passes, but I can't relax. I know it's not over. There will be more before it's over. There will be blood. There always is.

The good thing about not letting anyone get close is that no one pries no matter what state I come back in. Sure, I get a few stares. When I sit down by Blue at lunch, she raises a brow, but she doesn't ask. Mav asks if I'm okay when I walk by his table in the cafeteria. But it's not the first time I've shown up with bruises, though the scrapes are new. No one really cares what happened. They go on with their lives, their lunches.

I go on with mine, but I'm waiting.

Mr. Behr doesn't so much as look at me in class. He's probably waiting for the other shoe to drop, too, too freaked out about being exposed to worry about my battered face. As I sit in class on Friday, I start to get pissed about that. Who decided he's worth more than me? Just because he has a respectable job doesn't mean he's respectable. Me? I don't have far to fall. I barely made it out of the trailer park, so you can bet your ass the moment everyone finds out, they'll be calling me a homewrecker, even though I didn't know he had a family.

Why is an adult's reputation more important than a kid's? Yeah, he risked a lot, but I sure as shit didn't ask him to do that. And I went all-in, same as him. I bet it all on a chance to get out of Faulkner.

I'm in my last class when the familiar little black box with green letters pops up in the corner of my laptop screen.

MrD: Hello, Darling

Faulkner440: How TF do u keep finding me?

MrD: Magician never reveals, remember? :)

Faulkner440: What do u want?

MrD: The real question is, what do you want?

Faulkner440: For u 2 leave me TF alone

MrD: What else do u want? If I really was a magician, and I could make it happen, what would you ask for?

Faulkner440: I think genies r the 1s who grant wishes

MrD: I could be your genie.

Faulkner440: Gross

MrD: 3 wishes, Harper. What would they be? A car? A house on the other side of town? New school? What do you want?

I think about telling him to fuck off again, but what's the point? He keeps finding me. He must want something. I'd rather know what it is and get it over with. It's not like I'm giving him my home address. And who am I kidding? Dude already knows my name and hacked into the school's computers. If he wants my address, he already has it.

Faulkner440: a million bucks, a way out of here, 2 matter

MrD: You don't think you matter?

I wince, already regretting saying something so personal.

Faulkner440: I matter 2 me.

MrD: Who do you want to matter to?

Faulkner440: Maybe I want 2 do something that matters in the grand scheme.

MrD: What if I could get u all those things?

Faulkner440: U really think highly of urself

Faulkner440: R *U God?*

MrD: Sometimes

*Faulkner440: *eyeroll**

MrD: Let's start with the easy one.

Faulkner440: A million bucks? Do u need me to forward this email to 10 ppl in the next 10 minutes and they'll all send me back $? Lol

MrD: A way out of here. What does that mean? Out of your class? Your school? This town?

Faulkner440: yes

MrD: What if I said I could do that.

Faulkner440: I wud say ur a funny guy

MrD: You have to do your part, too.

Faulkner440: Here it comes. Let me guess. I have 2 meet u somewhere shady, alone, without telling anyone. Then ur going to tell me you have some job in another state, and next thing I know, I'm a junkie living in a trailer servicing truckers while u pocket the $. No thanx.

MrD: You have quite the imagination, Harper.

Faulkner440: Not imagination. I watch the news.

MrD: You saw that on the news?

Faulkner440: I see the truth. When ppl look at a woman's body, they see opportunity.

MrD: That's not what I see when I look at your body.

A shiver clings to my spine, and I want to turn around, to look at the other students, see who's engrossed a little too much in their laptop. I force myself not to move. Maybe he's fucking with me, or maybe he's seen me, but that doesn't mean he's here right now. If he has ten grand, he's not sitting in a flunkie class at FHS.

Faulkner440: Not going 2 ask.

MrD: I like your body type. It's the kind that looks all delicate when I'm on top of you, like you'd break with one good pounding. But turn you around and hit it from the back, and that ass looks like it could take the most brutal gangbang imaginable. And trust me, babygirl, that's pretty fucking brutal.

The hair on the back of my neck stands up, and I swallow hard, glad he's not here to see my face. I'm no innocent, but I'm also not used to men talking to me quite so crudely. Or candidly. I'm not sure which it is. Maybe both.

Faulkner440: I see a creepy old dude jerking off in his trailer while stalking teenager girls online

MrD: That's how you see yourself? Talk about distorted self-image…

Faulkner440: funny guy

MrD: I have my moments.

Faulkner440: As enlightening as it's been, class is about over. GG.

MrD: You haven't seen what I can do.

Faulkner440: Yeah, this app doesn't accommodate pics & since I've got 0 interest in meeting u…

MrD: You'll see soon enough. But like I said, you have to do your part. Take advantage of the opportunity I'm giving you. Don't throw this away, H. You'll be sorry if you do.

I close out of the browser and log out before shoving the donor laptop back onto the cart. My skin feels all crawly and wrong, and I bolt for the door when the bell rings. I shove my books into my locker without bothering to check if I have homework and take off. I just about run over Blue as we head out the doors toward the ancient, bleached out buses that take us home. The afternoon sun is blazing down on us, the heat rippling off the pavement and rising with the choking exhaust, making the air so thick you could chew on it.

"You okay?" Blue asks, glancing at me from the corner of her eye.

If we were the kind of friends who told each other shit, maybe I'd ask for advice about this online stalker I've gained. But we're not, and there's nothing she could do about it, so I just shrug. "Just ready to get out of here."

"Doing anything this weekend?" she asks, shuffling up to the edge of the crowd milling around the buses. Everyone is practically gasping for breath in the smothering heat. The diesel exhaust is so strong it's no wonder Faulkner High's student population is low on brain cells. A guy goes bounding past, his shoulder slamming into Blue and sending her reeling to keep her balance.

"What the fuck," I say, shoving him in the back. "Watch where you're going, asshole."

He spins around, already drawing back a fist before he sees it's me. His eyes widen, and he hurls a curse at me, then bounds onto the bus like it's somewhere he really wants to be.

Blue brushes her hair out of her eyes, muttering a curse under her breath. "Thanks," she says. "Sit together?"

"I think I'm actually going to walk," I say, backing up a step. I didn't bring my books home for the weekend, so I don't have much to carry, and even though the temperature is hovering around a hundred degrees, I just can't take the crowd on the bus right now. Blue doesn't push for an explanation, which I appreciate. We're both fatherless, and I get the feeling her mom's not much better than mine, but we have enough mutual respect to let the other keep her dignity by not getting up in her shit.

I head home to get ready for the one fun part of my week—the Friday night fight at the Slaughter Pen. It's a good way to blow off steam, not to mention to make a few bucks and stay out of the way on Mom's date night. I'd like to say that's all it is to me, that I don't need it like other people need a drink on the weekends, but I know better. The money's good, but it's not about the money, either. I'd do it for free.

Fighting reminds me I'm alive when everything else in this town seems determined to drag me under, to hold me against the grindstone until there's nothing left of me but my bad name. On Friday nights, I'm somebody. Right there in that moment, I'm more alive than in the rest of the week put together. Nobody cares if I have a future or where I live or what my real name is. There, I'm my moniker, the one given me by the man we call Dynamo, who gives everyone a name. And even if we all have stupid names, I like to be that girl.

A girl who speaks the language of knuckles, of the current moment when nothing else exists but the dirt and sweat and blood, the frenzied cries of few dozen fevered spectators, and the satisfying pain that races up my arm when I land a blow.

When it's over, I can think about the money. I can get myself a Coke and a bag of chips from the convenience store on the way home for a treat, something completely frivolous I'd never think of spending money on ordinarily. I can wonder if Mom's done fucking her flavor of the week so that I can go home, because even though I'm too old for her to lock me in the closet when her dates come over, that doesn't mean I want to meet them.

Men want a girl who's still tight, so do your mom a favor and stay out of sight. If they see I have a kid, they'll start imagining I'm loose, and who's fault is that? It's yours, Harper. So don't even think about coming out until I come get you.

I don't want to wake up to find one of her creepers in my room, or shake their hands and pretend I don't see the way they're eyeing my boobs like they want to put a dick there, or turn around from making coffee in the morning and find one of them with his hand down his pants as he watches me. I don't want Mom to fly off the handle and chase me around smacking me with a spatula and screaming at me that it's my fault my dad left her, that it's my fault her dates are pedos, that it's my fault her life is shit.

The feeling is fucking mutual, Mom.

The weekend passes too fast, and Monday morning, I'm back at FHS, still waiting. I can almost feel the charge in the air. Something's going to happen. I'm a month into sophomore year now. I almost start to hope. Maybe those boys will leave me alone, not spread the pic around. Anything is possible.

By the end of the week, the wait is killing me, so I decide to do a little digging. At lunch, I turn to the most boy-crazy girl at my table, a girl who might have been my best friend if I'd stayed in the trailer park. I lean in so she can hear me over the roar of voices in the huge, industrial room. Jolene's always looking for gossip, though she's never part of it—maybe *because* she's never part of it. She's been dating the same guy since middle school, and she hasn't gotten pregnant yet. Not much else is going to put a girl in our circle on the social radar.

"So, I saw these guys down by the tracks the other day," I say. "They don't go to this school, but they're definitely in the juvenile delinquent category. Any ideas?"

"Already graduated?" Jolene asks.

"Harper's looking to slum it with some high school drop-outs," says Earnhart, her boyfriend, laughing. "Way to go, girl. Get you some STDs."

"Does Willow Heights have any guys like that?" I ask, remembering their rich car. "Oh, also I heard them talking, and they had some kind of accent."

"That would be Colin," Skeeter Bite says, turning his camo hat around backwards and resting his elbows on the table.

"Not Colin," I assure them. For one, he goes to this school. For two, my "number" is far too low to have forgotten a guy on my list. Not that they need to know about that disaster. "Their accents were more like the Sopranos. And there were three of them."

"Ohhh," Jolene says slowly. "Are you talking about the Dolces?"

I shrug, pretending it doesn't matter, but I save the name in my mind to look up later. "Maybe."

"Oh, no, you're not getting away with that," Jolene says, staring at me with wide eyes. "Hold on. Did you actually *talk* to the Dolces? Oh my god, do you know the Dolce boys?"

Jolene should know I don't. I got to know her and her whole posse of boys from living in the trailer park, but since I moved out, I'm not really one of them. Still, we've known each other since we were kids, and she knows I'm only one unpaid bill from being right back there with them. I consider fucking with Jolene and telling her I know the Dolces just for kicks, but it might give her a stroke, so I resist the urge.

"Why would I talk to them?" I ask. "I don't even know who they are."

"They live in the same town as us," she says, pouting. "It's not impossible."

The same town, sure. The same universe? Not even close.

"Yeah," I say with a snort. "It is."

"Then why'd you ask about them? Usually only the popular girls here worry about the Dolces."

"Why would they worry about the rich Willow Heights boys? Don't they have enough guys here to knock them up?"

"Yeah, but they're Willow Heights guys," she says. "And they're the Dolces. Come on, Harper. Even you've heard of them."

"Not really," I say, dropping my flavorless burger onto my plate.

"Yeah, you have," she says. "That's why you asked. That's why all the popular girls want to get with them. Whoever dated one of them would be the queen bee of this school by default. They *own* this town. Can you imagine what that could do for your reputation?"

I can imagine exactly what they could do for my reputation. One leaked picture, and I'll be a lot worse than a poor nobody. I'll be a social pariah.

"Everyone knows they're trouble," Shiner says. "I heard they been arrested like ten times, but their dad paid off the cops."

"I heard they didn't just pay off the cops, but the judge," Earnhart says. "They made a deal so nothing they do goes on their permanent record, no matter how bad it is. Can you imagine what we could get into with that kind of immunity?"

"See?" Jolene bugs her eyes at me, as if I should be impressed by this disgusting behavior, while the guys go on talking about what they'd do if there were no consequences.

"If they got arrested, I'm sure they deserved it," I say, thinking about my record, which isn't exactly squeaky clean. I've avoided going to juvie, but I've been picked up by the cops more than once myself.

"They're so fine, though," Jolene says, leaning back in her seat with a sigh.

"Dude, I'm right here," Earnhart says.

"Oh, whatever," she says, swatting his thigh. "Don't even pretend you don't spin around so fast you get whiplash every time a Willow Heights girl walks by in her little plaid skirt."

"Carry on," Earnhart says, going back to his fries.

"Is anyone going to the game tonight?" Jolene asks.

We all look at her.

"What game?" I ask. "And since when do you care about sportsball?"

"The game tonight," she says. "The *football* game. Hello, it's the first game of the season, between us and Willow Heights. It's kind of a big deal."

"To who?"

"To everyone," she says, gesturing around the cafeteria. "The first game of the season will set the tone for the rivalry all season. We play them again for Homecoming every year—either theirs or ours."

"How do you know all this?" Dodge asks.

"Everyone knows," Jolene says.

"Why would we go to this thing again?" I ask.

"You just don't get it," she says, rolling her eyes.

"Have you ever gone to a game?" I ask.

"No," she admits. "But that's because I don't have anyone to go with, and I don't want to go alone like some kind of loser. If you went…"

"Then you can be losers together," Earnhart says. They've been dating so long she knows she can't convince him to go.

"Shut up," Jolene says, tossing a fry at him.

I sit up straight, knocking a ketchup packet out of the air as Earnhart fires back. "Do the Dolces play for Willow Heights?"

"Yeah," Jolene says slowly. "Duh."

"Okay, let's go."

"Really?" Jolene shrieks loud enough for people at several tables to turn our way.

I shrug. "Sure, why not?"

"Oh, my god. This is going to be epic."

"If you say so." I can't help but smile. Jolene wants to be popular, but she was dealt a crap hand when it comes to that stuff. She lives in the trailer park on the edge of town, for one. At least I don't care that I'm not popular. Honestly, it seems like a lot of effort. But I care about ending up on the internet, and if I can get those guys to erase that picture…

Phone Calls to New York

I'll have to call you back
I'm interviewing the new cook
I had to let Marta go
She cooked the same thing twice
Can you believe?
She must not have much in her arsenal after all
Probably thought I wouldn't notice.
It's so hard to find good help these days.

I'll have to call you back
When you're not being so insolent
I told you I don't want to talk about your sister
You know I can't handle it
There's a reason I didn't go to the funeral
I don't know why you insist on bringing it up
It's like you're rubbing it in my face.

I'll have to call you back
When you're done making up such outrageous tales
Do you know how upset your father'd be
if he knew you were saying these things about him?
I'm sure it's not as bad as all that
At least he's there with you
I'm the one he abandoned
Left me here all by myself
Barely even calls to see how I'm doing
And look at you
Just like him
Did you even ask me about the new art class I signed up for?

I'll have to—

You know what, Ma
Never mind
Don't even bother.

five

Harper Apple

Neither of us have a car, so that evening finds a dude named Tater Bug dropping off me and Jolene at the Faulkner High field. Jolene may not be popular, but she seems to have a small army of dudes wrapped around her finger and willing to do her favors when she needs them. It may have something to do with her chest size. I have only mad respect for her. A girl's gotta work with what she's got.

"Text me when the game's about over," Tater Bug says, leaning down to call out the passenger side window, which is ringed with tape where he had a trash bag until Jolene insisted he take it down.

"I will," she says, blowing him a kiss like she's forgotten that she didn't want anyone popular to see her getting out of his old hooptie. She leans in the window and smiles adoringly at the gawky guy. "Unless you want to go with? You can buy us popcorn."

"I ain't allowed in on account of a certain streaking incident that occurred last year," he says, grinning back at her and flipping his floppy mohawk out of his eyes. "But I got a Coke for my favorite girl." He hands her a can of Dr. Pepper, and she squeals with happiness. After a few more minutes of flirting, Jolene retreats from his window, and we head into the game, the soda hidden in Jolene's shirt.

"Oh my God, that's them," Jolene says as we sit down. "That's the Dolces." Her nails dig into my arm as she points to a bunch of guys in pads. They all look the same to me. "That's Royal, he's a star. Like, might go to the NFL one day, will definitely play college ball. And that's Duke, oh, and Baron…"

I snort. "That family certainly thinks highly of their sons."

"With good reason. Oh my god, together they're unstoppable. We don't have a chance. I mean, they creamed us last year, and Royal was only a junior." By the time she finishes her tirade, her voice is a squeak of excitement and she's bouncing in her seat.

"You do know that's not the team we're supposed to be cheering for, right?"

"I really need a drink," she says. "My nerves are already fried, and the game hasn't even started."

I'm familiar with the football lust that takes over our town for half of every year, but I wasn't expecting Jolene to be quite so into it. By halftime, I still don't get what the fuss is all about. I mean, sure, the guys look good in their tight pants, even with the pads. Royal Dolce can throw a pass, I'll give him that, but so can our QB. With the helmets on, though, I still can't tell if the guys are the ones who took my picture, and that's the only reason I'm here.

At halftime, we split the warm Dr. Pepper and watch the cheerleaders, Lindsey and Elaine and all the others, shaking their pompoms and smiling their perma-smiles. I try to imagine what my life would be like if football—or anything—meant that much to me. I remember Jolene trying to convince me to join the Pep Squad in junior high, but I knew we didn't have the money, so I said no. Turns out, they had loaner uniforms for poor kids, and she was on the squad all that year.

She was in heaven, even though she was never a cheerleader like these girls.

I glance over at her, trying to see if it bothers her to watch them, since she didn't make it onto the squad when we went to high school. Or I assume that's what happened. I wasn't in school much that year, and we drifted apart. I spent most of my nights fighting and gambling to earn money for paint or prowling Faulkner, hunting for Zephyr Hertz like a stalker, so I could watch him work and learn from him when I found him. And then I slept while everyone else went to school. Took almost being held back a year to knock some sense into me, for me to realize that graffiti wasn't going to get me anything but arrested. So, a year ago I stopped painting and started saving.

"I can't take this," Jolene says. "Let's go smoke under the bleachers."

We make our way down. I don't ask for a smoke because I don't spend money on them. I save every penny for a one-way ticket out. But I accept when Jolene offers to share one. I inhale the bitter smoke and let my head fall back, exhaling toward the stands above, where all the families in Faulkner mill about. At no other time could you see all the town gathered this way, but it's still divided. The Willow Heights side of the stands is full of all the rich people, the families with money, the important people.

Above us, it's a sea of black and brown and white faces, half of them bi-racial or tri-racial or some kaleidoscope like me; lots of poor and middle class with a few rich families mixed in. Our side is Faulkner. Willow Heights' side is another dimension, another reality, another world. And I'm about to cross the invisible, unspoken line, the one that keeps our schools apart. I'm about to break the barrier, to dare to speak to them as if we're equals. But I don't care about that shit right now. I care about saving my future.

When the game finally ends, I make a beeline for the parking lot. Fans of both teams stream out into the bright light of the parking lot. People are yelling about a party somewhere, and a bonfire, and swimming. I don't know if it's all at one place, and I really don't care. I'm not here for the afterparty.

I find the SUV I'm looking for, the Range Rover, and lean against the grill.

"What are you doing?" Jolene whisper-screams. "Whose car is this?"

"I hope it's Royal Dolce's," I say. "You don't have to wait if Tater Bug's here to pick you up."

"Royal Dolce?" she squeaks. "Why are you touching his car?"

"I need to talk to him."

She grabs me by the arm and drags me a few feet away. "You don't just go up to Royal Dolce and talk to him," she hisses.

People are looking at us with curiosity, lingering to see what happens. Apparently, I'm not the only one who knows what car the Dolce boys drive.

"It's not like they're the president," I say. "They're our age."

"Their dad is basically the president of Faulkner."

I shrug and resume my spot on the bumper of the SUV.

Jolene gnaws at her lip for a minute, then nods. "If you really want their attention, you should be lying on the hood naked when they walk up. Otherwise, what's to set you apart from all the other girls who chase after them?"

"Not a bad idea," I say, cracking my knuckles. "I'll save that one for later."

I spot two boys walking our way, and from the reaction, I have a feeling things are about to get interesting. People step back, looking unsure and almost afraid. Girls are obviously checking them out, but I notice that none of them throw themselves at the boys. So, they aren't rock stars at Willow Heights—not exactly.

I have time to take in the three of them and recognize them as the guys from the tracks. The one who almost killed me is taller than the other two, and from the height difference on the field, I know that one must be Royal. My heart skips a beat and then races to catch up when our eyes meet.

While the guys stroll toward me with the kind of natural swagger that must come with millions of dollars and the body of a god, I have a few seconds to consider whether I'm doing something suicidal. I force myself not to move. This is a different situation. At the tracks, they were out wreaking havoc. There was no one around to stop them. Now, they'll want to look cool in front of all their friends and peers.

They're not going to go psycho in the parking lot of the stadium with a hundred families around.

Are they?

They must be aware that all eyes are on them, but they don't even glance around. They don't slow when they see us leaning on their car, either.

Actually, it's just me. Jolene has disappeared. But whatever. This isn't her fight.

"Get off my car."

His voice is colder than I expected. There's no laughter or teasing in it, none of the playfulness I expect from guys who are all that and know it. His voice holds none of the taunting that Duke's held when he mocked Mr. Behr's authority, and none of the cockiness I expect him to show in front of a crowd.

Royal stops right in front of me, just inches away. His face is blank and hard as stone. I remember that dead-eyed blackness in his gaze from the tracks, and a shiver races across my skin.

My tongue is suddenly tied tight to the roof of my mouth, and no words come. I'm not usually intimidated by assholes, but I've never been around rich assholes. I swear the guy smells like money. His dark hair is still wet from the post-game shower, and he has a football bag slung over one muscular shoulder. The two others stand back from him, watching. Duke, the running back, wears a cocky grin on his face, and the guy with glasses—Baron Dolce, according to Jolene—stands with his head cocked, like he's curious to see where this is all going. Like the last time I saw him, he has a sucker tucked into his cheek, the stem poking out between his lips.

"I said, get off my car."

I swallow, forcing my eyes to Royal again. People are starting to gather nearby, waiting for a show.

"I want the picture erased," I say, my voice low but firm.

He draws back just a fraction of an inch, but it's enough for me to know. Probably no one else notices. Probably no one else sees the faint flicker of something—I don't know what—cross his face before it goes blank again.

"I don't know what you're talking about."

I press my palms against his bumper, steadying myself. "I think you do."

"If you know what's good for you, you'll walk away right now," he says, his voice as low as mine but edged with warning.

"Are you threatening me?"

"I don't have your picture," he says. "Now go."

"Not until you erase it."

He leans closer, so close I can smell that he brushed his teeth after the game. His eyes fix on mine, hard and mean. I lean back instinctually, trying to keep my space. He keeps leaning in. When I'm bent back against the hood of his Range Rover, he exhales a little snort of breath and pulls away.

"Suit yourself," he says with a shrug, heading around the car. He hops up in, and the others follow. A second later, the lights sweep across the lot, and the engine roars to life. I leap away from the car to the sound of their laughter inside. The windows slide down, as if to make sure I hear how funny they find all this.

The sound of their celebration seems to unfreeze the crowd, and everyone starts hurrying away to their own cars, whispering about the little scene. Baron hangs out the window when a group of girls in short skirts walked by, swishing their long hair.

"Here, kitty kitty," he calls.

Faulkner High's mascot is the Wampus Cat, and annoyingly, the women's teams are Wampus Kittens. But I have a feeling he's looking for a different kind of pussy.

The girls giggle and bump together, casting excited glances over their shoulders, nearly swooning that the richest guys in town just paid them some attention.

"Let's par-tay," Duke Dolce yells from the passenger seat, pumping his fist. "I'm getting anal tonight!"

Royal revs the engine, and the Range Rover roars away, leaving me in the parking lot with way too many people staring and no way home. I hurry away, my heart pounding. I'm not scared of the ugly side of Faulkner, of running the streets at night when the gangs come out. But put me on the spot, with everyone staring, and my palms start sweating and my heartbeat gets all erratic.

All the way home, I curse myself for this stupid plan. I missed Femme Fight Friday, which is my big money night. I can try to make up for it tomorrow at cards, but I'll have to pull from my stash to buy in. I usually use Friday's money as my buy-in on Saturday, then add it all to the stash together. Somehow it feels like less of a loss if it hasn't been tucked into my floorboard yet. And I'll have to win a lot bigger tomorrow to make up for missing a Friday night fight.

I don't look over my shoulder for gangs or hooligans on my way home. I only look over my shoulder when I hear the roar of an engine that could be the black Range Rover. Of course it's not. It's just a truckload of Faulkner High boys whooping about their win as they roar by, tossing empties and knocking over mailboxes in celebration. A beer bottle shatters at my feet, and they careen away, laughing hysterically at their cleverness. But they know who I am, and they won't fuck with me.

Monday morning, it's back to the grindstone. I'm in the middle of first period when the intercom crackles to life. "Harper Apple to the office," the secretary drones. "Have her bring her stuff."

Blue shoots me a questioning look, but I just shrug and grab my books before heading out. No one pays me any mind. At a school like Faulkner, if you're not the kind of kid in the advanced classes, you're the kind who's had your share of trips to the office.

"You're going to be about the happiest young lady in the world this morning," gushes the guidance counselor, Mrs. Peterson, when I arrive in the office. She gestures for me to follow her to her office. She's one of those ladies who talks like she's in a competition to be America's Most Smiley instead of a dead-end job trying to convince a bunch of derelicts to go to college. And even though she's fake as fuck—there's no way someone could genuinely be that happy dealing with the punks she does—I like Mrs. Peterson. She didn't laugh at me when I said I wanted to go to college out of town, maybe even out of state. She brought me brochures.

"What's up?" I ask. "You got me early admission to Yale?"

"Not quite yet," she says, holding up a finger as she circles her desk to take a seat. "You'll have to do that part on your own. But I just got you a heck of a lot closer."

"Really?" I ask, taking the seat across from her and accepting the papers she slides across to me, a fat stack with a cover letter bearing a gold seal at the top. The letters WHPA top a crest stamped into it, with some Latin words circling it.

"Well, now, if I'm being honest, I can't take a lick of credit for it," Mrs. Peterson says with a little laugh. "It just showed up in my inbox this morning."

I look at it for a minute before raising my eyes to hers, my heart beating crazily in my chest. "Willow Heights? That's a high school."

"One that sends a whole heap of kids off to universities," she says. "Even Ivy League schools." She wiggles her brows like we're in on some grand shenanigan together.

"I don't get it," I say, flipping to the next page in the packet.

"The Lord works in mysterious ways," she says. "Remember to thank him in your prayers tonight."

I sit there for a second, trying to take in what's happening. Why is she telling me to go to the rich kids' school, the one across town where people drive Bentleys and Porsches, not rusted out hoopties with trash bags taped over the windows. Those people live in the kind of houses that my mother cleans, not owns. Why would I want to go there?

I push the packet back across the desk. "I can't afford Willow Heights."

"You don't have to," the counselor says. "It's a scholarship. A *full* scholarship, Miss Apple. They only give out a handful of those every year, usually to freshmen who will be with them for the whole of high school. I don't know how they got wind of you, but I'll tell you what. If I were you, I'd sign that so quick the ink wasn't even dry before I had it on its way back to them. A girl like you doesn't get a chance like this too often."

I bristle even though she's right. It still sucks when even the nice teachers who want to help you think you're trash. *A girl like me.* If I had a fucking dime for every time someone used that phrase.

I think of Mr. D's words, and a shiver goes through me. He said I'd see how he could put his money where his mouth was, how he could grant my wishes and show how powerful he was. Is that what's happening? Is this all funded by some creeper with a savior complex… Or one who wants me to owe him?

So yeah, there's this part of me that wants to toss the packet in the trash and flounce off like a brat. But I'm not a brat. A bitch, sure, but I'm not spoiled enough to be a brat.

And I'm sure as fuck not dumb enough to turn down this scholarship, however it's funded. Hell, I've sucked teacher dick to get out of this town before. Signing my name on a scholarship? Piece of fucking cake. There's really no decision to be made. I wanted a way out, and now I have one… At least a hell of a lot better shot at one.

If this is Mr. D's doing, so be it. I'm not dumb enough to think he won't want something in exchange for this. Nothing in life is free, after all. But I'll pay that price when the tax man comes calling. Just because I know I'm in debt doesn't mean I'm not going to take a chance when it falls in my lap. I have nothing that's worth more than this paper right here. I'm already getting the better end of the deal.

Plus, I didn't promise him anything.

Hell, for all I know, it has nothing to do with Mr. D at all. It could be just a coincidence. It could be a million things. All I know is, I've spent my whole life feeling helpless and hopeless as I scrabbled to climb out of the lake of shit and into a boat that takes me to something better, and suddenly, someone threw me a lifeline. It doesn't matter what the cost is. I'm grabbing hold and holding on with all I've got.

"Mrs. Peterson?" I ask, sliding the form back to her with my signature accepting the offer. "Is there any way to know who paid for this scholarship? I'd like to send them a thank you card."

I add that last part just to increase the likelihood that she'll tell me, since I have absolutely zero intention of writing a card if it's Mr. D. I have a feeling the thanks he'll want can't be written on paper.

She frowns as she flips through the packet. "Well, there's a spot for a donor's name, but this one just says 'The rest is up to you.' I guess you just got lucky, didn't you?"

I'm not sure if lucky is the word for what I got, but I know better than to walk away from money when it's handed to me. So, I leave with Mrs. Peterson's words running through my head, wondering exactly what price I'll end up paying for my stroke of luck but also knowing that even if I was told the price, I'd still make the same choice. When you have no other options, you take the one that's available, no matter the cost.

I want to get out of Faulkner. If this is a path out, I'll take it. If it isn't a path out, then I'll make it one. My scholarship may be shady as fuck, bought and paid for by some rich perv, but once I'm in, I'll make it legit. I'll prove I'm worthy of putting their esteemed logo on my resume by working so hard that colleges will be recruiting my ghetto ass right along with all the straight-A rich girls who go there.

I'm not naïve enough to think it'll be easy. A school like that is competitive. Not to mention the fact that people there probably don't want trailer trash like me walking the hallowed halls of their palace of snobbery. But I'm not worried about them. Let those southern belles try to stop me. There's nothing they can do that seventeen years on the wrong side of the tracks hasn't prepared me for.

Who We Are

Outsiders
Who forced our way inside
We came, we saw, we conquered
Went in swinging
Came out grinning
That's how we roll—
The Dolce boys.

This town is ours
We own it
But it doesn't own us
They don't revere us
They fear us
That's how we rule—
The Dolce Boys.

We don't belong here
They don't want us
But they obey us
We three kings
Together alone
A brotherhood of blood—
The Dolce boys.

six

Harper Apple

It happens so fast. I don't try to slow it down, though. I'm halfway afraid someone's fucking with me, that I'll get to Willow Heights and they'll have no record of my enrollment. The following Monday, I'm walking up to the front doors of the most exclusive private school in the state, thinking surely I'm dreaming. The school motto stretches above the doors, some Latin shit I can't even read.

What am I doing here?

I've never set foot in this school or even driven by, but I've heard stories about the kids who go here, criminals of a different caliber than the ones at Faulkner High. I've heard about the legendary parties where pure cocaine is the drug of choice instead of dime bags of schwag. I've seen the kind of delinquents who take pictures of hopeless girls performing desperate acts in the back of teachers' cars.

What's a place like that want with a girl like you? Mom asked, a cigarette dangling from the corner of her mouth as she signed the transfer papers. *Isn't that a good school?*

This isn't the kind of place you want to look weak.

I walk in like I'm daring anyone to fuck with me, not making a scene or trying to draw attention but not hiding who I am, either. I march into the office, a quiet, carpeted reception area that looks nothing like the bustling office at FHS, always full of assholes arguing loudly about their tardies, detentions, and suspensions. Instead of dark blue plastic chairs with scarred edges sitting along the wall, this office has chairs with padding and wooden arms.

Everything in this entire school, from the marble-floored lobby to the dudes strutting by in khakis and buttoned shirts, says I don't belong here. I try not to care, to let it roll off me. But I can't help the anxiety nibbling at my nerves. I'm out of my element, and I hate that feeling.

The receptionist pushes a button and then tells me a student council member will meet me to show me around. I tell her I can figure it out, but she insists. A few minutes later, a big girl clomps in wearing a pair of combat boots with a plaid schoolgirl skirt, her curly red hair pulled up in a bun but already losing a few locks, like she can't quite contain it in the style.

She's everything I don't expect from a Willow Heights chick, and to be honest, it puts me at ease a little. I thought this was one of those snooty schools where every girl was a perfect prima-donna, but maybe it's more modern, one of the private schools that hides the snootiness behind an all-inclusive façade.

"Ready?" my guide asks, holding open the office door for me.

"You're showing me around?"

"Yep," she says, flashing me a smile. She waves to the receptionist before letting the door swing shut behind us. "What, you didn't expect a fat girl to be the first face you saw at Willow Heights?"

I shrug. "Rich kids must come in all sizes, too. It was your clothes more than your size that threw me."

"As long as it follows dress code—collared shirts and slacks for boys, skirts two inches above the knee or slacks for girls—you can wear anything you want. Oh, and jeans on Fridays, but no rips."

There's a lot more to the dress code than that, including no logos and even a list of acceptable patterns, but I can read that in the handbook.

"How'd you get stuck with this job?" I ask. "Detention?"

The girl stifles a giggle. "I'm on student council, and we're in charge of showing the newbies around," she explains as we head down the hall. "You're lucky, really. You could do a lot worse than me. I'm Dixie, by the way. I'm a junior. What grade are you in?"

"Same," I say. "And I really don't need to be shown around. I'm sure you have something better to do, and this school is like tenth the size of Faulkner."

"You're from FHS?" she asks, pointing out my first class. "I went there—well, actually, I left after Middle, but I would have gone there. That school is so freaking big! You probably have like a million friends. Do you know Chase London?"

I roll my eyes. Of course she wants to know that. "I know *of* him," I say. "But no, I don't know him. We… Don't move in the same circles."

Chase is a football god at Faulkner, while I'm more the type to hang out under the bleachers and smoke a joint than cheer for the team.

"Oh, right," Dixie says. "I bet you only know, like, a tiny fraction of the student body. I know everyone here. I'm a wealth of information. If you need anything, make sure you come find me, okay?"

"Sure," I say, already knowing I won't. I'm not here to make friends. I just want to get a report card, send off my resume, and sail out of this town. And hell, my first day is starting out a million times easier than I expected. This girl's not a snob or a bitch. If everyone at WHPA is this chill, it'll be smooth sailing all the way. If not… Fake it 'til you make it.

Dixie points out my last class and flashes a smile. "Now let me show you the cafeteria, and we'll be done. Think you'll remember where everything is?"

"Not a problem," I assure her.

"Okay, good," she says. "Now, they just remodeled the café, and the food's real good, and healthy, too. But it's still a high school cafeteria, if you know what I mean."

"Right," I mutter. "Even rich kids have a pecking order. What's it ranked by, how much your car costs?"

Dixie laughs. "You can sit with me and my friends. My cousin Quinn's new this year, too. We sit over there." She points to one of the round wooden tables in the big room. It looks about as far from the white linoleum and prison-style dining of Faulkner High as the office looked different. Instead of drop ceilings with long fluorescent lights, giant fans and modern lights extend down from the vaulted ceiling here. The chairs are almost standard school chairs, but even those are a sleeker model, like the school had to flex a little and splurge on even cafeteria chairs.

"I'm sure I'll be fine," I say. I realize I'm being kinda bitchy for no reason. This girl seems genuinely interested in helping me out—or helping the school or herself get a gold star in student council. Not that it matters why she's being nice. The point is, she could have been a total bitch to a scholarship kid, but she wasn't.

"I know," Dixie says. "Just don't sit alone, okay? We can always make room at our table."

"Thanks," I say, forcing a smile. I'm not used to people being nice to me for no reason. "I'm not really into the whole social scene thing. I'll probably find the other scholarship kids and stick with my kind. Don't worry, I won't sit alone like some charity case. I'll come find you if I have any questions."

"One more thing," Dixie says, her eyes earnest as we leave the cafeteria and head back toward my first class. "You're new, and you're pretty, and you're bound to draw some attention."

Her eyes flit to my clothes, and I cringe inwardly even as I raise my chin and give her a level gaze, feeling instantly defensive. "What's wrong with the way I look?"

In truth, I didn't know what to wear to a school like this. Despite what I'd heard, there's not even an official uniform here. I've already seen a few girls wearing plaid skirts, so it must be the trend, but it's not required, and thank fuck for that. My mother would have thrown the papers back in my face if I asked her to pay for a uniform. As I suspected, she's definitely on the party bus with this new guy. Her hands shook so hard she could hardly hold the pen when she signed my transfer papers.

But I don't have a plaid schoolgirl skirt to my name, which left me to cobble something together from my very limited wardrobe. I dreaded getting dressed this morning. At Faulkner, I never thought much about what I wore. I just threw on whatever was clean. But even a bitch like me can feel the burn of shame in my cheeks when I think about all those kids staring at me, knowing I'm a poor charity case, judging me for the way I dress.

"Nothing's wrong with your clothes," Dixie says quickly. "I'm just trying to warn you. Some people here can be pretty nasty to new kids. Girls and guys. It's best if you just stay out of their way, but it'll be hard for the first few days. This school is small. Any new kid gets noticed. Just get through that, and you'll be fine."

"Like an initiation?" I ask, cocking a brow.

"Nothing so formal as all that," Dixie says, waving a hand. "But the Dolce boys like everyone to know from the moment they set foot in here that they run this place. I bet you have guys like that at Faulkner High. Like Chase London. Well, the

Dolces are the kings of Willow Heights. Just bow at their feet and kiss their shoes and all that, show them you're not here to cause any trouble, and they'll forget all about you in a couple days."

I look at her incredulously. True, I'm not here to cause trouble. But kiss someone's shoes? Not if it's the last thing I ever do. And fuck if I'm bowing at anyone's feet. I bow to no one.

"Just tell me what to look out for," I say. "And I'll walk the other way when I see them coming."

Her eyes widen a bit. "You don't know who the Dolces are?"

"I know them," I admit, a flutter of nerves starting inside me. "I mean, I've heard the name around town. I don't *know* them. Who else do I need to look out for?"

I didn't know I was supposed to study up on the important people of this town before my first day, but obviously I'm underprepared in several ways.

"I was gonna say," she says with a little laugh. "You have to know the Dolces. They're the family who took down the

Darlings." She widens her eyes at me, her expression expectant, like it'll all click into place for me.

I shrug.

"You don't know who the *Darlings* are?" she asks, her voice squeaking a bit with shock.

"Of course I do." It's a small town, and the Darlings basically founded it. But as I said about Chase, I don't move in the same circles as powerful people like them. They seem faraway, a name thrown around like the mayor or the governor. One of the Darling daughters goes to FHS, but she's a cheerleader who dates Chase and takes AP classes. She's never said a word to me. I know their name, their importance, but besides her, I probably couldn't pick a single one from a lineup.

"Okay, well, the Dolces are… New royalty in this town. And they didn't get that way by being worshipped by the townsfolk for their benevolence." A soft chime sounds overhead instead of the jarring ring of a bell. Dixie glances toward the front entrance and back to me. "They're not nice people, Harper. They have their reasons for being the way they are, but that's not really important. Just steer clear if you see them or their little harem of Dolce girls coming, and you'll be fine."

"And how do I know which ones they are?" I press.

"Look for the hottest guys you've ever seen," she says. "You can't miss them. Tall, dark, full of muscles. Kinda thuggish, in a hot way. But try to admire from a distance. You really don't want to get mixed up with them. Trust me on that one. They're brutal."

I meant the girls, but my heart skips when her words call a picture to mind… A picture of the three guys at the train tracks, all of them sharing an accent and a name that doesn't belong in these parts. The students are strolling in now, though, and it's too late to ask more, so I thank Dixie and head back toward the locker she pointed out for me.

The wheels in my brain are already turning. I head into class, but I can't concentrate. I keep thinking about Dixie's warning, how it paints a different picture of the Dolces than the image Jolene had in her mind. They're more than the hot guys that every girl wants on her arm to increase her status. They're assholes. I could have told her that, but it's different for them to be assholes to me down in poor town than to be known for it in the halls of their own school.

How am I going to convince them to delete that picture? They haven't shared it with the world as far as I know, though that doesn't mean much. I don't exactly frequent the internet looking for homemade porn shot through the windows of parked cars. Still, it's not circulating at FHS, which means it hasn't traveled too far from their circle of privilege. I may not have any tight friendships, but that doesn't mean someone wouldn't tell me.

Hell, the entire population of Faulkner would probably harass me about it. I'd get the dreaded Slut Club invitation dropped on my desk, and no one would ever speak to me again except the other "sluts" in the club and the lowlife guys who sniff around them hoping to get some while pretending they're throwing the girls a bone. If the pic shows Mr. Behr, it'd be a scandal big enough to rock this whole shitty little town. Probably big enough to make Willow Heights retract my scholarship. This is the type of school that expects its students to behave even when we're not at school, to be examples to the community, not porn stars.

I still have time to do some damage control before that happens. If only I had someone to go to for help. Maybe I should have joined one of the gangs at Faulkner, after all. I never felt the need to have someone watching my back. I look out for myself, and I've always liked it that way. Plus, I don't want to owe anyone anything, and once you're in a gang, it's a life sentence. The only person I'll ride or die for is myself. It's easier that way. I don't have to wonder about ulterior motives, getting played, or being left. I trust the only person in life I know I can trust—myself.

But coming here is like stepping into an alien world, one where I don't know the rules, who's the enemy, or what's expected of me. By lunch time, I'm already regretting my dismissal of Dixie's offer. Still, I've never shied away from anything that can make me stronger, so I tell myself that toughing it out on my own is only going to put another layer of armor on me. I put my books up and head for the café alone, despite Dixie's warning.

I'm not three steps from my locker when a girl's bitchy voice cuts through my determination.

"Oh my god, who is that skank?"

"Why do they even let scholarship kids in here?" another equally bitchy voice muses. "They make the whole school look cheap."

I turn to see a trio of girls with straight-ironed blonde hair, perfect makeup, heels, matching schoolgirl skirts, and white shirts unbuttoned just enough to show a hint of cleavage. They all wear matching monogram necklaces.

D.

My mind immediately lands on the guy I think is responsible for my scholarship, and I wonder if I'm going to have to join the clone squad and wear his necklace like a brand because I'm now one of his kept girls.

But just as quickly as it comes, I dismiss the ridiculous thought. These must be the southern belles I anticipated, rich bitches who don't need a scholarship. The necklaces could be anything—a sorority or secret organization or the "harem" of Dolce girls Dixie mentioned. If so, those boys have a very specific type.

I ignore them and walk off down the hall because they're not worth it. I have no beef with them, and if they're smart, they won't start shit with someone they don't know. They have no idea what I'm capable of. I'm not in a hurry to show them, but if they fuck with me, I'm not going to lie down and take it like a pussy.

"Hey," one of the girls barks at me, but I keep on walking. "Don't walk away from me. I'm talking to you!"

I notice a few others looking our way, thirsty for drama. A cluster of nervous looking girls huddles back against their lockers, their eyes darting from me to the hall behind me. I flash them a peace sign and keep going.

When I reach the café doors, a hand clamps around my arm, sharp nails biting in. I turn to see the D girls, all of them looking a bit flustered and indignant, like they can't believe my audacity just because I wanted to get to lunch. I'm not about to miss a meal for these bitches. Not when I don't know if I'll have one at home tonight.

"You're going to want to take your hands off me," I warn the girl who grabbed me.

She jerks her hand back and smooths her hair, which is a bit out of place from scurrying down the hall after me.

Her lip curls into a sneer, and she looks me up and down. "Where did you even get that outfit?" she asks with disdain in her voice.

I can't help but snort at her sheer pettiness. "You chased me all the way down the hall to ask that?"

She huffs and glances at her friends for backup. "You can't just come up in here wearing that," she says. "It's against dress code."

"Oh no," I say, covering my mouth in mock horror. "Call security. That extra inch of thigh might cause a riot."

Her mouth drops open in a way that's too comical. I drop my hand from my mouth and crack a smile at her.

She doesn't smile back.

"Seriously," one of the others asks, giving me some serious stink-eye as she flips her hair back over her shoulder. "What are you wearing?"

"Your boyfriend's cologne," I say. I mimic her bitchy hair-flip, though my mess of hair has never seen a flat-iron in its life. Turning on my heel, I walk away again.

New Girl

They say her name is Apple
But she doesn't look like an apple:
Blonde hair to the shoulders
held back with a pastel headband,
A skirt to the knees,
a matching cardigan.
Sweet and bland.
She looks like black cherry:
Dark hair tangled from a roll in the sheets,
Skirt so short it shows a glimpse of tats on thick, juicy thighs,
Round little tits,
a waist to fit my hands around,
a nice big ass to bury a dick in.
Black cherry
When you bite in the juice runs
like blood down your chin,
Dark and bitter,
With just a touch of sweet
when you take the time to savor it good and deep
Where it hurts.

seven

Harper Apple

This time, the bitchy girls don't follow me. I head for the food at the front, a buffet style setup where people mill around instead of standing in an agonizingly long line like the one at my old school. There, the popular kids cut in front until the losers ended up at the back of the line every day, a place that gave them about five minutes to scarf down whatever tepid scraps were left by the time they got through.

Here, there are no losers.

I take in the room as I make my way across. I'm used to the public school clique system, though I always hated it. Now, I can see the advantages. I don't know who belongs where in this place, which means I don't know where I belong. It's not like there's a table in the corner with a sign proclaiming it the scholarship table. The school doesn't have a uniform, per se, but its dress code is almost the same as one, which makes it even harder to single anyone out. A sea of rich white kids mills around the food, with an occasional brown or Black person, as if they're trying to hide the painfully obvious truth that they in no way reflect the makeup of Faulkner, where about third of the population is not white.

Thank god you're not as dark as your father. Gary has certain opinions about that, and he's helping me move out of this place and into a house, a real nice house, because he's a nice guy, and he knows a guy who rents it out. You understand? You better be grateful and don't go stirring up trouble.

Yeah, Mom, this guy who calls people like my father 'mutts' is a real nice guy. But don't worry, I've never known any other side of myself, anyway, so I'll pretend it doesn't exist.

The smell of money practically makes me lightheaded as I wade into the lunch crowd.

I bite back my nerves, an ominous feeling settling at the base of my skull. I don't like not knowing how things fit, and it puts me on edge. Instead of a roar you can barely hear yourself think over, the room is hushed. I feel like everyone's waiting for… Something.

I use the stainless-steel tongs to pick up some lightly fried chicken, then put a roll on my plate with it. A second later, a hand snatches it off my plate.

I look up to find one of the brothers from the tracks standing there holding my roll, a smug smile on his face as he bites off a piece of it and chews, watching me. It's the one with glasses, Baron Dolce. Though I was so hopped up on adrenaline the two times I've seen him that I paid zero attention to his attractiveness, Dixie is right. The guy is gorgeous, no doubt. Dark hair with just a hint of curl, dark eyes you could get lost in, bone structure of a cologne model, body of an underwear model.

I sigh and get another roll, but just as quickly, he grabs that one, too.

"Really?" I ask, reaching for another.

"I'll just take that one, too," he says, plucking the third one away. "Freshmen don't get rolls."

"Good thing I'm not a freshman," I say, reaching in again. I consider just stopping, since I honestly don't give a fuck what I eat. My stomach is squeezing painfully at the smell of all this good food. I could eat nothing but rolls, or I could leave all the rolls, and it wouldn't make a lick of difference to me. I have no interest in fighting this guy for something as ridiculous as control of the rolls.

But I notice everyone watching already. It's too late to go unnoticed. Like Dixie said, they'll mess with me for a few days because I'm new, and then they'll move on. At a school this small, I guess all the new kids get noticed. Even if I can't win against the Dolces, I can show everyone else in the school that I'm not to be messed with. And I might as well have some fun with it if they're going to fuck with me. I take another roll, and another, and another. The guy takes them all, and pretty soon, his hands are so full he has to hold them to his chest with his forearm so they don't fall.

At last, I reach for the single remaining roll. Instead of putting it on my plate, I set it carefully atop the precariously balanced pile in his arms.

"The peasants can't afford bread, anyway, your majesty," I say with a wink. "But let us eat cake." I slide down the line, toss a scoop of roasted potatoes onto my plate, grab a square of applesauce cake, and head to the table where I spotted Dixie sitting next to a pretty redhead. My heart is hammering, and my knees feel shaky, but I hold my head high and meet everyone's eyes like a dare.

When I'm almost there, I see that there are no empty chairs. But Dixie waves frantically and scoots back to snag a chair from the next table. Bless her fucking heart. I could just about hug the girl, if I was the kind of person who did that sort of thing.

"Come sit with us," she calls.

I scoot into the chair and shoot her a smile. "Thanks."

"Everybody, this is Harper," Dixie says. "The new girl. Harper, everybody." She gestures around her packed table. Everyone sitting here is female, but none of them fit the stereotype of 'rich bitch' I had in my head, unlike the girls who accosted me in the hall. One girl even has blue hair, though it's a deep, rich blue that looks like she probably had it done at a professional salon rather than in her bathroom sink. Still, it sends a pang through me, and I wonder what Blue's up to right now. Probably choking down the prison food served in that cafeteria. I feel almost guilty as I bite into the warm, fried chicken.

"What did Baron say to you?" Dixie asks, her eyes sparkling with curiosity. Everyone goes quiet, like this is something worth gossiping about.

"Nothing," I say with a shrug. "Just stupid-boy stuff."

"Baron's not stupid," Dixie says. "He acts like a thug like the rest of them, but he's really smart. Like, genius level."

"I heard he got a perfect score on the SAT *and* the ACT last year," says another redhead.

"Oh, this is my cousin, Quinn," Dixie says. "The one I was telling you about."

Aside from the similar hair and eye color, the girls look nothing alike. Dixie's hair is curly and unruly, most of it hanging around her shoulders while the rest is still pulled up. Quinn's is straight and shiny, setting off a tan that's probably the result of some darker-skinned heritage than Dixie's pale, freckled face. While Dixie's big all over, Quinn is small and curvy.

"Huh," I say. "Never woulda guessed."

"I know, I'm the fattie of the family," Dixie says cheerfully. She bites into her roll, and I salivate at the look of it. Damn that stupid boy and his roll hoarding.

"You're not that big," Quinn mutters.

Dixie waves off her comment and pops a Brussel sprout into her mouth.

"We don't care what size you are," says the blue-haired girl, throwing an arm around Dixie's shoulders and kissing her cheek with a loud smack. "We love every inch. I'm Susanna, by the way." She flashes me a smile. "We like to mix things up around here, keep the school on its toes, if you couldn't tell."

I arch a brow, thinking it must be pretty quiet around here if dyeing your hair keeps the school on its toes. But I don't comment. If this girl wants to think she's a badass, who am I to stop her?

"Susie was new last year. We met the first day of school, and it was insta-friendship," Dixie says. "Quinn just started in August this year. How come you started a month in?"

"That's when they offered me a scholarship," I say, polishing off my chicken. An uncomfortable silence falls over the table, everyone concentrating on their food.

"We don't really talk about that here," Dixie stage-whispers.

"My bad," I say with a shrug. I'm poor and everyone knows it. There's no point in hiding it. It's not something I'm embarrassed about. "I figured it was obvious. Those bitches in the hall took one look at me and knew. So, where do the scholarship kids sit? I'll sit there tomorrow."

"They don't really have their own spot," Quinn says, her cheeks reddening through her golden complexion. "They'd just rather not advertise it."

"Got it," I say. Rich people are so weird. They don't want to talk about money, but they'll wear a thousand-dollar pair of shades with a brand name right on it for all the world to see. Maybe they have so much it makes them feel guilty to admit it out loud, so they let their clothes and cars do the talking.

On my side of town, it's the opposite. My mom and her friends can't *stop* talking about how broke they are.

Another uncomfortable silence falls, and since I'm the cause, I figure I owe it to them to change the topic and put everyone at ease again. "So, what's up with the southern belles from hell over there?" I ask.

Dixie and a couple other girls giggle.

"Those are the populars," Susanna says.

"Also known as the revolving door the Dolces go through every week," Dixie says. "Those are their girls. They're almost as mean as the guys."

"Worse," Quinn says. "Don't get on their radar, either. Especially the Walton girls."

"Which are those?" I ask, though knowing my luck, I already have an idea.

"The three who look like Barbies," Dixie says, pointing to the girls from the hall. "Gloria, Eleanor, and Everleigh. There's also a brother, Dawson. I personally like all of them, but then, I like everyone."

"She really does," Susanna says. "It's a little unfortunate."

"Hey," Dixie says. "It's not like I stop you from gossiping about them."

"Because then you'd have no platform," Quinn says.

"Anyway, about the Waltons," Susanna says, grinning as she goes back to the gossip that, apparently, Dixie approves of despite liking them. "I heard they're actually part of *the* Walton family."

"I heard they're just super rich and don't correct people who think that," Quinn says. "They *want* people to think they're Arkansas royalty."

Dixie leans in, her voice lowering as she relays the gossip. "Point is, they think because there are three of them, and three Dolces, that they're destined by god to end up together or something along those lines. They're… Territorial."

"Don't let me stand in their way," I say.

"Don't try to," Quinn says, casting a dark look at the Waltons. I take it she was a target of their vitriol, and I'm not eager to get more of it. I have zero time in my life for that kind of drama.

"I know they're mean, but I kinda feel bad for them," Dixie says. "I mean, they're obsessed with those boys, and the feeling is definitely not mutual. I think the Dolces just humor them so they can keep getting the milk for free, if you know what I mean."

"They're not the Dolces' girlfriends?" I ask.

Susanna snorts. "Definitely not. I hear Royal has a girlfriend in college, and the other two go through a different girl every weekend. Sometimes it's the Waltons, sometimes not."

"They haven't had a girlfriend since Mabel Darling, and I'm not sure I'd call her a girlfriend since they were just setting her up to take a fall."

"Last year was cray-cray," Susanna sings. "I hope there's as much drama this year. I love that shit as long as I'm not part of it."

"You really don't want to be part of it when the Dolces are involved," Dixie says. "I can't decide which one is scariest."

"Isn't it obvious?" I ask, cocking a brow. But I'm remembering those eerie, empty eyes of his, and I'm not so cavalier beneath the surface.

"You'd think," Quinn says. "But I heard Baron's, like, the mastermind behind everything they do."

"Yeah, and Duke's the kind of dude who would light you on fire and dance around while you burned," Susanna says. "My vote's on him."

They've obviously never spent any time staring into the abyss of Royal's eyes, or they'd know that he's the scary one.

He wouldn't even dance around while you burned. He'd just sit there watching with no emotion.

"I hear they have a little black book," Quinn says. "If they call, you can't say no. You have to go and let them do whatever they want to you. And it might be super twisted."

"Why would anyone agree to that?" I ask.

"Because they called," Dixie says, widening her eyes like I'm missing something obvious. "You can't say no to the Dolces. They take anything they want, and no one stops them. You couldn't if you tried. They run this town, Harper. I don't think you realize the influence they have."

Just then, the Walton girls come mincing past, each of them trailed by a nervous looking girl carrying a plate.

"Good morning, Gossip Girls," says the one Dixie pointed out as Gloria, though it's hard to tell them apart with all that flawless makeup and matching outfits. Looking at that much perfection is a bit blinding.

"Hey, Lo," Dixie says.

"Anything new on the blog?" Her voice is cheerful and sweetly accented with southern charm, but I can't tell if she's faking the benevolent smile.

"Not yet," Dixie says. "I'll have it up tonight."

"Looks like y'all forgot to take out the trash," says Everleigh, wrinkling her nose at me.

"You're so right," I say, imitating their sweet-as-candy tone. "Let me take you out right now."

Eleanor huffs with indignation. The girl behind her cowers visibly. All three of them are just standing there waiting, and I realize they're actually holding the Waltons' plates like little servant girls.

"I've got some advice for you," Gloria hisses at me, her eyes narrowing into ugly slits. She leans down, enveloping me in a cloud of sweet, flowery perfume that contradicts the savage look in her eyes. She grits out three words, each one coming slow and fierce. "Know—your—place."

With that, she straightens and swishes off, snapping her fingers for her minion to follow. The other sisters and their servants fall in behind her, the six of them trailing over to the tables where the Dolce brothers sit with three other guys and three girls. The Waltons sit, and the three nervous girls set their plates down in front of them and scurry away.

"What the fuck was all that about?" I ask.

"You really don't want to get on their bad side," Quinn says, wiping her palms on her thighs.

"You're friends with them?" I ask Dixie.

She shifts around, looking uncomfortable. "Not friends, exactly. We have a symbiotic relationship."

I narrow my eyes at her.

"What?" she asks. "What can I say, I'm a nosy bitch, and I like gossip."

Susanna takes over, grinning as she recounts the story. "One day last year, she was moaning about how she'd never hear all the gossip because we're not exactly popular. But then she decided she'd become popular, not so she could hear all the gossip, but by relaying all the gossip she did hear."

"It just kinda snowballed from there," Dixie says. "People started coming to me for gossip, or to tell me gossip. I'm not really popular, but I don't care anymore. It's not like I'm famous, but everyone from Willow Heights reads the blog and knows me. And no one messes with me the way they did before that, calling me fat and stuff."

"Because you can destroy them," Susanna pronounces with a triumphant smile.

I watch the three girls who were trailing the Waltons scurry back from the food line and set plates in front of the Dolce boys.

"They have servants?" I ask.

Dixie nods. "Sort of. The Dolces pick freshmen or newbies and make them carry their plates and clean up after them—and their flavors of the week."

"So fucked up," I say, shaking my head.

"At least it doesn't last long," Dixie says, giving Quinn a sympathetic smile. "When the Darlings ran this place, you could be their whipping boy for a whole year. The Dolces have a much shorter attention span. No one holds their interest for more than a week or two at a time. The Walton girls are just enjoying the perks while they have them."

I turn to Quinn. "You were their slave?"

"For a couple weeks," she says, her face reddening. "You probably will be, too. New girl and all."

I turn to look at the table where the three boys and their entourage sit. A jolt goes through me when I find Royal staring straight at me. I quickly turn away, shaken by the funny flutter of my pulse.

"Don't count on it," I mutter.

"I heard Mr. Dolce pays pretty much everyone's salary at this school," Quinn says. "Some people say he gets his money from *the mafia*." She whispers the last word like she thinks the mob might overhear and come whack her.

"I heard they just let people think that, like the Waltons," Susanna says. "They want people to be scared of them, but just because they're Italian doesn't mean they're mobsters. Jenna said when she was sleeping with Duke, she asked him, and he said they weren't."

"Either way," Quinn says. "He's still super rich and besties with the mayor."

"I can attest to that," Dixie says. "The mayor is my step-uncle, and they're always golfing together, going to the country club, all that." She keeps on about her uncle, but my mind is stuck on the name of a man influential enough to make a snooty school add an extra scholarship a month into the school year. A man whose last name starts with a D.

But if Mr. Dolce is Mr. D, and he's the man who brought me here, I can't help but wonder. Why? And why me?

What We Hear

Go ask your mother,
Can't you see I'm busy?
Somebody has to earn the money around here,
And you know your mother isn't going to earn a dime.
The least she can do
Is take you off my hands.

Go ask your father,
Can't you see I'm busy?
There's this party downtown,
A benefit for the children.
Don't you want me to help
The unfortunate children?

But before you go,
Did you see my new earrings?
Your father got them for me,
Ten thousand-dollar diamonds,
Aren't they pretty?
Maria Giancursio will eat her heart out.

Speaking of…
Did you see her dress at the gala last week?
Who wore it best,
Maria or the dime-store whore
Down on the corner?
I'd vote the whore.

A decent woman saves it for the bedroom.

BAD APPLE

Make sure you pick a nice girl
Who leaves something for the imagination.
If she lets anyone see it,
She lets anyone touch it.
My sons deserve better
Than someone who's already been used.

Now go on,
That's all the time I have for you today,
I've got to finish getting ready.
I can't wait to see their faces when I walk in
With diamonds dripping from my ears
And a perfectly exquisite, tasteful dress
To save the unfortunate children.

eight

Harper Apple

By Thursday, I've pretty much settled into school. I still don't fit, but I try not to care. I'm not here to fit in and make friends and all that shit. I'm here to get an education that Faulkner High can't come close to offering. Just two years, and I'll leave this place and never look back. I'll never have to see these people again. What does it matter if they think my shorts are too short or my midriff too scandalous?

I'm just sitting down at lunch that day when an ear-piercing whistle echoes through the room. Conversations die, the room falling silent.

"They're calling you," Dixie says, her eyes glimmering with excitement as she cuts them toward the Dolce boys and their girls.

"Yeah, well, I don't answer to dog whistles," I say. "If they want to say something to me, they can come and say it."

"You have to go over there," Susanna says, like it's the perfectly obvious thing to do.

I shrug. "What are they going to do, lasso me and drag me across the room? I don't *have* to do anything for them."

"It's not that bad," Quinn whispers. "I mean, they say some rude stuff about your boobs, and everyone laughs at you, but then it's over. You don't have to have it hanging over your head, wondering when they're going to single you out and what they'll do. You bring them their lunch for a few days and do a couple other demeaning things, and then they move on. It's better to get it over with."

I shrug. "I'm not going over there. If they want me, they can come and get me."

"Hey." A deep voice cuts through the expectant silence in the café. "New girl. I know you heard me."

There's no point in making a bigger spectacle by ignoring them. I turn in my chair. All three of the Dolces are looking at me. Baron, looking at me through his glasses like he's examining a cadaver in biology, a sucker tucked into his cheek yet again. Duke, the brother who mouthed off to Mr. Behr in the parking lot, is the one who spoke. He's a bit bulkier than Baron, his hair a bit shorter, but they look like twins anyway.

And Royal.

His shoulders are broad, filling out the collared shirt that must be custom tailored to his huge frame, his muscles showing even through the fabric. His big hands rest on the table in front of him, his fingers long and thick and tanned. Damn. Even his hands are sexy.

I let my eyes travel back to his face, the sculpted jawline that could cut glass, a strong, straight nose, lips that would make any girl melt. But it's his eyes that really get you.

I don't like to meet Royal's eyes. There's too much there to unpack. It doesn't help that when he looks at me with that quiet, intense stare, I feel like he can see right through me. It also doesn't help that all three of the guys are fucking gorgeous, the kind of gorgeous that makes butterflies swarm in your stomach and gets your mind all confused because you're not sure if you're hot and flustered for them or terrified of all that strength and power coming at you. Even though Royal doesn't say much, I can tell he's the one in control, the one with the most power of all of them. And now he's staring at me like his eyes want to consume my soul.

My soul wants to let him.

I jerk my gaze from his, offer a little wave, and turn back to my table.

"Get your ass over here," Duke says behind me.

"I'm good, thanks," I call over my shoulder, but I don't turn back to them. I answer to no one but myself.

"It wasn't a request." Royal's voice is quieter than Duke's, but it carries across the room even better, everyone going dead silent to hear when he speaks.

"Go," Dixie says, her eyes wide with alarm. "They're going to kill you."

I do a double take when I realize she looks genuinely scared, her face pale beneath her freckles.

"Yeah, go," Susanna says. "Before they take it out on us."

"Really?" I ask, skeptically cocking a brow.

"Yes," Quinn says, staring down at her crostini toast. "You don't know how things work around here yet. But you just have to do what they want."

"Well, I wouldn't want the big bad bullies to mess with you because of me," I concede.

"No, you wouldn't," Susanna says. "I'm fine with you sitting with us, and Dixie sees the good in everyone, even the Waltons, and she can't resist a charity case, but if you bring down the wrath of the Dolces on her after everything she's done for you—"

"Whoa," I say, holding up a hand to stop her. "I'm no one's charity case. I didn't realize that's what this was."

"It's not," Dixie says, but her cheeks are bright pink.

I feel my throat tightening in a horrible way, and I push back from the table before they can see how much that stings. "Let me just make this easy for everyone," I say. "I'll find somewhere else to sit from now on."

"Harper—" Dixie starts, but I stand and turn away, avoiding her eyes. I've known these girls for all of four days, and I hate to think how much I've come to rely on their company if nothing else. But I know it's not just that. I liked them. It was nice to feel like I had a place, even if I didn't truly belong. I was no closer to them than anyone I sat with at Faulkner High, but it was still nice to be welcomed. Now I have to face the truth, though. They were just being nice because I was new. They don't know me or even like me for who I am. No one does.

And that's the way I like it, I remind myself. I've made sure of that because I had to, because it was the only way to survive. I trust myself, rely on myself, because I'm the only person who can be trusted. No one else really cares, no one looks out for me or has my back the way the Dolces do each other. I'm an island, a girl alone.

I feel it more than I ever have as I cross the café toward the table where the Dolce boys and their girls sit waiting. I don't like attention. I don't want any of this. My knees threaten to wobble, but I force myself to stay steady, to be strong. As I walk, I notice that the table I left is in the minority. Most of the girls in the café are looking on with jealousy and longing, as if being singled out by these beautiful monsters is an honor.

I reach the table where they sit waiting expectantly, because apparently it's beneath them to come to me and harass me. I have to come to them like I'm asking for it.

"Here I am," I say. "Do your worst."

Duke wets his lips and looks me up and down the same way he did by the tracks. "Yes, you are," he says, making no secret of the fact that he appreciates what he sees.

I may not care about boys and dating and all those complications, but I'm not a total stranger to men hitting on me. Still, it's different to be hit on by a guy who looks like this—gorgeous, my age, with the scent of money oozing from his every pore—than when it's a dirtbag on the street or a sleezy asshole trying to sneak a grope in the hall.

Royal holds up a hand to put a pause to whatever's going on. He stares at me a long second and then speaks, not turning around to address the teacher standing at the door. "Give us the room," he says. "This is a student affair."

The small woman glares at the back of his head, her lips tightening. Royal doesn't turn to see if she'll obey.

He knows she will.

God, watching him in action, seeing his power, makes me just about wet.

After a second, she turns on her heel, muttering under her breath, and walks out. I've seen a hundred assholes defy a teacher, but this is not defiance. It's command. I try not to show I'm impressed, but damn. These boys really do run this school if they're ordering teachers around. Not only that, but Royal never once bothered to even look at her. He knows he has the power here.

All the while, his eyes stay locked on me. Though I have a poker face that pays the bills some months, I suddenly feel like he can see past it, like his dark daze has pierced straight into me. Like he's bypassed knocking down my walls and simply stepped over, where he's fingering every secret shame and stroking every hidden desire.

"Now," Royal says slowly, his lips twisting into the slightest smirk, one that makes me want to squirm and press my knees together. "Where were we?"

"What do you want?" I ask, ignoring the traitorous ways my body responds to being the object of his intense attention. Power is sexy, I remind myself. It's not about him at all.

"Oh, we just want to get to know the new girl," Duke says. "Maybe have a little fun. You like fun, don't you, new girl?"

I narrow my eyes at him. "I doubt we have the same definition of fun."

"Don't be so sure," Baron says, a glint of humor in his eyes. His gaze holds mine, and my heart starts to pound. I knew it was wishful thinking, maybe even downright stupidity, but a part of me had hoped against hope that they didn't recognize me. It was evening when we met before, dark by the time we'd left the railroad. And it was dark at the football game. It had been in a different environment, and maybe some part of me had thought, when they didn't confront me right away, that they didn't put two and two together and realize I was the same girl.

But of course life never goes that smoothly.

"What do you want?" I ask quietly, the attitude gone from my voice this time.

"That's better," Royal says, his voice a deep, smooth purr. "You can start by dropping the bratty attitude. You think you're special? Not here. Here, you're no one. We are kings in this place, and there's no room on this throne for the likes of you."

"Fine by me," I say. "I'm just here for the education. I have no interest in your power games."

He cocks a brow. "Then kneel and kiss our feet."

I stare blankly at him for a second. Dixie said something along those lines, but I didn't think she meant it literally.

Royal's phone is lying face down on the table, his big hand resting casually beside it. He taps a finger lightly on it, a gesture so subtle that probably no one else even notices. But I know what's on that phone. I notice.

The blood drains from my cheeks when I realize the choice before me. I have to literally kneel on the floor and kiss someone's feet like he's a fucking king, or he's going to show the whole school a picture of me sucking dick.

They've got me where they want me, which is exactly the place I hate worst—at someone else's mercy. And it's clear these boys have no mercy for anyone.

"This is blackmail," I hiss through clenched teeth.

Royal crosses his arms and leans back in his chair, his brows raised and a smile on his face that's so smug I want to reach across the table and clock him, knock him right the fuck out. He stretches his legs out, wiggling a foot at me.

My blood burns with rage as I stare at it. Why should I care if someone sees me blowing a teacher? It's better than kneeling in front of the entire school to kiss this guy's feet like he is worthy of worship.

But fuck, this is a small town. If that pic gets out, I'll never be anything but the girl who blew her teacher in the back of his Corolla. Yes, I'm already trash to half the town because I live on Mill Street, but I'm not trash to myself. I know why I did it, and I don't regret it. To get out of this town, I'd do it all over again. But no one else will understand that. No one else will see it as anything but the juiciest gossip to hit the town in years. I'm only here for two more years, but those two years will be a living hell.

And that's *if* any college will take me. I can't afford to pay for school, so I'll need a scholarship. I'm already going in with a hand out, begging for help. When a college looks me up, and the first thing they see is an image of me sucking dick to get ahead, are they going to want to help me out? Or will they move on to the next student, the one without a blemish like that on her record?

Bowing to the Dolces is one moment, and it will be gone forever once I do it. Like Quinn said, it's better to just get it over with. Sure, everyone will laugh at me, but if they do it to everyone, it can't be terribly exciting. Once it's over, people will stop talking about it in a day or two. A pic of a student blowing a teacher in a parking lot? That'll be talked about all over town for months, maybe even years.

Gritting my teeth, I swallow my pride and lower myself to my knees. What did pride ever do for me, anyway? It's a pointless virtue, and my instinct for survival is stronger than any silly notion that I have dignity. I was born in a trailer, and only by the grace of one of my mother's slimy boyfriends did we ever get out.

"Think about this next time you think what you want is more important than what we tell you to do," Royal says. "When we say come, you come."

There's something in the way he emphasizes that word that makes it take on the sexual connotation, and my cheeks heat a bit as I lean down and quickly press my lips against the toe of his shoe.

Duke and the three other guys at the table snort with suppressed laughter and elbow each other. But I survived, and it's over now. Baron pushes back from the table, turning his chair to face me, which puts me at eye level with his crotch.

Ignoring the bulge I can see in his slacks, I force myself to bend. My body rebels, my spine stiffening, as if it can keep me from doing this humiliating thing.

"Let this be a lesson," Baron says as I perform my duty. "We're the kings of this school, and you've chosen to be our subject. As long as you walk the halls of Willow Heights, you will bow to us, and worship us, and serve us in whatever ways we see fit."

Is he fucking serious?

"Look, I've played your little game in front of the school," I say, sitting back on my heels and keeping my voice low enough that only their table can hear it. "I understand your need to assert dominance or whatever little power plays get you off. I'm not here to disrupt anything or get in anyone's way. Carry right the fuck on doing what you do. But understand this. I will never kneel for you again. So take a picture with that phone you like to use so much, because this is the last time you'll see me on my knees."

Duke stands and steps over to me. "We require one more," he says, a cocky-ass grin on his face. He adds a wink. "For that picture you're promising."

Gritting my teeth, I bend and kiss his shoe. It's not so bad the third time around.

When I sit back on my heels, his dick is in my face. For a second, I'm too startled to move. Not like I've never seen a dick, but to have a guy whip one out while I was so preoccupied I didn't even notice the sound of his zipper, that's new. Plus, it's a pretty impressive dick. Before I have a chance to come to my senses and react, Duke grabs his dick and slaps me right across the face with it.

I don't even think about what I'm doing. It's instinctual. Someone slapped me. I slap back.

The Duke

The duke in his fine home
Enjoys the fire
That consumes the curtains, the carpet, the silk tablecloths.
He sips his whiskey and laughs,
So everyone laughs along,
Pours more whiskey,
And pretends the house isn't burning all around them.

nine

Harper Apple

Blue is sitting on her stoop next door, smoking a cigarette when I pull up on my bike. I'm not the only person who bikes to school, though the other bikes on the rack at Willow Heights probably cost more than Mom's car. Mine was five bucks at a garage sale because it's missing most of one pedal.

Unlike FHS, my new school is too far to walk, so I rode home in the soup of September humidity. Willow Heights doesn't have a bus, since they probably never took into account people who might not have cars of their own. I know how to drive, but Mom had to work the early shift at the gas station this week. Not that she'd let me take the car.

What, you're too good for our hometown school now? Don't go getting any uppity ideas in your head, Harper. You think you're hot shit now, but just wait. You'll see how they treat the likes of us at that high-fallutin school. Mark my words. They'll take one look at you and know you're bad news. That school won't do one thing to help people like us.

Blue holds up a hand in a wave, and I hop off my bike at the curb and mop my forehead with my arm. Southern Arkansas air is heavy as a blanket you can't throw off even when you're burning up, and it traps all the sweat on your skin to make you even more miserable. I pull my damp shirt away from my body and fan myself with the edge before walking the bike up the walkway to lean it against the side of our house.

"Hey," I call to Blue. "Haven't seen you in a minute. What's up?"

"You suspended?" She's wearing a jean jacket despite the heat, and I wonder, not for the first time, if her mom is even worse than mine. My mother may be a regular gem, but she knows better than to lay hands on me.

"No," I say, trying to laugh even though I'm still catching my breath. Exercising in this weather is like trying to run through bathwater. "I transferred."

"Oh, yeah?" Blue asks, turning her head to squint up at me in the afternoon sun as I make my way over to her stoop. "Where to?"

"Willow Heights, believe it or not."

"What's that like?"

"I got dick-whipped in the face today."

She laughs, but it's not the mean kind, the kind that followed me out of the room, roaring through the café when I jumped up and bolted out of there today. "Sounds about right," Blue says. She holds out a crushed pack with a few cigarettes left. "Smoke?"

After the day I've had, I could use it. I even manage a smile as I pull out one, dropping onto the concrete step next to her. "Thanks."

For some reason, even though she doesn't say anything else about it, her reaction makes it bearable somehow. I've spent the whole day walking around in a kind of traumatized stupor, but five minutes on Blue's stoop brings me back to myself. This is who I am. This is where I belong. When I try to claw my way out, look what happens.

Somehow, Blue's quiet laugh makes me feel better, like I'll be okay, and it wasn't that big a deal. Maybe it is a little bit funny. Yeah, what Duke did was fucked up, but I gave back as good as I got. At least I hope he'll think twice before trying that shit again. I don't have a dick, but I'm guessing it's not a pleasant place to be slapped.

"I'd better take off," Blue says, crushing out her cigarette and tossing it into the rusted tin can on her porch where a thousand butts have drowned in rainwater, turning it the color of swamp water with a thin oil-slick glaze.

"Picking up Olive?" I ask, standing as well.

"Gotta go clean the landlord's house," Blue mutters, looking down at her knock-off Converse sneakers and avoiding my eyes, as if cleaning houses is something to be ashamed of. Any job short of selling drugs, your body, or hawking stolen goods is downright respectable in these parts. Hell, even those jobs command some respect. At least those people are resourceful, unlike Blue's mother, who's never had a job since we moved in next door.

But it's none of my business what they do or how they pay for food, I remind myself. For all I know, her mom gets a disability check and food stamps, and Blue has a roll of savings wedged under the musty carpet at the back of her closet that she counts when she's alone and dreaming of the day she'll leave this town and never look back.

I don't know their story any more than Blue knows ours. Maybe if we had enough for ourselves and could spare a little to help the other, we'd give each other more than privacy. Maybe we'd be better friends, and I'd tell her the hollow, shell-shocked feeling I walked around with all day, and thank her for just making me feel better and for being someone who understands what it's like to live our reality. Maybe she'd tell me why her mother can't work and if the rumors last year were true, that she fell down the stairs at Faulkner High on purpose because she couldn't afford a baby *or* an abortion.

But we don't do friendship that way, so I watch her walk away, her head tucked down and her hands in her pockets as if she's trying to make herself smaller, to take up less space than the tiny fragment of the world left for her when the important people were done carving out and claiming their space at the top.

Inside, I fire up the old desktop and root through the fridge for something to eat, since I didn't get to finish half of my lunch. I find some old heels of white bread and a few condiments and make a mayonnaise sandwich before sitting down at the desk. Just as I've settled into my assignment, the dreaded little black box pops onto my screen. I'm not surprised. I've been waiting for this with a heavy feeling in my gut just like I waited all day for the Dolce boys to seek revenge.

I know it's not over with them, and it's not over with Mr. D.

MrD: How's your first week of school?

BadApple: As expected.

I realize a second after I type in the words that I should have asked how he knew, but then, nothing he knows surprises me anymore. The guy—or girl, who the hell knows?—is a serious stalker and seems to know everything about me. Considering I'm pretty sure he's responsible for the move, there's no use in playing coy.

MrD: Anything exciting happen today?

That crawly, cold feeling moves along my arms, making the hairs stand up. Does he know? Does he go to Willow Heights? Or have spies there?

I start to push the thought away, scolding myself for being paranoid and ridiculous, but am I? The guy has found me on multiple computers, and if he's powerful enough to get me a scholarship that quite probably didn't even exist until he decided to add another one to WHPA's scholarship count for the year, he could definitely have spies. I suspect I know exactly who he is, and if his sons tell him everything that goes on there… It's creepy as fuck to think about some guys telling their dad how they dick-whipped me, but I'm not sure what other explanation there is.

Unless…

I swallow hard, remembering Dixie gushing about Baron being a genius. Is he a computer genius? Is he the one sending me all these messages?

But that doesn't make sense. Why would he care about some FHS kid *before* he saw me with Mr. Behr? At the time, that seemed random, just some kids out wreaking havoc. Was it random, though?

MrD: Can't be that hard to think of something…

BadApple: Nothing special.

MrD: That's too bad. It's such an exciting place, isn't it? Surely something notable happened this week.

BadApple: Not really

BadApple: It's pretty hard tho. Better go do homework.

MrD: I want to hear about your day.

BadApple: Same old. Hard classes, clueless teachers, stupid social politics.

MrD: Tell me about that.

BadApple: Sorry, really gotta go

MrD: Awww, after all I did for you, I don't even get a thank you???

BadApple: Thx

MrD: That's it?

BadApple: Yep

MrD: Surely you can spare a few minutes for the man who put you on the path you wanted so much.

BadApple: Guess that's what u get when u don't negotiate before giving someone what they want.

MrD: I'm not worried about it. I'll get what I want. I always do.

BadApple: Good luck with that

I close the chat box and get back to my work, trying not to think about why some creepy dad won't leave me alone. Fuck, I hope they didn't show him the picture of me blowing Behr and give him the idea I like old guys.

But no, that can't be it—at least not all of it. He started talking to me before they even took the picture. It leaves me feeling so paranoid I go and close the blinds, glancing at the corners like I might find a hidden camera. What if it's not all a coincidence?

What if he started talking to me, and then his kids showed up and took a picture of me, and then he put me in the same school with them for a reason?

It gives me the shivers, and I can barely do my homework. For once, I wish I had someone to talk to. I wish I had a friend.

And that's a dangerous thing to wish for. I learned a long time ago not to wish for what I don't have, not to rely on anyone but myself. Not the men who came and went from our lives like the turning of a calendar page. Not the teachers who didn't have the energy or patience or time to coax something real out of every single flunkie they got stuck with, or the neighbors and classmates who couldn't help even if they wanted. Not even the man who spawned me or the mother who blames me for all the disappointments in her life.

I have me, and that's all that's guaranteed, so it's safer not to count on anyone else. I don't—and can't—need anyone else. Sooner or later, they'll all give up, walk away like men do when they're done with my mom, like the first guy I ever slept with, who never talked to me again but talked all over school about how easy I was. I learned a valuable lesson that month. I'm the only person who cares enough not to let me down.

So, I'll have to figure this out on my own, just like I figured that out on my own, like I'll figure out how to eat tonight and how to get out of town in two years and how to get to school tomorrow.

I'm a smart girl. What do I need friends for?

I am enough.

I am enough.

*

The next day, I walk into science and find Royal Dolce sitting at the table in the back corner where I've made my unobtrusive home all week. He doesn't sprawl casually like some of the jocks, but just sits there, still and empty-eyed, staring into the middle distance. I walk back and stop when I reach the table.

"Is this some kind of joke?" I ask.

Royal takes his sweet time turning his attention to me. "All of high school is a joke," he says. "Haven't you figured that out yet?"

"So, what? You got transferred into this class just to fuck with me?"

He snorts. "I've been in this class, sweetheart. You're the one who transferred in."

"You weren't here all week."

"I'm a senior," he says. "I work at my own pace."

"Which is why you're in a junior science class?"

"We don't worry about grade levels here," he says. "As long as you get everything done, you can take the classes whenever you want."

"Lucky fucking me that we both took the same one this period."

"You gonna stand there all day or sit down?" Royal asks with a smirk.

"I'd rather stand all day."

"Don't worry," he says, pushing a chair my way. "I don't bite… Hard."

His eyes flit down me, and I feel my nipples harden inside my shirt. Ignoring the sensations in my body, I roll my eyes and take the seat, since I'm the last one standing and the irritated teacher is glaring at me. Royal scoots my seat in right next to him, though I would have preferred the end of the table. "You did my brother wrong yesterday," he murmurs. "You're going to pay for that, Harper Apple."

"No, see, I think what happened is that he did me wrong," I say. "And then he paid for it."

He gives me a cool look. "That's not how it works around here."

"Maybe it is now."

We stare at each other for a long moment. His eyes are dark and inscrutable. His forearms rest on the lab table in front of us, his sleeves rolled up to reveal olive skin over thick, corded muscle. I try to ignore the heat coming off him, caressing my skin, shimmering over me and making me want to squirm in my chair. Electricity crackles between us as we stare each other down.

His eyes are as dark as twin pools of obsidian, and they draw in everything around him like a black hole absorbing light and energy, sucking in everyone's darkest hidden truth, the ones we won't admit even to ourselves.

At the same time, they're somehow empty, as if they destroy everything he absorbs, as if no matter how much he feeds that empty, insatiable pit inside him, it's never enough. Nothing fills it. He's perfectly, purely hollow. It makes me ache, makes some stupid, primal part of me want to reach out and touch him, wrap my arms around him, fill him with all he's missing.

"You don't make the call about how things are around here," he says at last, his voice low and his eyes still sucking me in.

"Fine by me," I say. "But you should thank me for bringing you a taste of the real world. One day you're going to have to graduate, and there will be consequences to your actions out there. You can't rely on your family's money to get you a free pass to do whatever the fuck you want for the rest of your life. You can't major in being an entitled prick, and you can't get a job as a king."

Royal just smirks and cocks his head. "Are you sure about that?"

I want to say I am, that in the real world, it's each man for himself. That we all start from the bottom and claw our way up, that we are judged on our merits, our intelligence, our skill. But I'm not that naïve. There is no American dream where we're all created equal, where we all have the same opportunities to pull ourselves up by our bootstraps and become the next Bezos or Walton.

I'm the one who needs a reality check, not Royal or Duke. In the real world, some people start on the bottom of the heap, and everyone steps on them to climb. Some people aren't just at the top, they have a fucking rocket waiting to launch them into space from the top of the heap. And somewhere up in space, on some other planet, is their world, while my world is down here in the gutter. In their world, people don't face the consequences of their actions or pay for their crimes. The Dolces might as well be majoring in being entitled pricks because they'll probably need that skill to survive life up there.

I'm the one living in a fantasy. In the real world, a name means something, and cash means even more. I'll never be anything but a bad apple, a girl from the wrong side of the tracks who got lucky and had one chance to drag herself up from there. I have to do what I have to do. Kissing feet, sucking dick, it's all part of the climb. Girls like me, we do whatever's asked if we want to get up, get out of the gutter. We can't be picky or proud. We're beggars. We don't get to choose the cost of getting out.

And the Dolces, they'll never be anything but what they already are—kings of the world. Guys who get away with anything in school and will get away with anything in business when they leave here. This is a taste of the real world, a hell of a lot more sobering and more accurate than the bullshit they tried to feed us at Faulkner, telling us we could be more, we could have as much.

The Dolces were born on thrones, with silver spoons in their mouths. I was born on a stained mattress with a plastic spoon in my mouth. Guys like them die as kings, laid to rest in their riches, with big obituaries on the national news to recount their glory. Girls like me die unnoticed somewhere, maybe in the weeds down by the tracks, and if we're lucky, we get a line in the local paper.

This is reality. Slapping someone's dick doesn't change it. It just pisses off the people who can leave me in that ditch and walk away with a slap on the wrist at worst.

I don't even bother trying to talk to Royal the rest of class. I do the lab we're assigned even though I have to touch giant hissing cockroaches. I don't complain when he does nothing. He doesn't have to do anything. He could probably turn in blank pages for every assignment and get a better grade than me. His father paid for my scholarship, and he no doubt pays for their grades.

I hear my mother's voice in my head.

That's just the way the world works, Harper. The sooner you accept it, the sooner you'll stop trying to change things that will never change.

This is our place in the world. You might as well have some fun before you die.

It's not fair, but no one ever claimed life was fair. Maybe once, Mom had dreams to get out, too. She grew up hearing and probably believing the same lies we're all fed, that she could be a doctor or an astronaut or a rock star if she just worked hard and believed in herself. I'm sure she didn't grow up thinking she'd work at a gas station when she was forty.

Maybe one day, I'll let go of my dreams and wind up like her, with a kid she never wanted, a drinking problem she can't afford, and a string of boyfriends that for a night or a week or a month, make her laugh and hope and feel alive again before she comes crashing back down to earth, and her dreams are shattered all over again.

*

At lunch, I'm torn. I want to eat, but I'm not keen on facing the whole school at once— Duke with his revenge scheme, Baron who might be Mr. D, and the girls who told me I couldn't sit with them if I was planning on standing up for myself.

In the end, it's the Waltons who convince me. They mince by in their red-soled stilettos, stopping to stare at my garage sale jeans and fading black tee.

"Oh my god, weren't you wearing that shirt yesterday?" Gloria asks.

I wasn't, but I only have so many plain tee shirts, and we can only wear jeans on Fridays, so my wardrobe choices are severely limited.

"Don't you have anything that doesn't look like you found it in someone else's trash can?" Everleigh asks, wrinkling her pretty little nose.

"What are you even wearing?" Eleanor says. "Those jeans were in style, like, ten years ago."

"I didn't realize school was a red-carpet event," I shoot back. "But if you really want to know who I'm wearing, my shirt is probably Faded Glory, and my jeans are by Levi. But your stylist might have to get on the waiting list for a pair—apparently, it's like *ten years* long."

The girls huff and exchange looks, probably because they've never heard of that brand. I roll my eyes and turn away, exiting through a short hallway off the café and finding my way outside instead of sitting through another lunch with a bunch of insufferable snobs. At least that's what I tell myself as I cross the grass toward the football stadium. In reality, maybe it's starting to get to me—the looks, the cutting remarks, the insults. I have thick skin, but it's still skin.

The truth is, it sucks to walk around feeling like everyone's staring at my dated, thrift store finds. At Faulkner, they were invisible. No one batted an eye. Lots of girls there shopped at thrift stores just to be quirky and cute. Once, I ran into Zephyr Hertz at a Goodwill. He complimented me on my find—a real leather jacket—and suddenly, we were co-conspirators, searching for steals in the shoe aisle. I actually felt cool for being there.

That would never happen here. First off, I'm sure even the other scholarship kids aren't as dirt poor as we are, and even if they are, it's the kind of place that magnifies your shame for being poor, so we'd probably just hide and hurry away, pretending we'd never seen each other.

A sweet, earthy aroma finds me when I'm almost to the bleachers, and I can't help but smile. So maybe I won't hang out with the scholarship kids or the gossip girls. But apparently there's one more group I hadn't considered, a group I didn't expect to exist at ritzy Willow Heights. Stoners.

I round the end of the bleachers and stop short, colliding with a pair of big, soft tits. I stumble back, and Dixie stumbles the other way.

"Dixie?" I ask incredulously. "You're a stoner?"

"What? No," she says quickly.

"What are you doing here?" I ask.

"I—I'm on my way to my student council meeting," she says, smoothing her skirt and rubbing her lips together like she's smoothing out her lipstick.

I narrow my eyes. "You meet on the football field?"

"I just came out to get a minute in the sun, okay?"

Total lie. She came from under the bleachers.

"What are you here for, anyway?" she asks.

"Needed a break from the assholes," I say with a shrug.

"Well, I'm going to be late if we don't hurry, but I'll walk in and get food with you," she says. "No one bothers me."

"Right," I say. "Because of the blog."

As tempting as her offer is, I already accepted that I'm not eating lunch. I'm pretty used to skipping meals, and I've been eating breakfast here, which means skipping lunch isn't a huge deal anymore. Besides, just because no one messes with Dixie, that doesn't mean they'll leave me alone. I was at her table yesterday, and they pulled me away and gave me the royal treatment.

"Thanks," I say. "But I'm good."

She glances under the bleachers and back to me. "Okay," she says. "See you around, Harper."

As she walks away, I get the feeling I just fucked up any chance of being her friend. Part of me wants to fall into step with her, tell her that I could eat after all. But another part wants to know why she doesn't want me to go meet the smokers.

I wait until she's almost at the building before I step around the bleachers, out of the sun and into the dimness under the metal seats. I blink a few times, waiting for my eyes to adjust. The smoky scent of burning tobacco and weed under here makes me feel at home for the first time all week.

I don't usually buy pot or cigarettes, but I've definitely had days where I headed for the bleachers, knowing that someone would be willing to share either for a couple crumpled bills. Zephyr, Maverick, Blue, Jolene and her fanboys, and some of the Slut Club girls were all good for a hit when I had a really rough day. A couple times when I didn't do so well in a fight, Mav would even let me bum a whole joint for the pain.

When my eyes adjust, I find a blond guy standing against one of the supports for the bleachers, watching me. Something's familiar about him, though for a second, I can't place him. One hand is resting casually in the pocket of his jeans, and the other holds a joint to his lips. He takes a slow drag and watches me approach, his eyes narrowed so I can't read them. A little shock goes through me when I get close enough to see the tattoos covering the backs of his hands, his forearms, disappearing under the sleeves of his dusky blue t-shirt and appearing again on his neck, extending all the way to his chin and jawline.

"Dynamo?" I blurt, gaping at him. He's about the last person I'd ever expect to attend a preppy private school. Not only does he help coordinate the fighting rings, he's all tatted up and hard looking. I never really wondered about his age. I've wondered how he lost a finger on his left hand, which is now hidden in his pocket, or what left the back of that hand and part of his forearms mottled with ugly scars he's covered up with tattoos. I've wondered how much all that ink cost. If I'd thought about his age, I would have put him a few years out of high school. There's something about him that makes him look older than your average high school kid.

"Appleteeny," he says in his slow, southern drawl. I never paid much attention to it at the Slaughter Pen, when I'm busy getting my head in the right place. But now I notice that he doesn't talk like me, like the other people at Faulkner High. He has a southern accent, but it's more like something out of an old movie, like he's auditioning for a *Gone with the Wind* remake.

"You go here?" I ask, still not quite believing my eyes. Maybe he's just here to sell drugs under the bleachers to high school kids.

"Yeah," he says, dispelling that theory. He gives a little smile that doesn't reach his eyes and holds out the joint to me. "But I'm not Dynamo here. I'm just Colt."

Colt Darling

"Colt, Darling,"
Her voice drifted in from next door,
Sweet and high as songbirds.
Her peels of laughter
Falling to the floor
Like magnolia petals.
"I'm so happy to see you.
Sit down and tell me all about
School, your friends—Do you have a girlfriend?—football…
Let me get you some pecan sandies,
And sweet tea,
And we'll make an afternoon of it."

"Colt, Darling,"
Her voice drifted across the hospital waiting room,
Hoarse and ragged with worry.
No peels of laughter
Falling to the sterile linoleum
Like ash.
"I'm so happy you're okay,
You can tell me what happened later.
We've been up all night praying.
Let me get you some ice,
And talk to the nurse.
We'll get you in to see a doctor right away."

"Colt, Darling,"
Her voice still drifts across the lawn.
The concern of a mother,

BAD APPLE

The ghost of her laughter,
The specter of her love,
Haunts us like the smell of smoke
When the wind is right.

ten

Harper Apple

"How do you deal with it?" I ask Colt. We've emerged from under the bleachers and are sitting in the stands, sharing a bag of potato chips. I feel comfortable with him, like I've known him for years, though in truth I didn't know his name until a few minutes ago, and I don't know anything about him. Still, he's the one familiar face I've seen all week. I didn't know how much I needed that, didn't realize I actually miss Faulkner High, until I saw his sleeve tats and lazy grin.

"Deal with what?" Colt asks, shaking the open end of the bag at me until I take a small handful.

"The Dolces, the Waltons, all the other rich, entitled pricks around here…"

Colt cracks a small, humorless smile and flexes his left hand. The skin is so tight his fingers don't extend the last fraction of an inch. "You get used to it," he says. "Eventually, you stop fighting it and accept that it is what it is. You know it could be worse, and that really you're lucky, and you can't change it. So you just live with it."

I'm not sure if he's talking about his hand or Willow Heights, but it makes perfect sense to me—probably because I've heard that same shit from my mother since I was old enough to talk.

"I don't buy it," I say, reaching for a chip.

Colt holds the bag away. "Then no chips for you."

I laugh and hold up my fists. "Do you really want to mess with the mighty Appleteeny?"

Colt laughs and hands over the chips. For the first time, his smile reaches his eyes. Just a little, but it makes me feel better somehow, as if I've paid for the joint we shared or the half sandwich he insisted I take.

"Seriously, though, I'll pay you back for this," I say, taking a few chips and handing back the bag.

"Don't worry about it," he says. "They're just chips."

"Yeah, but food costs money," I say. "So does weed."

"I make money off your ass every Friday night," he points out, munching on a chip.

"You make it sound like you're my pimp."

"I could be your pimp."

"Why is everyone trying to turn me into a whore lately?"

Colt looks me up and down. "Because you're hot and you'd make lots of money for them?"

I roll my eyes. "Don't flirt. I've seen what relationships do to a girl, and I'm not going down that path."

"Relationships?" Colt asks, cocking a brow. "Who said anything about a relationship? I was talking about pimping you out. Sure, I'd sample the goods first, have a little taste of that sweet ass, but my only relationship would be as your… Booking agent."

I laugh and shove his shoulder, feeling lighter than I have in weeks. "I knew you came up with terrible names for us, but I didn't know you were equally terrible with words. Never try your hand at poetry, that's for damn sure."

"Sadly, you'll never get to see my poetic brilliance," he says, shaking his head. "I took comp last year."

"What year are you, anyway?" I ask.

Colt tips back his head, tilts the chip back upside down, and lets the crumbs cascade into his mouth. He chews before answering. "Senior."

"Lucky," I say. "I'm a junior. Two more years of this hell. I knew the work would be hard and everyone would be snobs, but I didn't know there would be guys like the Dolces."

Colt grimaces and crumples the chips bag, tossing it back into the paper bag from his lunch. "You smoke squares?"

I shrug. "I'll share, if you have extra. And again, I'll pay you back."

He shakes his head. "Don't worry about it."

"Oh my god," I say slowly, pulling back to look at him. "I thought you must be a scholarship kid like me, but you're not, are you?"

He gives me a big, smug grin. "Nope."

"Ugh, is that why you go here? You're one of the rich, entitled assholes?"

"I used to be," he says with a shrug, still smiling. "Now I'm just rich."

"And not an asshole?" I ask. "I'm not convinced."

"Aw, and here I thought we could be friends," he says. "I shouldn't have told you."

"I would have found out and been pissed, not just disappointed," I say. "Besides, I don't do friends."

"No friends, no relationships," he says, nodding. "Just no strings sex. I like that."

"No relationships of any kind," I say. "Friendship or romantic. Sorry."

"What about a business relationship?" he says, pointing to his chest with his good hand. "Booking agent, remember?"

I notice that he slides his left hand into his pocket whenever he's not using it, but I don't know if he's hiding it unconsciously or by habit, if he's doing it because he thinks other people will be uncomfortable with it or because he is.

"We'll see," I say with an easy smile back at him as I turn and walk away. I can feel his eyes on me, and I don't even mind. It's nice to be appreciated, even if I don't want anything but an occasional smoke under the bleachers.

I cross the field and push open the doors to the school, only to run smack into Royal Dolce's stone chest. Talk about being dunked in the ice water of reality. Colt was a nice escape, but now it's back to this shit. My heart takes off in my chest, and I try to push past Royal, but he grabs my arm, his dark eyes boring into mine.

"Stay away from that guy," he says, his words clipped and deliberate.

"Excuse me?" I ask indignantly. The first time I've even come close to making a real friend, or even talking to someone who knows the tiniest fraction of my life, and he's trying to fuck it up?

"You don't know who he is," Royal says, glaring out through the glass door.

"Trust me, I'm well aware. I've known Colt for years."

"If you knew who he was, you'd stay away from him," he snaps.

"Thanks for looking out for me, Captain America," I say, giving him a mock salute. "But I can choose my own friends, and last I heard, you were looking to get revenge on me, so I see no reason to trust any advice you give me."

I push past Royal, but he grabs my arm and spins me around. "He's involved in some bad stuff," he says, his voice low.

"I know," I say, yanking my arm free and smiling up at him. "I *am* that bad stuff."

I turn and walk away before he can fuck with my head any further. Why is he suddenly acting like he cares, warning me about Colt? Is this just another one of his games, part of a mission to make sure I have zero friends?

That only makes me more sure that I've found an ally, one who isn't into the Dolces' twisted power games. If Royal doesn't want me hanging out with Colt, there must be a reason. And since he hates me, and he apparently hates Colt, it seems only natural that Colt and I become… If not friends, then at least friendly.

What possible reason could Royal have for wanting to keep us apart? Does Colt know something about him that he doesn't want me to find out? He shouldn't care or even notice if a couple outcasts find each other. If I'm friends with Colt, that has zero impact on him. So, why is he threatened by it?

I can't help feeling like I'm missing something, which pisses me off. I head to my next class, wondering who I can ask. Maybe I'll have to wait until Monday and ask Colt.

As I head for my locker, I mull it over, because I'm an impatient bitch and I want to know now. I hate being the last to know. It puts me in a vulnerable position, and that's not somewhere anyone likes to be.

I'm so busy thinking over whether I can ask Dynamo tonight, or if that violates the unspoken rules of the Slaughter Pen, that I almost miss the snickering behind me. I turn to see the Waltons and their equally pretty, equally white, equally indistinguishable friends standing there, six of them in total. They're just watching me, laughing behind their hands.

A pit opens inside me, but I clench my teeth together and try not to show anything. These bitches don't deserve a reaction. Still, I lean back just enough to let my back graze the locker because these bitches are just immature enough that they might think they could get to me by sticking a note on my back.

No paper rustles on my back, though, so they can't be laughing at that. I don't have my period, so I know I didn't bleed through my jeans and hand them a reason to make fun of me even more. Deciding they're just fucking with me, I turn back to my locker. That's when I see it. Along the bottom of the polished wooden door, someone has carved the words *WHITE TRASH*. The grooves of the letters are deep, sharp and a little jagged.

I clench my teeth and finish turning the combination. That was carved by someone who wanted to do more than laugh at me. There is hatred in those slashed grooves, cut with a box cutter or a knife instead of just scratched into the varnish with a pin. Maybe they even imagined it was my skin as they slashed those letters into the wood. Someone here has a knife and wants to hurt me. Unlike Faulkner, there are no metal detectors here. Hell, kids even carry backpacks to class.

Guess it's time I start carrying my own knife.

It had to be Duke, I think as I spin the combination. He's pissed because I hurt not just his dick but his pride.

I pull open my locker. A squirming mass of black cockroaches covers my books. I yelp involuntarily and jump back. I've lived with my share of roaches, but that doesn't make me like them any more than a Walton in a fancy mansion. And something deeper than that, a disgust as deep as the primal fear of snakes, coils in my belly when I see them. These ones are huge, as long as my fingers, their squirming bodies black and greasy looking as they scuttle over each other, letting out disgusting hissing noises.

One fat, black insect plops to the floor, missing my toe by half an inch. I jump back, blood rushing in my ears. All around me, I hear laughter and gagging noises and even a few shrieks, but I register them as if from far away. It's not just the Waltons. It's everyone. A crowd has gathered, all of them wanting to see me lose my shit.

I want to. I want to turn and run, away from the disgusting sight, away from the cruel laughter, away from this fucking school where I don't belong and where a good education suddenly seems like the least of my worries. Pressure mounts behind my eyes, but I won't cry. Not even when my throat tightens until I can barely draw a breath because it hurts so much just to keep breathing.

"What's going on here?" asks a male voice. Mr. Harris, my science teacher, comes pushing through the crowd, past one of the Dolce boys.

Royal.

He stands there staring at me, not laughing with the others, but watching me with a cool smirk on his lips and burning hatred in his eyes. I swallow hard, wanting to look away but trapped in the paralyzing inferno of his gaze. Royal's a closed book, and this is the first time I've seen any real emotion in his eyes.

Before I can tear myself free or think about the unwarranted hatred in Royal's eyes, the teacher steps up on me, right in my face. "Are these my cockroaches?" he demands.

Of course they are. Where else would someone get a bunch of giant hissing cockroaches? I examined them in class with Royal just yesterday. And now, conveniently, they've turned up in my locker.

"What is this?" Mr. Harris demands, his voice rising with anger until he's yelling at me and everyone else. "You think this is a joke? These are not for you to play pranks with. They're rare, exotic pets shipped all the way here from Madagascar!"

"Are you sure?"

It's Royal's voice cutting through the hushed murmurs. The chatter stops, and everyone turns to see what their head thug has to say. "Those probably crawled into her backpack last night at her trailer park."

"Yeah," Gloria pipes up. "They probably live in her hair, too, like head lice. Do you ever even comb that mess?"

"I don't live in a trailer," I say. "And the only sneaky, disgusting little creatures I've seen lately are right here in this school, and they aren't cockroaches."

I give her a pointed look, and a few people murmur and shuffle their feet, excited to see what she'll do next.

"Enough," Mr. Harris roars. "Someone get me something to put these in. Harper, close your locker to keep them contained."

"She probably stole them to sell on the black market," Eleanor says, clutching her books to her chest and meeting my eyes with haughty triumph. "She's poor, you know."

Mr. Harris turns to me, his face red with anger. "Is that true?"

"Or maybe to eat," Everleigh says.

"Yeah," I say slowly, glaring over Mr. Harris's shoulder at the girls. "I stole your nasty roaches and put them all over my books where everyone could see them when I opened my locker."

He splutters in anger and goes chasing after one of the roaches that's careening down the hall, everyone jumping back to get out of its way.

"I may be poor, but I'm not stupid," I say to Devil Barbie. "If you're going to try to get me in trouble, you'll need to be a little more clever. That's not even convincing."

"I wasn't trying to get you in trouble," Royal says, his voice a low rumble that draws my attention and everyone else's. His eyes lock on mine, and he waits a second, making sure everyone will hear it when he cuts me down. "I was reminding you where you came from."

My throat squeezes, and my eyes ache again. If there was any doubt about being an outcast here, any doubt about getting by without being noticed, it's gone now. Royal's put a target on my back for the whole school, giving them permission to treat me like trash because that's what he says I am. That's probably what they all see already, but it still cuts into me deeper than I want to admit. I'm used to being ignored, being nothing. I'm comfortable with that. I don't need attention. Especially not when it comes in the form of an entitled thug calling open season on me.

"Why don't you go back to your trailer park and cry to your own cockroaches," Gloria says. "No one wants you here."

Someone does. I just don't know why. Maybe it's time I find out.

"I've got it," Mr. Harris says, returning with the bug cradled between his hands. One creepy little antenna pokes out between his fingers, testing the air. My stomach hitches. "You'd better not have lost any of them, Ms. Apple. This is a very serious matter. Don't think you're getting away with tampering with my equipment."

"See, even our roaches are expensive," Everleigh says with a smirk. "Obviously you're out of your element."

"They probably cost more than her clothes," Eleanor says, giggling behind her hand.

"Her clothes?" Gloria asks, giving me a haughty look. "They probably cost more than *her.*"

I spot the giant roach that fell near my shoe, still huddling behind the heel of my cheap sneakers. I bend, snatch it up, and throw it in her face.

eleven

Harper Apple

Pandemonium erupts. The roach hits Gloria square in the face, and she shrieks like a banshee, slapping frantically at her cheek. The roach goes flying, and everyone scatters, running and screaming like it's going to attack them. Mr. Harris is yelling to save the cockroach, but no one listens or probably even hears him. Gloria is flailing like she's dying, screaming, "I can still feel it on me! Where is it?"

She dives at me, her fist pulled back like she'll hit me.

So not happening. This bitch can cut me down all day long, but fuck if she's going to lay a finger on me. Before she can swing, I do.

I throw a low, sharp jab into her ribs, and she doubles over.

I start to turn away, but before I've taken a step, she tackles me.

"You bitch," she screams as we crash to the floor together. My head slams into the thick wooden lockers, and blackness blots my vision. I hit at her, jabbing her with my fists every chance I get, at the same time cursing myself for letting her catch me off guard. I know better. I just wasn't expecting a rich bitch like her to fight back. By the time my head's stopped spinning, she's busted my lip and landed a couple good punches.

People all around us are chanting "Fight! Fight! Fight!"

I grab a handful of her hair and yank her to one side, thrusting my hips up and rolling at the same time. I manage to get my head away from the lockers and roll onto her, but just as quick, Gloria bucks her hips and flips us again. We go rolling down the hall, punching and pulling hair and cussing at each other. I have to give it to this girl—she's not the simpering little southern belle I took her for.

By the time a couple teachers and a principal drag us apart, half the school is there cheering, their excitement palpable in the air. It just amps up my own excitement, feeds it like gasoline to a fire. I want to dance on my toes, throw a few more punches, but the principal is holding me back.

Maybe it just proves their point, that I am trash, but I fucking love a good fight. I'm still hopped up on adrenaline, my pulse racing, excitement charging my veins like electricity through a wire. That was just a taste. I want a real fight, itch for it the way a junkie itches for a fix when they just get a taste to whet their appetite. I've got a split lip, a loose tooth, and blood pouring from the wound on the back of my head, but I've never felt better.

Gloria's nose is already swelling, and blood is pouring from both nostrils, not to mention the clumps of hair I tore out, but she looks fucking gorgeous, better than she ever will when she's all coifed and painted. This is the real girl, a savage, and I have mad respect for her when her hair is all wild and her eyes crazy with bloodlust.

"My dad will sue the pants off you for busting up my face," Gloria snarls at me, straining against Mr. Harris's hold. "You better be glad it's not our homecoming game tonight."

I can't help but snort at that. One minute she's throwing down like a champ, and the next, she's worried about her pretty face.

"Don't worry, I saved some for later," I say, flexing my hands and grinning at her, though I can taste blood from my split lip. "We can have a rematch in two weeks."

"Dude, that was *sick*," DeShaun Rose yells.

"Best fight of the year," Baron Dolce agrees, phone in hand. Some others have their phones out, recording the scene, too.

So much for keeping my head down and staying off the radar. It's not like the Dolces left me much choice in the matter, though. They've already made me the center of attention. And even if they hadn't, I'll be damned if I'm going to let anyone push me around.

In the office, I sit on one side of the door while Gloria sits on the other, both of us in the plushy chairs they have set up. Gloria crosses her arms and works her jaw, sticking her nose in the air and pointedly refusing to look my way. I almost laugh at her pettiness.

A nurse calls us in individually to look at our injuries. Gloria comes out looking almost normal, her hair smoothed back under a headband, every blonde strand in place again. She's wearing a new white shirt tucked into her designer jeans, and aside from the swelling nose and a hint of what might be two black eyes forming from the blow, she looks normal.

"I hope I knocked your teeth loose," she says as she walks by.

"You can really throw down for a prissy little bitch," I reply. "I'm impressed."

She huffs and turns away while I go in to get my face looked at. We both got a few shots below the neck, too, but nothing's broken. The nurse tells me I'll need stitches in my scalp if I don't want a scar, and I almost laugh. No fucking way is my mom taking me to get stitches. If we had that kind of money, she'd buy herself some crystal and go party with her flavor of the week.

I let the nurse tape some gauze to it, even though it'll hurt like hell to pull it out of my hair, and I take the ice pack she offers. When I get back out to the office, Gloria is gone, and the receptionist motions for me to go into another office. My first thought is that of course Gloria got away with it. She's rich.

But when I walk into the office, she's sitting at a round table with the principal and another admin person I don't know who introduces herself as a counselor. They motion for me to take the fourth seat, an even cushier chair than the ones in the reception area. Prints from a local artist adorn the walls, and the heavy walnut table makes the room even more posh. Still, I can't help but feel like I'm in an interrogation room, like one of the walls should be a one-way mirror.

"We don't discipline students often around here," the principal starts out, adjusting his tie and giving me a pointed look, as if he wants to add, *At least we didn't until you came along.*

"Our philosophy leans more toward working out our conflicts and differences without punishments," the counselor explains.

Shocking, I think to myself. *And you wonder why your school is run by delinquents.*

Or maybe they don't wonder. Some things are the same for adults as they are for us. Money is power, whoever you are. In a place like this, most of the teachers have fancy degrees from

Ivy League schools, and they might be smart as fuck, but they aren't rich. Not like the donors, alumni, and parents. They know not to bite the hand that feeds them.

"We rarely have altercations of this severity," the principal goes on, his accusatory gaze still on me. "Of course, there are legal ramifications in most instances like this, but we've spoken to both your families by phone, and both have declined to press charges."

My heart lurches in my chest, all my snark gone.

Press charges? Fuck. I hadn't even thought of that. At a school like this, they call fighting "assault." No one at Faulkner—or very few—would press charges over something like this. The gangs fight on the daily, and sometimes it can't wait until after school. So when anyone else fights, it's not exactly shocking. Yeah, everyone buzzes about it for a hot minute, but it dies down and is forgotten by the end of the day.

"Can I go, then?" Gloria asks, crossing her arms and sulking.

I glance sideways at her, surprised she's not protesting and saying I should be thrown in jail. Of course my mother isn't going to press charges. She probably laughed in their faces when they asked. She doesn't have the money to hire a lawyer or the authority to punish me. But I'm surprised Gloria's esteemed parents aren't pursuing it.

"We don't want this school to become a place where people resort to violence to work out their conflicts," the counselor says. "We'd like the two of you to resolve this issue before leaving here today."

"Fine," Gloria says, glowering at the wall. "I'm sorry I tried to knock your teeth out, Harper."

I roll my eyes and play along with the charade. "I'm sorry I busted your nose and probably gave you two black eyes, Gloria. I throw a mean punch."

"Noted," she says icily.

"What prompted this attack?" the principal asks, still looking at me, because of course it must be my fault. A precious Walton would never start a fight.

"I threw a roach in her face," I admit.

"And why would you do something like that?" the counselor asks.

I feel like I'm on fucking trial here.

"Because I was tired of her bullshit?" I offer.

"Let's keep things civil," the principal says, looking downright disgusted by the scholarship kid he allowed into his school, only to find out she dresses like a slut and fights like a lowlife.

"I'll try," I say with a tight smile.

"I don't understand why you even let people like her in here," Gloria says. "If I wanted to go to school with thugs, I would have gone to Faulkner. People pay good money for their kids to get an education with other good, southern families."

"Oh, *I'm* the thug?" I ask. "What about the assholes who run this place—your boyfriends? Is your Sopranos squad from a good *southern* family? Or are they exempt because they brought truckloads of laundered money to town?"

"Watch your language, Ms. Apple," the principal warns. "We welcome students from all over the country, not just the South. And we try to avoid baseless accusations and stereotypes based on people's region of origin."

I roll my eyes. "So, you admit they're thugs, but it's okay as long as the money keeps flowing this way. Let's just not assume they're in the mob."

"Why don't we stick to the topic at hand," the principal says, licking his lips nervously and adjusting his tie again.

So, I got it right, and he doesn't like it.

"This has nothing to do with them," Gloria agrees.

"It always has to do with them," I say with a sigh. After all, it was Royal who put the roaches in my locker and started this fight. But Gloria wasn't even involved in that. She put herself in the middle to get his attention off me.

"That's why you hate me, right?" I press. "Because you're threatened that I'd dare to wear clothes you wouldn't, and it might catch the attention of the guy you've been trying to land for the past year. You're frustrated because you can't keep his attention and terrified that someone who can will come along and grab him out from under you."

Gloria huffs. "I have bigger concerns than who some guy likes," she snaps. "Royal's not my boyfriend. He can do whatever, and whoever, he wants. This is about you not knowing your place."

"Oh, and you know my place?" I ask. "Please, enlighten me. And then I'll tell you yours."

"This is impossible," she says, appealing to the admins. "Can't we just go back to class? We said we were sorry. Neither of us have serious injuries, and neither of our dads want legal action. What they want is for us to get an education."

The principal sighs. "Go back to class, Ms. Walton," he says. Then he turns to me. "We still need to address the issue of the stolen cockroaches with you."

I want to laugh. Who the fuck would want to steal a cockroach? They can go to our old place in the trailer park and get all they want for free. But I know better than to run my mouth to these assholes. They might pretend they're treating us fairly when the daughter of one of their top donors is in the room, but now they're going to lay it out for me. I'm not here because someone paid them millions. I'm here on a scholarship. I'm a charity case. If I fuck up, they can rip that away with a snap of their fingers.

They proceed to tell me just that, but in slightly more subtle terms. Only slightly, because a dumb bitch like me from the ghetto side of Faulkner couldn't possibly understand if they're too obscure. They could save their breath. I know way more about how the world works than half the kids at their posh school. But I shut my mouth and let them wealth-splain to me like I'm the uneducated white trash they take me for.

At last, I agree to write an apology letter to Mr. Harris for stealing his cockroaches for a prank—why I would prank myself is a question the school doesn't want to address—and to work off any loss of money caused by missing cockroaches. Because I can't resist, I have a little fun with them by telling them I can bring them a whole jar full of roaches from my house on Monday. They react as expected.

By the time they're done lecturing me, it's time for my last class of the day. Thank fuck they don't keep me until class has started and force me to walk in with everyone staring. I still get plenty of stares, and everyone starts murmuring to each other when I walk in, mostly because Gloria is in the same class.

It's a relief to slide into my seat at one of the round tables in my comp class. Since the first day, when Dixie welcomed me at their lunch table, I've been sitting across from Susanna and Quinn in this class. A third girl I don't know well, who also sits with them at lunch, rounds out the four-person table. That's the thing about a small school. It's hard to avoid anyone. I've only been here a week, and looking around, the room is full of already-familiar faces. The three people in my group, Baron and the Black guy who sits with them at lunch, and one of the Walton girls are all in this one class.

"Have y'all talked to Dixie since lunch?" I ask my table.

"She has student council on Fridays," Susanna says.

"I know," I say. "I ran into her out near the bleachers."

The girls exchange looks, and I know I hit on something. "Did she say what she was doing there?" Quinn asks.

I shrug. "I think she was talking to Colt."

"Oh, well, you know Dixie," Susanna says with a forced laugh. "She's nice to everyone."

"Even social pariahs like me and Colt," I say lightly.

"Just… Don't mention Colt Darling again, okay?" Quinn says, lowering her voice and casting a furtive glance over her shoulder to where Baron Dolce sits with his buddy and Gloria Walton. "Dixie's had it pretty hard at this school, and she's finally in a really good place. And that… Situation… Wouldn't go over well with some people."

"Got it," I say. "Didn't see a thing."

Colt is a Darling. Damn. So many fucking puzzle pieces to fit together.

"So, anyway," Susanna says. "Who's going to the game tonight?" They go on talking while we work on our assignment, and I turn over the information in my head, trying to piece together all the tidbits I've gotten since I started here. There's so much history between everyone, so much I don't know. It feels like I'll always be two steps behind, always trying to solve a puzzle without all the pieces.

Part of me knows that I should try harder here, and not just academically. I should make friends. I could use them. I could find out the answers to all the questions cluttering my brain. I could find someone to have my back instead of melting away when shit goes down, leaving me standing alone. I could go to the football game with these girls, slowly working my way into their group.

But I could also use the money I'll get tonight. To be honest, I could use the fight, too. There's nothing quite like the feeling of fists on skin, the shock that races up my arm, the burning of my muscles when I fight hard. I need my fix at the end of the week, and what I got from Gloria was just a taste.

After school, everyone else goes running off toward the stadium for a pep rally, bouncing around and whooping with excitement. Football rules our town, like a lot of southern small towns. I guess even stately schools full of snobs are not immune. I've never been into the whole sports scene, so I've never cared. My friends and I showed our school spirit by skipping the pep rallies and ditching school for an hour. But here, it feels different somehow. For the first time in my life, not participating makes me feel left out, like I'm missing something important. And not just the game. It's not about that. It's about bonding, about community.

What is this school doing to me? Why do I fucking care about being part of their community?

I shake my head at my foolishness and climb on my rickety bike and start for home. I can hear the roar of the crowd, a chant starting up as everyone gets their fill of school spirit.

The sound carves out a hollow inside me, one that stays long after the cheers have faded behind me.

But that's okay. The Dolces don't need another fangirl, and I don't want to be one. While the whole town cheers them on, I'll quietly kick ass in a much less obnoxious, attention-seeking way. It doesn't matter if there's a thousand people at their game and only a hundred at the fights. I don't need a whole town to lift me up. I don't need friends to show up for me and show their support. They can go gawk at the boys like everyone else.

I'll cheer for my own damn self.

Fucked Up Football

Dad knew what it took
To buy the soul of the town.
All the money in the world
Couldn't get us a key to the city
But a Hail Mary pass
Might.
Dad knew what it took
To win the heart of this town.
Risking his son's life
For the love of football
Was a move the whole town
Respected.
Dad knew what it took
To claim the crown in this town.
Everyone was watching
To see if we were villains or heroes
It all depended on whether we
Scored.

twelve

Harper Apple

MrD: I heard you got in a little tussle at school today.

BadApple: Who the fuck r u?

MrD: Tsk tsk. Your first week and you're already fighting.

I know I shouldn't be surprised. This guy has stalking down to a science. But damn. I'm becoming more and more suspicious that it's not the father but one of the guys themselves. How else would he already know I got in a fight? The Dolce boys are still at school, at the pep rally. As soon as I came home, I saw the little message up on the screen of the computer, which Mom left on.

BadApple: no comment

MrD: Don't you want to thank me for getting you out of trouble?

BadApple: Gotta hear this. How exactly r u taking credit for this one?

MrD: No one's pressing charges, are they?

BadApple: I'm guessing u already know the answer 2 that

MrD: I do.

BadApple: fishing 4 compliments much???

MrD: You're welcome.

BadApple: U R insufferable

MrD: Glad I could help.

BadApple: Again, what?

MrD: I told her father I wouldn't press charges if he didn't, either.

I stare at the screen for a long moment. The school told me my parent had agreed not to press charges. Obviously, I assumed they meant my mother, since I don't have a father. A chill wraps around me when I think about just how much influence this guy must have. He has himself on my contacts for school? They called him instead of my mom?

Which means Mom might not even know I was fighting at school, and I'd like to keep it that way and spare myself an ass-chewing. I'm glad I walked in and saw the chat box open on the computer before she did.

BadApple: U told them u were my dad? Pervy.

MrD: Call me daddy ;)

BadApple: barf

MrD: Aside from the fight, are you settling in okay?

I think about the hollow feeling in my chest after school today, when everyone else was doing something together, and I walked away. I'm not used to that kind of unity in a school. Faulkner High is so big that there were always lots of kids like me, more interested in skipping school than going to a pep rally. I'm not going to whine to this weirdo about that, though. Coming home was my choice. I could have stayed.

BadApple: Yep.

MrD: Took you a while to answer.

BadApple: Don't psychoanalyze me. Maybe I was taking a dump.

MrD: Are you ready to work for me?

BadApple: Sry, not a cam girl

MrD: I need you to get inside one of the most exclusive groups in WHPA and report back to me.

BadApple: wut

I stare at the screen, the little green rectangle cursor blinking back at me like a sightless eye. So, this is where all this was heading all along? I knew he wanted something, that nothing in life is free, but damn. I thought he'd want nudie pics or to meet up and fuck. I could have said no to those things.

I suppose I can say no to this, too.

Or…

Or I could stay the full two years at Willow Heights. Maybe some part of me knew I'd say no to the sex deal, and I knew he'd pull the scholarship. That's why I held myself at a distance, didn't pry too much into the history of everyone around me. I could have asked Susanna and Quinn. I could have asked Dixie from day one. I could have asked Colt more questions today.

But I didn't. I was curious, but some part of me thought I wouldn't be here for long, so it wouldn't matter. It was better not to hear the full story, not to get invested, not to be part of the community, the school spirit. I honestly never understood what that meant before. It was kind of a joke between me and the people I hung out with.

Rah-rah, shake your pompoms, look at the herd cheering when they're told, moooo…

We wanted to believe we were above it because we knew we didn't fit with the people who did that kind of thing.

Maybe we knew we were missing out, if only subconsciously, so it was better to make fun than to admit we were on the outside looking in. Today, I caught a glimpse of that. The feeling of togetherness, of pride, of being part of the larger whole. And yeah, there's a herd mentality component, but maybe that's not such a terrible thing. Maybe it would be okay to be part of the herd. Together, that herd is strong. It's always the animal that gets separated from the herd who becomes prey, after all.

MrD: Are you in?

BadApple: Do I have a choice?

MrD: You always have a choice.

BadApple: ok

MrD: Are you in?

BadApple: Yes

MrD: I knew you were a smart girl.

BadApple: But this is the only thing I'm doing. This is the trade. You got me the scholarship, I get you this information. There won't be any other added tasks later. No pics. No sex.

MrD: Not even a bj?

I swallow hard, remembering my earlier suspicion that this guy's sons shared the pic with him. Gross. Nothing I can do about it, though.

BadApple: no

MrD: I was kidding.

BadApple: sure u were

MrD: So, let's talk about this.

BadApple: the answer is no.

MrD: Not that. The assignment. Ready to hear the details?

BadApple: ok

MrD: There's a secret society at Willow Heights. Most people don't know about it, or they've only heard whispers. By the time you're done, you're going to know everything.

A scholarship in return for a badass assignment infiltrating a secret society? Sign me the fuck up. I'd do that shit for free.

Not that I'm going to tell him that.

BadApple: And u will 2

MrD: Exactly. I used to know, but things have changed.

BadApple: Give me all the info u can. I need more to get started.

MrD: The group was founded by the original backers of the school because they felt the parents and new donors were affecting policy too much, and the school was losing sight of its mission. Their sons were still students at the school, and they became the founders of the secret society. They met in what was originally planned as a storm shelter under the school. It was a secret weekly meeting at midnight. They called themselves the Midnight Swans.

I sit forward in my chair, a shiver of excitement going through me. I feel like Lara Fucking Croft—minus the tits. Secret societies? Dungeons under the school? This is literally the coolest thing that's ever happened to me. Not that I've set the bar very high, but still.

MrD: The Swans kept their membership small, secret, and very exclusive. I'm sure you know about the big changes that took place a few years ago, in town and at the school. The Swans were not exempt. With the new memberships, everything changed. I want you to be my eyes and ears in the halls of Willow Heights, not just the Swans. But I want that, too.

BadApple: u were kicked out

MrD: You don't need to know about my personal involvement. You only need to do your job and report back to me. I want to know everything about the Swans and how the school is being run, and I don't mean by the administration. I want to know about the boys who run that place, what they're up to, how they behave. I expect weekly briefings staring Friday.

BadApple: ur right. Will do. Signing off.

Damn, he got me to break my own rule, to get invested in the outcome of this. But it doesn't matter what his personal stakes in the matter are. It doesn't even matter who he is. All along, I thought he was Mr. Dolce, the boys' dad. But now I'm not so sure. Why would they kick him out of their secret society? Just because he's old? And why would he want to spy on his own sons?

I remember Dixie telling me this family took down the Darlings. I don't personally know any Darlings, but a couple went to FHS, and I saw them around. They're the kind of people everyone sneaks glances at, wondering what it's like to hold that much power. The Darling name is synonymous with Faulkner. They're town royalty, the way the real Waltons are state royalty.

They were definitely around for the founding of Willow Heights. If this guy got kicked out of his own secret society after the Dolces took down his family, it makes more sense that he's another Mr. D altogether—Mr. Darling.

I push back from the computer, startled to see that it's time to get ready for my fight. It doesn't matter who he is, I remind myself. He gave me a scholarship, and what he's asking in payment is far less degrading than what he could have asked. This isn't personal at all. If he wants me to spy on some assholes, so be it. They're entitled little shits and I don't owe them anything.

It's a job, the same as a fight or a poker game. Instead of money for my stash, it's a scholarship—worth way more than anything I could earn. If I graduate Willow Heights, I'm almost guaranteed to get into a decent school.

The only thing standing in my way is that fucking picture. It nags at the back of my mind, always there, always a threat. The shoe that never dropped. I need to get the picture. And now I need to get into the Swans. Lucky for me, I'm certain the people who took over the Swans and kicked out the olds are the same people who have my picture.

Not so lucky? They think I'm trailer trash who doesn't belong at their school, and I'm the absolute last person they'd let into their exclusive inner circle.

The question is, how do I convince them I'm worthy of being a Dolce girl?

Add More Weight

The coach says,
Are you sure, son?
I'm sure.
Add that shit until my muscles ache,
Until leg day is pain day
Until I can barely walk to my car after practice.
I'm sure.
Sure I'll never be caught unprepared,
never be smaller than anyone in the room,
never be outnumbered
or overpowered.
I'm sure.
Sure I'll work harder
Until I'm bigger and stronger
Sober and alert at all times
A better fighter
A faster runner
With more control
Than anyone.
I'm sure
Even if I have to stay up all night
While my brothers party
Lifting
Until there's no more weight to add
And I'm holding up
The whole world
And I'm so much better
Than everyone else
That they can't even
Touch me.

thirteen

Harper Apple

"So, can we talk about... You know," I say as I wait for Dynamo to unlock the gate and let me in. "Real life? Or is that one of the rules of *Fight Club*?"

"Best movie ever," he says, swinging the gate open for me to pass.

"No arguments here," I say.

"And yes, it's one of the rules, Appleteeny," he says with one of those slow, empty smiles. "We suffer all week for this. Why bring the bullshit here?"

"Fair enough," I say, hooking my thumb into the strap of the tiny duffle where I keep a change of clothes, pepper spray, a knife, and a box of tampons to stash my money in. "Want to hang out after?"

"Are you asking me out?" he says, his smile growing wider.

I shrug, sparing a glance at the handful of dudes waiting impatiently at the gate. "Sure."

"Ah, now, that wasn't very convincing," Dynamo says. "Aren't you gonna butter me up a little first?"

I thumb the rough edges of a cigarette burn in the nylon of my bag. "You have that whole tatted up, smoking under the bleachers bad boy thing going for you," I say. "I'm sure you get plenty of pussy."

"Which is why you're going to have to work a little harder to convince me," he says.

I sigh. I knew it would take some work to get in with the Dolces, but I naïvely forgot it would also take work to get any info. But nothing in life is free or easy.

I wait while Dynamo goes to the gate and lets the guys in. Then a group of couples comes in, the guys with trucker hats and shirts with the sleeves torn off to show their tats, their big-breasted girlfriends wearing T-shirts with roses and rhinestones, their roots growing out and their thick makeup trying to hide their age. These are my people, the ones who'd rather watch me beat the shit out of someone than go to a football game.

Dynamo closes the gate and comes back over to me. "Thought up anything you could tempt me with?"

"Greasy diner," I offer. "I'll pay."

Dynamo looks me up and down, then reaches out and curls his hand over the button of my jeans, pulling me in. I can feel his fingers on my bare skin, almost grazing my pubes. "I hear you give pretty good head."

I don't pull back, even as his first finger moves back and forth against my soft skin, teasing me. I bat my lashes up at him. "Oh yeah? Where'd you hear that?"

"I've got ears all over town, baby."

"I bet you do," I say. "And you bet I do."

"Oh really?" Dynamo bites his lip and tries to dip his hand further into my jeans, but I twist away.

"Yeah," I say, hardening my voice. "But I've never in my life been so desperate for a date that I promised a blowjob, and I'm not about to start now."

I flash him a peace sign, turn, and walk away. It's not that I don't like the guy. Aside from the money and the name, he's a lot like the other bad boys I've had things for. I'd probably go out with him if he asked, maybe even blow him, if I was feeling it. But I'm not bargaining blowjobs for information. That's a slippery slope I've had to avoid too many times lately. Apparently, rich people see a poor girl with an ass, and that's all they can think about. I have nothing else they want, so they ask for sexual favors.

But I'm not just an ass. A bitch, sure, but not an ass. There's plenty more to me than my body, and if someone is worth my time, they'll work for it. I don't have to get information from him. I'm sure Dixie would be happy to spill the gossip for free. I just thought Dynamo was more… My people.

But I wonder where he heard that rumor about me giving good head. If Mr. D is Mr. Darling, and he knows about it, did he tell Colt?

But no. I have no proof that Mr. D knows about the pics. Or Colt. Or are they the same person?

I shake my head, pushing away all thoughts as I head into the Slaughter Pen. Now is not the time for distractions. I clear my head, and I fight well, and I get my cut.

When I walk out at the end of the night, my bag slung over my shoulder, Dynamo calls to me from across the lot. I stop and watch him toss a few empties before jogging over.

"You headed out?" he asks.

"Yep."

"So, how about that diner you mentioned?"

"I thought you only ate if a BJ came in your Happy Meal."

"I hope nobody cums in my Happy Meal," he says with a grin.

"Then you'd better not ask for a BJ from me."

He falls into step beside me as we walk out the gate of the tall, chain-link fence that surrounds the warehouse where the Slaughter Pen is housed. "Damn, girl. You are not making me want to reconsider."

"You've reconsidered?"

"I'm going to get pancakes with you, aren't I?"

"Even if there's no BJs involved?"

"Can't blame a guy for trying," he says, tucking his left hand into his pocket. "If you had a dick, and you knew how good it feels to have it sucked, you'd ask for one, too."

"I'll have to take your word for that."

"You don't like your pussy sucked?"

"That escalated quickly."

"That's not an answer."

"I wouldn't know," I say. "My hookups were much more concerned with their dicks than my pussy."

"You're obviously dating the wrong caliber of dudes," he says, following as I steer us toward the all-night diner downtown, not far from the Slaughter Pen.

"And I'm sure you're going to tell me you're of a different caliber," I say.

"Well, I am pretty concerned with my dick," he admits.

We pass the tattoo shop that Mav's brother owns and step into the 1950's style greasy spoon diner. It smells like French fries and cigarettes, since this is the kind of place where you can still smoke inside. We slide into a corner booth and order pancakes and coffee. When the waitress leaves, Colt racks his laminated menu and fixes me with his guarded, cornflower blue gaze.

"What you want to talk about, Teeny?"

"I thought out here, we were going by real names."

"You said you wanted to talk about life."

"Yeah," I say, dropping the bratty attitude. "Thanks."

"What do you want to know?" he asks. "Now that I know you're not lusting after my dick, my patience might wear thin a little sooner, so ask me now."

"Okay," I say, liking his direct approach. "I need some insight into the rich side of Faulkner, I guess. You didn't tell me you were a Darling."

"Born and bred," he says, accepting his Coke from the waitress.

I take mine and thank her before going on. "So, Dixie says you ran this town until the Dolces came along a few years ago."

"Sounds like you know everything already."

I snort. "Hardly anything."

For a minute, neither of us speaks. Our tall, clear, red plastic cups sit on the checkered tablecloth between us.

"So, what happened?" I press. "That wasn't like, three generations ago. More like three years. You were part of it, right?"

"Yeah," he says. "We were all part of it. They came to town, those three guys at Willow Heights, plus one more and a sister. My cousins and I thought we were big stuff, you know? And they proved us wrong."

"How?"

Colt sighs and shifts in the booth, pulling at the knees of his jeans. "Well, one of my cousins fell for their sister. Hell, I guess we all kind of fell for her. But she fell for him back. Our families weren't having any of it, though. They hated each other. They wouldn't let them be together. My cousin and her ended up going missing during that flood on New Year's a couple years back. The cops and the whole town looked for them. We thought they'd run away at first, but they found the car a few days later. Said they died fucking in the back seat."

"Damn."

I remember that New Year's. In passing, Zephyr mentioned he was having a couple people over if I wanted to join. I was crushing on Maverick, so I'd walked over, hoping he'd be there. Because it was freezing cold and raining, no one but Mav and Zephyr's girl showed up, but I remember the electric high of hanging out with cool older kids and realizing they thought I was cool, too. We couldn't do a bonfire in the backyard, but his dad said we could burn shit in a barrel on the front porch.

At one point, his dad left to get beer and came back without the car. He said he'd sold it to get more beer. He and Zephyr got in an ugly fight about it, and I left with Maverick to save Zephyr the embarrassment. Mav asked if I wanted a tattoo, and we went to his house.

"That was just the beginning," Colt says, bringing me out of the memory of my world and back into his.

The waitress arrives with our pancakes and a carafe of syrup. We thank her and busy ourselves unwrapping the gold foil from the butter patties and spreading it.

"So, what's the rest?" I ask at last, drizzling syrup over the pale stack of pancakes.

"Our families had been feuding, but when we lost Devlin, it kinda crushed us," Colt says. "You know, he was the golden boy, the favorite son. Our grandpa had it all set up for him to be mayor one day. Maybe he would have been, I don't know."

I want to touch him, to take his hand, but I don't.

Colt goes on. "When he died, we were ready to throw in the towel, call a truce. It's all fun and games until your brother winds up dead."

"I'm sorry," I say, stacking the tiny white containers of creamer while he talks.

"We didn't have any fight left in us," Colt says, his expression darkening. "At least most of us didn't. Gramps would have kept going, but the rest of us were done. We just wanted to grieve."

"I'm sorry," I say again, because what else do you say when someone tells you they lost a brother and weren't allowed to grieve? One look at the guy says they were close—more than close. They were family. Blood.

Colt shrugs and slices viciously into his stack of pancakes. "That wasn't good enough for the Dolces. They blamed us for Crystal dying, for pretty much all the shit wrong in the world. And they made us pay."

I swallow hard, eyeing his hand. "Is that what happened there?"

"Some people like playing with fire."

I can't tell if he's talking about himself or not. I shake my head and smooth back a loose lock of hair that fell out of my messy updo. "Sorry. None of my business."

"Nah," he says, setting down his fork and grabbing a few blocks from my creamer pyramid. "I'd rather you ask than keep staring at it and then pretend you're not."

"Shit," I mutter, my face heating.

"Don't worry about it," he says. "Everyone does it. You know, I used to be a big shot like the Dolces. Played football. Had all the girls. And not just the ones who like bad boys who smoke under the bleachers." He gives me a lazy wink as he repeats my words.

"I'm pretty sure all girls like that. Even the ones who pretend they don't."

He shrugs. "They fucked up our family pretty bad, Harper. In one year, they systemically destroyed everything our fathers, grandfathers, and great grandfathers built over hundreds of years. You might not feel it on your side of town, but Faulkner's different. The small-town America vibe isn't quite the same when there's mafia men running it."

"Oh," I say, remembering calling them the Sopranos. Maybe I wasn't so far off. Not that Colt is an unbiased source. But still. It's hard not to feel for the guy who lost so much. He's right about me, though. On our side of town, we already had nothing to lose. How could we lose more? In some ways, maybe it's better to be someone who never knew any different, who hungers for a way out, a taste of something more. A guy like Colt who had it all, he knows what it tastes like, and all he has left is the bitter aftertaste.

His eyes are hard with it as he goes on. "Sometimes I wish they'd just killed us all instead of letting us live to suffer, watching them strut around like kings, seeing them continue to chip away at everything this town stands for and infect it all with their rottenness."

"Damn."

"I'm not talking little shit, like getting me off the team. I'm talking about murder and mayhem, sick shit you can't even imagine."

"Sounds like my kind of fun," I say, trying to lighten the mood.

"They got away with it, too," he says. "Ruining people's lives, their livelihoods. I guess we could have kept fighting. We did, for a while. But they were always just a little meaner, a little crazier. It was like, when they lost Crystal, they had nothing left to lose. We still cared about each other, about the town. They don't care about anything. They ran us into the ground, humiliated us, destroyed our family. They paid off the cops if they came looking, paid off judges if things went to court, paid off the mayor to look the other way." He shakes his head and wads up a napkin. "The mafia has endless pockets."

"But you're still rich."

"Not that rich." Colt lowers his voice and leans forward. "There are still Darling loyalists, though. Not everyone forgets their history when new money comes to town. We're not done fighting. We might look beaten, but one day…"

I think of Mr. D wanting info on the Dolces. Now I'm sure it's one of the Darlings, but I don't think it's Colt. Mr. D talked about the Midnight Swans, about the founding of the town, and how it had changed. I should be happy to do his bidding, to help him after what the Dolces did to him. And I do feel for Colt. But it still feels dirty. No one wants to be a snitch, and that's exactly what he's asking me to be.

I push the thoughts away, though. I don't owe the Dolces anything. I owe Mr. D.

Colt has only made my job a whole lot easier. Why should I feel guilty about spying on some people who sound pretty damn evil? Helping Mr. D take down a family that destroyed his and is destroying this town isn't a bad thing. I'm pretty sure Colt has no idea someone in his family is behind my inquiries, though.

I consider telling him, consider bringing him into this scheme to take back Faulkner, but when he reaches for his coffee with his scarred hand that's missing the middle finger, the words die on my tongue. This isn't a game. Or maybe it is, but it's a dangerous one, and it's not fair to involve him. He's played with Dolce fire, and he's been burned. He's no longer a player in this game, and he probably doesn't want to be. He might be bitter he lost, but he's accepted his defeat.

"So… Now what?" I ask Colt, mopping up syrup with a forkful of fluffy pancake. "You're the rebel who hangs out under the bleachers and runs an illegal fighting ring, and they're the kings of the school?"

He nods. "They got what they wanted in the end—to destroy our family. I hope they're fuckin' happy."

I think about that night at the tracks, about the look in Royal's eyes when he had his hands around my neck and I couldn't breathe. He looked capable of murder. He didn't look happy about it, though. I shake my head and take another bite of the sticky sweet pancakes, washing it down with the bitterness of cheap, scorched coffee before answering. "I've never seen a dude who looks less happy than Royal Dolce."

Colt shrugs. "They won the game, but they lost their sister."

"Sounds like they lost her before they won the game."

"If you'd met her, you'd know it wasn't worth it. Not even to destroy the Darling legacy."

"She must have been really something," I say, finishing off my food and pushing the empty plate away.

Colt tosses some money down on the table without even counting it and stands. "She was."

I'm surprised at the disappointment I feel that I won't have an accomplice, and the twinge of sadness at his words. It's not that I'm jealous of some dead girl I've never met. It's more that I'm jealous of what she meant to someone—to a lot of people. Not just to her family, but to a guy whose family was destroyed by hers. If I was gone, not even my mother would mourn. She loves to tell me how much easier her life would be if I wasn't around.

I try telling myself what I always do, that I don't need anyone. Not my mother, not friends, not an accomplice. But a little voice inside whispers the truth—even if I don't need them, I still want them.

"Her brothers, though?" Colt says. "Straight psychos, all three of them. After what they did to my sister… She'll never be the same. None of us will."

I want to ask what they did, but it's clear he's done with this conversation. "Thanks for the warning," I say instead.

"Just giving you the info you asked for," he says, as if remembering he doesn't know me or owe me shit. "Do what you want with it. Just know that whatever you can imagine in your worst nightmare, it wouldn't even phase them. They've seen it and done it—and laughed while they did."

What They Say

Did you hear about the fire?
The one that burned the man?
No, the one that burned the girl.
Did you hear about the girl?
The one they drove out of her mind/ off the bridge/ out of town?
No, the one that disappeared.
Did you hear about the disappearance?
The one that took the car and the couple?
No, the one that took the boy.
Did you hear about the boy?

There never was a boy, Helen.
You must mean the monster.

fourteen

Harper Apple

"What do you think you're doing?"

I pause, momentarily caught off guard by the ice cold tone of Royal's voice. I work up my courage and remind myself I belong here just as much as they do. There are no assigned seats. I have as much right to sit here as anyone else in the school. I have no real plan. I'm just jumping in with both feet. Whatever they throw at me, I can take it.

"I'm eating lunch," I say, giving them my sweetest smile. I set my plate down and take a seat across the round table from Royal. He stares at me with such incredulousness that I want to laugh out loud. His brothers flank him on either side, two buddies off to their sides, and the Dolce girls filling the remaining seats. All but one.

"You can't sit here," Royal grits out between clenched teeth.

Baron holds up a finger, as if telling him to hold that thought. And though I'm sure Royal is the leader of their little posse, he obeys. He crosses his arms, which makes his muscles bulge in all the right ways, and stares down at me with hooded eyes.

I try not to let that asshole pose make me hot, but god, he's fucking sexy when he's trying to intimidate me. I'm not sure if I should be scared or aroused, but I'm pretty sure I shouldn't be both at the same time.

Baron takes a sucker out of his pocket and unwraps it slowly. The crinkling of the plastic is the only sound in the room. My heart hammers against my ribs, but I force myself not to move. When Baron finally speaks, I swear everyone in the café leans forward to hear him.

"What do you want?" he asks.

"Oh, are we negotiating already?" I ask. "That was easier than I thought."

"We don't negotiate with trailer trash," Royal growls.

"Why are you here?" Baron clarifies, tucking the sucker into his cheek and nodding at my plate.

"Didn't you say everyone had to bow and scrape and kiss your ass?" I ask. "Well, here I am, all puckered up."

"Leave," Royal says flatly.

"No, no, wait," Duke says, leaning across the table toward me. "I want to hear this. So, you're ready to fall in line?"

"Already in line," I say. "Straight and narrow, single file, all that shit."

"You're going to do what we want, when we want it?" he asks, positively leering at me.

"If I can be your little Dolce girl," I say, batting my eyes at him.

"No." Royal stares me down, his dark eyes seeing right through me, the way they always seem to. They all know I'm full of shit. I'm not hiding it. But he's the only one who looks like he knows it's more than that.

Duke sighs and reaches across the table, snagging my plate and spinning it toward himself. "Thanks for bringing me my lunch," he says.

I reach toward him, but his hand clamps on mine, his grip crushing even though his mouth is still smiling. "I'm not your servant," I snap.

"Now you are," he says. "The next time you put something in your mouth in this school, it'll be my dick."

"Remember that next time you come begging for crumbs," Baron says. "Now leave, before you piss off the important people."

"But I'm one of your little concubines now," I say. "Don't they all sit here so they can fan you and feed you grapes?"

"That's not how it works," Royal says. "Now if you know what's good for you, you'll walk away and don't look back."

"And remember what I said," Duke says, casually adjusting himself in case I've forgotten about his dick already.

I stare back at Royal, still sitting there with his arms crossed, his shoulders filling out his buttoned shirt so well I can see the definition in his shoulders, his chest, his biceps.

For a long minute, neither of us move. At last, he stands. Everyone at the table stands a second later, and as one, they turn and walk away. They descend on another table, and the few people sitting there scatter to find other seats so their royalty can take their place. I sit frozen, suddenly aware of every eye in the cafeteria on me. I don't move, hardly dare to breathe. I don't even have food to occupy me. I am alone, exposed for the pariah I am.

Suddenly, my throat is tight, and it's all I can do not to get up and run out. I won't give them the satisfaction, though. I blink hard, forcing away the stinging in my eyes, glad my back is to the room so no one can see how close to tears I am. I sit, emptyhanded, not daring to move a muscle and break the careful, fragile control I have on myself right now.

All around the room, I hear the whispers. Then the conversations. Laughter. Giggling.

I don't turn to see what they're laughing about. I don't want to see who's still looking, who pities me, who thinks I'm pathetic, and who thinks I'm as repulsive as the Dolces make me out to be.

They don't matter. The laughing people. The scornful ones. The ones with friends. The guys who won't date me now, the girls who won't be my friends. Everyone who sits by quietly, not wanting to draw the wrath of the town's most powerful bullies, and the ones who gleefully participate in their sickest schemes. None of them matter.

I matter. Getting out of this town matters. What I tell Mr. D matters.

I've never been so relieved to hear the scrape of chairs when people start getting up to return their plates. I stand, my legs feeling wooden as I walk out the door without looking back. As soon as I reach the hall, I start walking faster, determined to make it to safety before I cry. When I think of going to my next class, though, I know I won't make it. Instead of going to my locker, I veer off, pushing out the door and heading for the football field.

I'm not even halfway there when I see Colt emerge from the shadows. He stops when he sees me, though, leaning on one of the supports and watching me approach. When I reach him, he holds out a pack of cigarettes. Without a word, he takes one out and sets it between his lips, lighting up before handing me the lighter.

Neither of us speak for a few minutes. At last, I realize I'm still holding his lighter, and I hand it back. "Thanks."

He slides the lighter in his pocket and keeps his hand there. "Dolce drama?" he asks.

"How'd you guess?"

He raises a brow while he takes a drag. "I didn't," he says, grinning and letting smoke drift out of his smile like some ghoulish Halloween mask. "It's already on the blog."

"You read Dixie's blog," I say. It's not even a question. Everyone reads it. She told me the name of it, but I haven't looked because I don't really want to see what's on there. I probably should, but considering my infamous dick-slap is probably front page news, I'm going to skip that one. I'll have to get gossip the good, old-fashioned way.

"Everybody reads Dixie's blog," Colt says.

Still, I didn't really expect my tatted up, fight-ring ready, new friend to read a gossip blog.

"You know her or something?" I ask, blowing smoke out the corner of my mouth, enjoying the charge of nicotine through my veins.

"No," Colt says, scowling at me.

I give him some side eye. "Really? Because I saw her coming out from under the bleachers the first time I came out here, and you were the only one here."

"It must have been someone else," he says. "I barely know the girl."

I start to argue, then shrug it off. If he doesn't want me knowing his business, I can respect that. I'm not here to spy on him. So, I thank him for the cigarette, and we finish up in silence before heading inside. I'm glad I'm late to class. It means I don't have to face anyone in the hall.

I dread going to school the next day, but I know I have to suck it up and keep going, keep trying, until I get the job done. Mr. D expects that report.

So, at lunch the next day, I go straight to the café without going to my locker. I arrive early and waltz in like I own the place every bit as much as the other Dolce girls, the ones given that title by the Dolces themselves. I'm the only self-proclaimed Dolce girl.

After getting my plate, I take a seat in the same spot as yesterday, directly across from where Royal sits. No one ever sits here. At first, I thought it must be reserved for someone, but now I've realized that he likes to be able to sit with his back to the wall beside the door and see the entire cafeteria. He doesn't want my big head in the way.

A minute later, he walks in with his posse. His step falters for just a second when he sees me there, but I notice. He steps up to the table and glares down at me.

"What—the fuck—are you doing?" he asks, his dark eyes burning with that aching emptiness that makes me shiver, makes me want to run away but at the same time, to go closer, to let myself be sucked in by the darkness of his soul that calls to mine.

"This is the best table," I point out.

"That's why it's *our* table."

"There's room for you," I say, gesturing to all the empty seats around us. A crowd is gathering behind his squad, bottlenecked in the door of the café, but no one moves to make way.

"Get the fuck out of our table," Royal warns.

I shrug. "I don't see your Dolce crest stamped on it," I say. "In fact, I don't even see a plaque saying your big daddy donated it. So, I think it's fair game."

"It's not."

"Honestly, I didn't expect you to come back," I say, staring him down across the table. My heart is beating wildly in my chest, but I won't back down. "I thought I scared you away yesterday."

"I'm not scared of you," he says, his posture tense, like he's about to spring across the table and throttle me.

"Hm, I seem to remember you running away yesterday," I say. "I must be pretty intimidating to make a big man like you run scared."

His big hands curl around the back of his seat, the two of them almost covering the entire top of the chair. An absurd thought enters my mind, a flash of all the guys I've heard say "more than a handful is a waste." If that's the case, it would take some pretty huge tits to satisfy this guy.

"How do you expect us to eat with your fuck-ugly face right in front of us?" Royal asks, his words low and laced with venom. "It's enough to make anyone lose their appetite."

For a second, I can't think of a response. It's the lowest cheap shot a guy can take, calling a girl ugly, and I know that. But it's easy because it works. It hurts. I want to say it doesn't bother me, that I know I'm more than a pretty—or ugly—face. But I've heard the echo of my mother's words so many times they're in my cellular makeup. In a world where looks are all a girl has, being ugly is the worst thing she can be. If I don't have beauty that a man can recognize, I have nothing. I am nothing.

But I know my worth, even if they don't. Even if my own mother doesn't.

"Be that as it may," I say carefully. "This is clearly the best table in the café. Which means this is where I belong."

"Let's show her where she belongs," Baron says, stepping around one side of the table.

"Time to take the trash out, girls," Gloria says, hovering behind Royal's shoulder like an annoying mosquito. Her double black eyes give me some satisfaction.

Baron reaches for me, but I'm faster, and I'm out of my chair in half a second. Duke grabs me from behind as I back away from his brother. I throw an elbow into his ribs, and he grunts, grabbing my arm and twisting it behind my back. He rips my arm up, expecting me to bend over the table so he can make a joke about fucking me in the ass, undoubtedly.

Instead, I spin out of his hold and drop to the floor, landing on my ass. While he's busy laughing, I brace myself on my palms and swing my legs around, taking his feet out from under him. He stumbles forward and grabs for a chair but falls to his knees anyway. I start to move in for a good kick to the groin, but someone grabs my hair from behind, yanking me backwards across the floor.

"That's enough of that," Baron growls in my ear, yanking both my hands behind me and holding them pinned against his chest with his forearm. He wraps his other arm around me, hoisting me to my feet. I kick at his legs, trying to get a heel to his kneecap, but Duke hops to his feet and grabs my legs.

"Let's do this shit," he crows, pumping a fist in the air before grabbing one of my ankles in each hand.

I buck and twist, slamming my head against Baron's chest, but they're both twice my size, and there's no breaking free now. Everything in me is screaming in panic, but I force myself to go still, be a deadweight in their hands. I need to save my energy for escaping whatever they have planned when they put me down.

A crowd has gathered to watch, chattering excitedly at the prospect of entertainment. The Dolces march me out of the cafeteria and down the short hallway to the door that leads outside. I've gone out these doors to escape to the bleachers, but they turn the other way once we're outside. I have no idea where they're taking me, and terror knifes through me, but I don't move a muscle, even though adrenaline is spiking through me, making my whole body shake with anticipation.

"Good girl," Baron says. "See, it wasn't so hard to be obedient, after all. Was it?"

They carry me around the corner and stop at a pair of Dumpsters and a recycle bin.

"Really?" I ask. "This is the most original thing you can come up with?"

"Open her up, girls," Duke says, starting to swing my feet.

Baron gets in on the action, the two of them swinging my body back and forth to get momentum. Okay, I can deal with a Dumpster. Not my favorite place to be, but better than what I thought was about to go down.

One of the girls steps forward and unlocks a padlock hanging from the front of the thing, since apparently even

Willow Heights' trash is so fancy it needs to be protected. Dawson Walton and DeShaun Rose step forward to throw open the lid before stepping back. The twins are about to send me flying when a familiar, tattooed figure comes strolling up beside the Dumpster.

He leans an elbow on it, watching the proceedings with casual disinterest. "Is that really necessary?" he drawls.

"Fuck off, Dynamo," Royal snaps. "This has nothing to do with you."

"Hell, yeah, it's necessary," Duke yells, and with a final heave, they send me sailing into the bin. I crash onto heaps of black, plastic bags, warm and reeking of spoiled milk and rotting food. My head hits the back wall with a thud, and for a second, all I can hear is a loud, metallic ringing in my ears.

"What's it to you?" Royal asks.

Colt ashes his cigarette over the edge of the bin. "Nothing."

"Let's toss him, too," Duke says. "Trash with trash."

I'm just getting my head clear enough to struggle upright when they grab Colt and heave him over the side. I try to jump up before he lands on me, but he slams into me before I can stand, and we both go sprawling. I kick at him, struggling frantically to free myself while he groans and rubs his head. The rubber lid of the bin falls closed, plunging us into dank darkness. I shoot out from under Colt, jabbing at the lid. It pops up about a foot, but someone crushes it back down. Scrambling on the sliding, hot bags of trash, I shove at the lid, but it only jounces a bit.

"Let me out," I yell. Outside, the guys laugh as I throw my shoulder at it, trying to get out. This goes on for about five minutes.

"I'm bored," Royal grumbles. "Let's go."

For a second, relief washes through me, and I sink back, wiping my hair off my sweaty face. And then I hear the horrible click of finality as the lock snaps closed.

"Let's roll it," Duke yells, pounding on the lid with his fists.

Oh god. I'm going to die in here, suffocated under bags of rotting trash. "Let me the fuck out," I yell, banging on the lid again.

"Leave them," Royal says. "They deserve each other."

Someone bangs a fist on the lid one more time. "Rape her once for me," Baron calls, and they all bust up laughing. The voices move away, and after a minute, we're left in silence.

"You couldn't have helped me out there?" I ask, jiggling the lid, trying to see if I can bend up one corner.

"It's better not to fight them," Colt says. In the sliver of light that comes in when I push up the lid, I can see him reclining on the bags of garbage like it doesn't bother him at all. Meanwhile, I'm trying hard not to lose my shit. Let's just say small spaces and I don't get along that well. I press my nose and mouth to the opening, trying to suck in a breath of the clean air outside. In here, it feels hotter by the second, and I can't seem to get my lungs full without wanting to gag at the smell. I can feel a layer of damp, nasty sweat breaking out on me.

"Are you just going to lie there?" I snap at Colt.

A second later, he flicks his lighter, and I think he might help. Instead, he lights up a cigarette. Just what this sweltering, smelly, tiny space needs—smoke.

"Do you mind?"

"Nah," he says. "It's not my first dumpster dive. Chill out there, Appleteeny."

That's when the smoke hits me, and it's not the acrid scent of tobacco. When he holds it out, I nearly fumble it I'm in such a hurry to get it to my mouth. I'm *this-close* to freaking the fuck out, and I know that's not going to help anything. I take a few deep hits before passing it back. Fuck weed etiquette right now. Desperate times.

Colt doesn't seem to mind. He's scrolling on his phone.

When the cannabis sinks in, I can breathe again, even though it's hotter and smellier than ever. "Thanks," I say, sinking back on the warm, disturbingly soft bags. "Sorry I was being a bitch. Not my first dumpster dive, either."

I don't add that mine were voluntary, that I've scavenged food this way when things were bad, mostly the year I skipped school. The year before, at the end of my eighth grade, Mom had gotten a decent job and a halfway decent boyfriend and moved us out the trailer park, and for a while, I'd thought it could be better. She spent most of her time at her boyfriend's house, but I'd take that over the ones she dragged home to bang her headboard against the wall and keep me up all night, then leer at me over coffee in the morning.

And then came the end of summer, and with it, the inevitable. I'd been holding my breath waiting for it even as I hoped it would never come—the moment Mom stumbled in sobbing in the middle of the night. I took care of her as she ranted and raved about how evil he was, how evil all men were. That night was followed, as always, by all-nighters with her friends and whatever guy was drunk enough to bang her, then the loss of her job, this time accompanied by the confession that the only reason she got the decent job in the first place was that she was already seeing Mr. Hot Shot. Still, that was one of her longest relationships, and one of the worst breakups.

Hence the attempts at finding food, which didn't go too well at first. But then one night after I'd been out with Zephyr, he wanted to stop by a store on the way home. I told him it was closed, and with no shame whatsoever, he shrugged and said it was one of the best places to Dumpster dive. After that, he showed me the places that had good food like dented cans or ones missing labels, and those that locked their Dumpsters, and those that would call the cops if they saw you on their security cameras. Apparently some people would rather the poor starve than get anything for free—even expired food they couldn't sell and considered trash.

Colt nudges my shoe with his. "What you thinkin' about there, Teeny?"

"We're getting high in a Dumpster right now," I say. "Reclining on our throne of garbage."

"That's what you were thinking about?"

"Nah," I say. "Just some guy I used to know. But what we really should be thinking about is how to get out of here before we bake into a garbage casserole."

"Ah, relax," Colt says, tugging at my elbow when I start to rise. "Don't you want to know what I was thinking about?"

"Sure. What were you thinking about?"

"About that blowjob."

I can't help but laugh. "You can't be serious. We're in a literal dump surrounded by rotting garbage. That turns you on?"

"No," he says, grinning at me with slow, stoned eyes. "You turn me on."

"Be serious," I say. "And you better not be thinking about raping me just because Baron said that."

"Not a rapist," he says. "Even if I was, I wouldn't fuck with you."

"Good," I say. "Because I have a knife."

"I've seen you fight without a knife," he says. "I wouldn't fuck with you even if you didn't have one. You're a crazy bitch, you know that?"

I jerk my chin in a nod. "Thanks."

"No worries, Teeny," he says.

"Well, we've got some worries," I say. "I can't break the corner of this, and it's too thick to bend."

"Someone will come," he says, toking on the joint and thumbing through his phone.

"Seriously?" I say. "That's your solution? What if they don't come? Do you know when the trash truck picks up?"

"No," he admits.

"And do you have a plan for when they dump the whole bin into their truck and compact us?"

When he doesn't answer, I take out my knife and start trying to saw my way out. It's ridiculously hard and agonizingly slow. At last, I hear the rush of students as school lets out and everyone comes outside to hang around and talk or rush to their cars and peel out of the lot.

I hear the scuff of shoes on pavement and freeze, suddenly sure that someone will come tell me I'm destroying city or school property by trying to cut myself out of a death trap. Instead, I hear the jingle of keys, and a second later, someone throws the lid open. I blink against the sunlight, blinded after so long in the dank inside of the bin.

"Not again," comes a familiar sweet, southern voice. "I thought they were done messing with you. What'd you go and do this time?"

Colt jumps to his feet and vaults over the side of the bin, reaching a tattooed arm over the side for me. I grab it and jump down with him and Dixie, our savior for the day.

"See, someone came," Colt says, waving his phone at me. "Patience, Teeny. Sometimes that works better than brute force."

"Tell that to my fists."

"All I know is, I didn't break a sweat," Colt says. "I was just chilling in there while you freaked out and tried to cut your way out with a pocketknife."

I narrow my eyes at him. "You could have told me you knew someone with a key."

"If you'd gone all *128 Hours* on me and tried to saw off your arm, I would have stopped you."

I roll my eyes at him. "Thanks."

"Why were you in there?" asks Dixie, who's been following our conversation like she was waiting for a place to interject.

"That's where I live," I say. "Seeing as how I'm the white trash queen and all."

"I'm sorry," Dixie says. "Those boys have more power than they know what to do with. I swear, they used to be real nice. Or, at least kinda nice. Somewhere deep inside, they're just lost little boys who need someone to love them enough to tell them no."

"Is that what we're going with now?" Colt asks. "I thought deep inside they were sociopaths who ruin everything they touch just for the fun of it."

"Well, that's another way to put it," Dixie says. "My way was just a little nicer."

"As much as I'd love to stand around debating the merits of the guys who threw us in the trash like we're garbage, I missed some classes, so I should probably go catch the teachers before they leave for the day," I say, pulling my damp shirt away from my skin.

"Wow, you're like a nerd, aren't you?" Colt asks.

I fix him with a look. "Yeah, pretty much. What about it?"

"Nothing," he says, holding up his hands. "It's cool. Go get that extra credit."

I narrow my eyes at him, trying to figure out if he's saying that because he knows something. Something about Mr. Behr. That life seems far away now, after only a few weeks, but I have to remember it's still there. The Dolces could release that picture any day. After the way I've been antagonizing them, I'm surprised they haven't already.

Colt was right. I do attack everything head on, with brute force, and this was no different. But these boys are sneaky. They hold their cards close to their chest. They'll play that trump card when they're ready. Which means I need to be more careful, more clever, if I'm going to get anywhere with them.

I start to turn away, then go back to something that's been nagging at the corner of my mind for hours. It pops to the forefront all at once, smacking me in the face.

When Colt showed up, Royal called him *Dynamo.*

"Hey, Colt," I say, backpedaling toward the building. "Does Royal fight?"

Colt shrugs, and his gaze flicks to Dixie for just a fraction of a second. It's so fast she misses it because she's looking at me. But I don't miss it.

"How would I know?" he says. "It's not like I follow the guy around to see what illegal shit he's into."

"Right," I say, giving them a wave before heading inside, still sweaty and reeking of garbage. But nothing is going to stop me from keeping my scholarship, and if that means I have to go to my teachers smelling like sour milk and rotten lettuce, then that's what I'll do. I don't even mind. Because finally, I have something.

Royal either fights or goes to the Slaughter Pen to watch. I've never seen him at my fights, which makes sense. He's off doing the whole Friday Night Lights thing while I'm fighting. But he knows Colt by his fight club name. Which means that on Saturday nights, when the guys fight, he's either on the sidelines placing bets or in the ring fighting.

Fight Club

The first rule
Hit harder
The second rule
Hit smarter
The third rule
Make them bleed
The fourth rule
Make them pay
The fifth rule
Leave them broken on the floor
The sixth rule
Leave them wanting more
The seventh rule
Drive to the bridge
The eighth rule
Stand on the edge
The ninth rule
Watch your sister die
The tenth rule
Never, ever cry.

fifteen

Harper Apple

I gape at the computer screen, not quite believing people live like this. I tried to look up the Dolce house at home, but Mom didn't pay the bill again, so we're sans internet. But I had to know where they lived, so I did a quick search at the beginning of class. Risky, since after a little scheduling mishap where I had to have my classes shuffled around a little, I now have a Dolce boy in every single one of my classes. But I sit in the back corner, and though people are milling around me because the heat's finally broken for a day and the windows are flung wide, no one is paying attention to me.

A quick search brings me what I need. A sprawling white Confederate mansion set back from the road, dual staircases curving up the front of the house to the second-floor veranda, which circles the entire house. It looks like something out of a movie. It's not exactly what I expected, though. Stupid that my brain conjured a picture of a modern house just because they're from a city, but so it goes. I pictured something with tons of glass and maybe some natural wood and stainless steel, something masculine and tasteful like their clothes.

I knew there was a rich area on the north end of Faulkner, but I've never been there. Seeing a house, even one that looks nothing like I imagined, makes it so much more real, just how far from my universe these boys live. Hell, until today, I didn't even know there were schools whose windows could open. I'm used to the narrow, rectangular windows set high in the walls at FHS, like it's a prison. I've stepped into someone else's world, and I don't know the rules, and seeing this house only makes me more aware of how carefully I need to tread.

Colt was wrong about them. They have a lot to lose.

Warm breath curls into my ear, sending a shiver racing through me. "Stalk much?"

I nearly jump out of my chair, my cheek colliding with Royal's. He chuckles against my neck, and another shiver races through me, this one charged with electricity. I try to scoot back, but his hand is on the back of my chair. He slides into the seat next to me, even though it's not where he sits. I can still feel the heat of his skin against my cheek, and it's all I can do not to lift my hand and run my fingertips over my skin, see if it was real. I try to come up with an excuse for why I'm sitting here staring at a picture of his house, but nothing comes.

He doesn't look pissed, though. He smirks at me instead. "It's okay," he says. "If you're desperate enough to walk across town for a pity fuck, I'd slum it for a night. That room's mine." He points to a window on the top floor of the house.

"I thought you had a girlfriend in college," I say, recovering myself.

His brows quirk. "Who told you that?"

"I don't remember," I admit. "Probably Dixie."

A flicker of something slips over his expression, and then he gives me those hooded eyes, his chin raised just a bit so he can stare me down just a little better than he could from his usual six and a half feet. "And you think that would stop me from fucking a tight little piece of ass like you?"

I roll my eyes and repeat something I've heard one too many times. "A hole's a hole, right?"

Quinn, who usually sits with me, hovers a few feet away until Royal sees her. He gives her an annoyed flick of his fingers, and she scurries off. Guess we're sitting together and talking about fucking, then.

"Don't believe everything you hear, sweetheart," Royal drawls in his New York accent.

I'm used to people calling me sweetheart and honey and darling. It is the South, after all. But when he says it, it's different. It sounds straight up gangster, like a threat a mobster says before putting cement shoes on you.

Hope you're ready to swim with the fishes, sweetheart.

Okay, they probably don't say that, but it's still different to hear that word in his dangerous, accented voice. Again, that little shiver of fear and excitement prickles my skin. Yeah, it's fucked up. But for a girl like me, whose only lasting possession is the body she was born with, money is seductive. For a girl like me, who's had to carve out respect with her fists, power is intoxicating. And he has both—in spades.

"What is it I shouldn't believe?" I ask, resting my chin in my hand and giving him a look that's somewhere between a challenge and an invitation. "That you have a girlfriend, or that you think one hole's as good as the next?"

Royal reaches up, slowly brushing the hair back from my cheek. I freeze. My breath catches in my throat, and I know I should slap the shit out of him for thinking he's entitled to touch me, but oh fucking hell, it feels like my whole body is being lit up when his fingertips brush my skin. He watches his fingers moving against my face, collecting an errant lock, winding it behind my ear with painful, agonizing care. When his fingers skim around the shell of my ear, barely brushing my earlobe, a tremor starts deep in my core, and I'm so lightheaded I think I'll topple right out of my chair.

"Neither," Royal whispers, leaning closer. His gaze dips to my lips, and he wets his own lips, and fuck me, but all I can think about is kissing him. If he can touch my cheek and make me light up like it's fucking Christmas, what would those lips feel like on mine? What would those big hands feel like on my body?

God, I need to stop, but he's fucking intoxicating. His touch, his voice, the animal heat of his body pouring over me like warm honey, the dark, spicy smell of him when he leans close, and most of all, his eyes. There's something about them that pierces me straight to the core, like he's shining a light on my darkest shames, cataloguing each of my deepest fears. His gaze strips me bare, and I feel all the vulnerability and eroticism of the first moment a man lays eyes on my naked body, even though I'm sitting in a class full of people, fully clothed.

His fingers graze my jawline, his gaze holding mine. It's not a feeling like being pinned, but one that draws me in, pulling me closer, sucking me into his world. The darkness I can see hidden behind those eyes calls to mine, invites me to come and play his sick, twisted games, invites me to turn away from the light and dance in the darkness with him.

He lifts my chin, and I can't hear the teacher or anything in the room anymore. All I can hear is my heart racing in my ears, his heavy breaths against mine. Nothing else exists. He skims his thumb slowly across my lower lip, and a shiver rolls through my body, pinching my nipples tight and making my knees squeeze together and my lips part as an inaudible gasp escapes.

Royal leans even closer, until our foreheads are almost touching, our mouths only an inch apart. "You really made up a girlfriend for me so you could pretend that's why I'm not interested in ridiculous high school girls and their petty drama?" he purrs, his voice warm across my skin like velvet.

"What?" I snap, yanking back from his touch, my heart racing and my head spinning. How could I let him get to me for even a minute?

The teacher gives us an annoyed look. Royal chuckles and slouches back in his chair. And even though he's pretending to be all cool, I can see a ridge in his pants that makes my thighs quiver.

Touching me made him hard. It's not just me who's feeling the crackling heat between us, then.

He doesn't do any of the silly things boys do to hide it when they get inappropriate erections in class. He just sits there, letting me look at the thick shape pressing up against the fabric of his fine navy slacks. A smug smile pulls at his lips, like he's very much enjoying the fact that I'm eye-fucking him in the back of the classroom. I can't help it. The dude is probably six and a half feet tall, and let's just say, his cock is not out of proportion with the rest of his body.

"As to your other question," he says slowly, waiting for me to drag my gaze away from his crotch, "It's too stupid to answer."

I shrug, trying to fight my way through the fog he blew into my brain. "It wasn't really a question. Just something guys like you say to make girls feel worthless."

"Or maybe it's something girls like you say to make themselves feel like they *aren't* worthless," he says with a smirk. "But we all know the truth, don't we? Saying every pussy is equal is like saying every bank account is equal."

"Oh, so you only fuck the twenty-four karat gold ones," I say.

"Exactly. You're not my caliber."

"Sounds hard, cold, and dry to me," I say, turning to my laptop and forcing myself not to check his crotch again. We're supposed to be doing partner work, so at least we're not the only ones talking. "But hey, to each their own. If that's what you're into, no judgment here. Guess I won't be climbing through your window anytime soon, though. I'm all flesh and bone and blood. No Midas pussy here."

"You're a cum dumpster," he says flatly. "As long as I double bag it so I don't catch any of your diseases, I'll throw a girl like you a bone once in a while. Helps me appreciate it more when the pussy's good."

"Sorry, not interested."

"What?" he asks, looking annoyed. "*I'm* not interested."

"If that's what you need to tell yourself."

"I'm not," he grits out.

"You're the one trying to convince me to come to your house."

He snorts. "I thought you were trying to convince me you were worthy of our table at lunch. Shouldn't you be telling me you're secretly as good as all the other girls, I just have to work really hard to see it?"

"Nope," I say.

Royal crosses his arms and narrows his eyes. "Why not?"

"Maybe I've decided your table isn't worthy of *me*."

Royal shakes his head and chuckles. "I gotta hear this."

"You guys think you're scary, but you're basic," I say. "Throwing the losers in the dumpster? Come on. That's in every teen movie since the eighties. Are you going to give me a swirlie next?"

Royal's jaw works back and forth, but he doesn't say anything.

"And just now, you're trying to insult me by telling me my pussy wouldn't be up to your standards. That's like me saying you have a small penis. It's not hurtful. It's pathetic."

Royal smirks at me, his brow cocked as he glances down at his lap before giving me a meaningful look. "Go right ahead," he says. "You think I'm insecure about my dick?"

"Exactly my point," I say. "I'm not insecure about my pussy, Royal. We're not fucking, so why would I care what you think of it? And even if we were, don't you think it's sad that the only way you can think to hurt me is to disparage something that only affects *you*? I don't care if it's good by a random guy's standard. I know exactly how good it is."

Royal scoffs and leans forward, resting his elbow on the table. "The fact that you don't care that you're loose as a whore and probably smell like the inside of that dumpster proves *my* point."

I feel heat creeping up my neck, and I want to punch the guy's teeth out, but I remind myself he's talking shit. He doesn't know the first thing about my pussy. Fucking two guys hardly makes me a whore, even if the first one told everyone I was. I'm sick of assholes telling me what I'm worth based on who's been between my legs.

"That's supposed to bother me?" I ask. "Are you ashamed of being a whore or smelling like a locker room?"

"The difference is, I could fuck a hundred girls, and my dick wouldn't be any smaller."

I laugh and shake my head. "Maybe not smaller," I concede. "But it would be a lot less special to a girl who wanted to matter to you."

"She'd never know," he says smugly.

"I'm pretty sure everyone knows you're a whore."

Darkness flickers across his gaze, and his jaw sets. "Everyone already thinks you're a whore, Harper. Once they know you're so loose that after you fucked every guy at Faulkner, you went for the teachers, you'll be so ruined not even a desperate bottom feeder will fuck you in a dumpster again."

His eyes are hard, his voice low and vicious.

Damn it. Why'd I have to provoke him? I can't let myself forget that he has that picture. I couldn't care less whether the guys here want to fuck me. He thinks he can destroy my life by releasing it, but he's not thinking ahead. He'll also destroy my future.

I want to say something about Dynamo. It's the perfect opening.

But I can't risk it.

"We didn't fuck in the dumpster," I say. "Or anywhere else."

I don't know what their deal is beyond the family politics, but I know they hate each other, and I don't want to give him any more reasons to hate me right now.

"That's too bad," Royal says. "You should have fucked someone while you had the chance. That maggot takes the fuglies that no one else will look at, but even he won't touch you when we're done with you."

Damn. I hit a nerve, and I'm not even sure where I went too far, what tipped him over the edge from casual disdain and rude insults to threatening to destroy me.

"Wow, all this because my pussy doesn't need your seal of approval."

"All this because you're pissing me off. Why are you such a freak, Harper? You don't react to anything like you're supposed to."

"Who says I'm supposed to?" I ask. "People aren't your dolls, Royal. You don't get to control how they react and what they say. Not everyone is here to be your plaything."

"But you are."

We stare at each other a long moment. Butterflies of fear and uncertainty and excitement flutter against my insides. He slides his arm toward me on the table, straightening in his chair as he leans even closer, his glorious body looming over me.

He's intimidating as hell, but I don't back down. He's so close he could kiss me—and wrap his big hands around my waist and lift me onto the edge of the table, push up my skirt, spread me open and pin me like a butterfly with that big, glorious—

I push the runaway image from my brain and lean forward to meet him, so close I have to rest a hand on his thigh to keep my balance. I arch my back a little, letting my tits just brush the front of his shirt. My nipples instantly harden, and heat pulses between my thighs when the corner of my lip brushes his chin, his skin the slightest bit scratchy with stubble. I squeeze his thigh, letting my nails bite into the fine, navy fabric. "If you're going to toy with me," I whisper, letting my lips brush feather-soft against his earlobe. "You better up your game. I play with the big boys."

Her Eyes

Damn, she's got a pair of eyes on her
Eyes that are windows to a hurricane soul
That threatens to suck you in and hold you captive
until you forget what light tastes like.
Eyes like a mirror
That shows you all the fucked up, twisted desires in your heart
Where your sickest fantasies
Are promises fulfilled.
Eyes that challenge
Eyes that have seen shit
Eyes that see shit.
I'm not afraid
Let her see.
Baby, you've never seen darkness like this before,
And I could use the challenge.
I look forward to destroying her,
Crushing her tight little body,
And shattering her deep, dark soul.

sixteen

Harper Apple

I have pathetically little to tell Mr. D on Friday. I haven't made any inroads with the Dolces. He makes it clear exactly how he feels about that.

The problem is, I don't *know* the Dolces. I know they're rich, and I've heard the rumors and tales from everyone at school—there's a dozen versions of the fate of Colt's sister alone, and half the time, people seem to be mixing them up with what happened to the Dolce sister. I've heard that they pushed her off a balcony into a swimming pool and she drowned; that it wasn't a balcony but a bridge; that she didn't fall off the bridge but ran into the water and was swept away; that she didn't run in but was swept away in a car; and that she didn't die but went to a mental institution.

Everyone has their own version of every rumor about the Dolces, but the one I never hear is the Dolces' version. I need to know them, need to figure out what guys like them could want, what they need. Not just for Mr. D, either. I like figuring people out, and I can't figure out these guys. They have this air of mystery around them, as if they've drawn a circle around themselves that both attracts everyone and yet never lets them inside it. People are scared of them, but they also can't help but flirt with that danger.

I remember Dixie's words. *They need someone to love them enough to tell them no.*

That ain't gonna happen.

Even if I told them no, if anyone told them no, they'd take what they want, anyway. They have money to buy anything under the sun, to buy off anyone who might stop them from doing anything under the sun. They have the power to get what they want and take what they want, everyone else be damned. They have more power than anyone in the school—not just the kids but the adults, too.

So how is a girl like me, who has no power over anything on this earth, going to give them anything they need? And if I don't, why would they let me in?

I stood up to them, and it didn't get me a lick of respect. It only put a target on my back. Royal called me trash, so now everyone calls me trash.

The next week is worse. On Monday, I open my locker to find it filled with garbage—brown banana peels, moldy yogurt dripping over everything, and slimy, rotten mushrooms that smell like fish. Even after cleaning it up, my books reek. Guess Royal got what he wanted—I smell like trash when I walk around carrying the stained books.

On Tuesday, I walk into the café, and his posse starts drumming and chanting, "There's a whore in this house, there's a whore in this house." And then everyone else starts chanting it, too, until the whole room is deafening.

That day turns out to be more of a weed-and-cigarette under the bleachers kinda lunch.

Wednesday, the Waltons take my clothes in PE, and I have to walk around for the rest of the day in the gym uniform. It's a little annoying that the girls take every opportunity to point and snicker at me every time we pass in the hall or they see me in class, but their prank is too juvenile to really bother me. The gym shorts and T-shirt they gave us at the start of the year were new, so they're better than my regular clothes, anyway.

Thursday, someone has written on my desk in every single class when I get there.

White Trash.

Go back to the trailer park.

BJ $20 Creampie $50 Gangbang $100

And on throughout the day. I start wondering why they haven't released the picture, and I come to the conclusion that they must not really have it. It's probably just a reflection on the glass of Mr. Behr's car, or a blurry head in a guy's lap. If they could tell it was me, they would have spread it around already.

By Friday, I skip even the pretense of getting food and head outside right away, even though it looks like it might rain at any moment. Colt doesn't care if everyone calls me a whore. He sits with me in the one class we have together, and at lunch, he's always willing to share a joint and some easy conversation. Even though he's rich, I feel comfortable with him. Maybe it's because we share the same social position at this school.

I'm almost to the bleachers when I hear a girlish giggle from the shadows underneath, and I pause. Damn it. I've come to rely on our lunches as my refuge from the school drama, but I've also made it clear to Colt that I don't think of him that way. I'm not jealous of whatever girl wants a piece of bad boy, but she's taking the one moment of solace I have in my whole day.

I hover for a minute, feeling like a creeper, and then I hear Colt say my name. I freeze, shifting between feet, trying to decide if I should hide or go back inside or try to sneak closer and eavesdrop. I hear Colt's murmuring deep voice, and then the unmistakable sound of a slap. I tense, but the girl yelps and then giggles, squealing something unintelligible. Before I can decide what to do, Dixie emerges from the shadows.

Okay then. I suspected something was going on the last time, but now I'm sure. I remember Royal saying something about Colt getting all the skanks, but he's obviously getting at least one 24-karat girl, too. Dixie may not be a Dolce girl, but she's about as popular as a girl can be without being one. She's on student council, she's pretty—if a bit eccentric in the fashion choices—she has money, and she's got loads of friends. Literally everyone in school talks about her blog the day after she posts.

I still haven't logged on, for obvious reasons, but a few people actually said I was brave after the roach incident went on the blog.

"Hey, Dixie," I say, giving her a smile that I hope is the equivalent of a high-five. Just because I don't want to bone Colt, that doesn't mean he's not obviously hot. If she wants to slum it with the tatted bad boy, more power to her.

Her face goes beet red, and she shuffles her feet and glances at the building. "I should go…"

"Right," I say, nodding. "Student council meeting."

"Yeah," she says with a relieved little laugh.

"I'm just out here to escape the mob," I say. "You know there's nothing going on with me and Colt. We're just friends."

"Oh—me, too," she says. "I mean, we're just friends, too. Nothing going on."

I shake my head. "I'm not going to tell anyone, Dixie. It's none of my business. You're the one with the gossip blog."

She swallows and nods. "Right. Hey, I'm sorry about that. If it made it worse. It's just, everyone was there, so I kinda had to do a blog about it."

"I know."

"Just… Be careful, okay?" she says, genuinely imploring me. "There are rumors that the Dolces are in with the mafia. They're not the kind of high school boys you're used to at Faulkner."

I quirk a brow. "Faulkner has gangs. I'm pretty used to that type."

"And were you in a rival gang?"

"No," I say, frowning.

"Exactly," she says. "Don't piss them off. They're the only gangsters here, and they run this place. And you're like a member of a rival gang moving in—the only member."

"Damn," I say. "And here I was, waving my colors in their faces and flaunting it."

"Right," Dixie says, sounding relieved. "If you can't fit in, keep your head down and stay off their radar. What you did last week, sitting at their table, that was really stupid. I know that sounds mean, but I'm saying this for your own good, okay? You need to understand how things are here, or it will only get worse."

After she leaves, we eat and smoke, but too soon, it's time to head back inside. The moment I step back into the little side hallway that leads past the cafeteria and into the main halls, Royal grabs me and slams me up against the wall.

I cuss and swing my fist before I have time to think. Royal ducks, and the blow only glances off his cheekbone. He grabs my hands and pins them to the wall, his big body caging me in as he leans close. "I thought I told you to stay away from that guy," he growls at me.

"Yeah, you did," I say. "And then you locked me in a dumpster with him for three hours and told us to fuck. It's hard to figure out what you want."

"Don't fuck with me," he warns.

"Don't fuck with you, don't fuck with Colt," I say. "Anything else, Your Majesty?"

I smile up at him. I can't help myself. I want to just obey, but he makes it so hard. He glares back at me, his dark eyes inscrutable. His face is so close I could count his long, thick, dark lashes, could memorize the perfect angles of his cheekbones, his jawline, his strong chin and masculine nose. Damn, he's too fucking gorgeous for his own good. Add money and power, and it's no wonder the guy thinks he's a god and we're all his playthings.

"Why are you smiling?" he snaps.

"Well, I'm pressed up against the wall by a big, strong man," I say, squirming my body against his. "Seeing as how I'm such a whore, obviously I'm enjoying this."

"Cut it out." He backs off a few inches, and I lean back against the wall, leaving at least six inches of space between us. That's more room to work with, and less chance of me losing my head over how good he looks or smells or feels. I may have only said that to be a brat, but it's not untrue. I'm starting to understand my mother, always controlled by her emotions and hormones. Guess I'm more like her than I want to be.

"What do you want from me?" I ask. "I knelt and kissed your feet like an obedient little slave. I sucked up and tried to be your fangirl, but you tossed me in the garbage. And now when I stay out of your way and give you the whole cafeteria, you hunt me down to demand to know what I'm doing."

"What are you playing at?" he asks, his voice sharp.

"Who said I'm playing?"

"I can spot a knock-off from a mile away," he says. "And you're a certified, authentic fake."

That makes me laugh. "I'm the fake? Have you seen your Dolce girls?"

"You don't want to be a Dolce girl," he says, sounding almost bitter about that, like I've offended him by not joining his fan club.

"So? You wouldn't have me if I did."

Royal leans in again, and I curse myself for not escaping when I could have. The last of the kids have left the café, and it's just us in the hall and a few stragglers talking by a water fountain down the hall. He stares at me a few seconds, and then the corner of his mouth pulls up in a smirk.

"You do want to be a Dolce girl," he purrs, leaning in again. He pulls my hands over my head, moving both my wrists into one hand so he can pin them against the wall while he brushes my hair back with his free hand. "You want me to fuck you up against this wall right now, don't you? I could, you know. No one would stop me."

"I'd stop you," I say, but I know it's bullshit. We both know he's right. He has so much power here it's dizzying. And as fucked up as it is, the allure of that power pulls me in just like all the other Dolce girls. It's sexy as hell, even when he's threatening me.

"You wouldn't stop me," he says, running his fingertips along my jawline, where a slight tenderness remains from last Friday's fight. "You want me to. You'd spread your legs and moan for me."

"Then do it," I say, my voice coming out breathy. "Take that big cock out and show it to the world, show them all how you can fuck a girl who has no choice in the matter, like that proves what a big man you are."

I can't deny that his dirty words have my heart pounding, but I'm not my mother.

I won't be controlled by my body.

Royal lets out a quiet breath, a smile playing at his lips. He strokes that spot on my jaw again, as if he knows that's where it hurts, as if he knows that even when he touches the tender place, it still feels good. Maybe even better than when he touches me anywhere else. He takes my chin and pulls it up so I'm looking right into his eyes. "Are you wet?"

"Dripping," I say, arching my body against his again. "It gets me so hot to think of being one of your many, many, *many* conquests."

He slides a hand between my thighs, all the way up, in one quick motion. He pushes a finger under my underwear and swipes it over my bare skin.

I'm so shocked I don't even react until he's already pulling away. I buck and squirm to free myself, but he doesn't seem to notice. His grip on my wrists is unbreakable. He smirks and brings his hand up, examining his finger like he couldn't tell if my pussy was wet by touching it. And then, if it wasn't humiliating enough to have him violate me in the middle of the hall, he gives his finger a sniff.

My face burns with embarrassment and fury, but Royal only cracks a grin and watches me squirm. I've known a lot of assholes, and I've had my ass and tits grabbed by immature high school boys plenty of times. But this is different. He didn't just goose me to cop a feel.

He went under my clothes, and the worst part of the whole thing is the detached, casual way he did it, like it was no big deal, like it never even crossed his mind to stop and consider whether he had the right to put his hand under my skirt, inside my underwear, and touch the most personal place on a girl's body. It was a cursory touch, just enough to check my story, but the fact that there was nothing sexual about it makes me feel dirtier than if he'd slid a finger all the way inside me.

"I knew you were fucking with me," he says, wiping his hand on his jeans. "You better be glad, too. I would have been pissed if you got your diseased slime on me."

I'm too seething mad to even come up with a response. I go for a knee in the groin, but Royal sidesteps easily. Thankfully, he seems to be done with the topic of my repulsive vagina. His hand tightens around my wrists, and his eyes go serious.

"No more trips to Green Meadows," he says. "That asshole's lucky we let him go to this school at all. Now he's plotting against us, and you probably bought his sob story and jumped right in to help."

Paranoid, much? I think to myself. But this isn't the time to smart off to him. The whole school revolves around his family, so why would he think this is any different?

"No," I say, all my bravado gone. "We're not planning anything against you. We're just two losers hanging out being losers."

I know they fucked up Colt's family, and what it cost him, what he's been through. At least, I know a little. It's more than enough. I'm not having any blame for this fall on him. If that means we can't be friends, then I'll give him up. This is why I don't have friends in the first place. They're a liability, and this time, it's not me who will get hurt. I can't have that. It's one thing to risk myself, but I won't put someone else at risk.

"Tell me what you're doing with him," Royal says slowly. "If you're not fucking him, then why are you out there with him every day?"

"Because you make my life hell in here," I admit, my throat tightening, as if it knows that letting out the truth will give him ammunition. "I tried to follow your rules, but I'm just not good at them. So I took myself out of your path of destruction, okay? That's why I'm out there. To keep from being where I am right now."

Royal blinks at me for a few seconds, like he can't comprehend that I might not want to be a part of his twisted games, that I really was just trying to escape him, that I don't want to be around him. That my main reason for going out to the bleachers isn't to be with Colt, but to avoid being with him.

Maybe my dry pussy convinced him, though, because he drops my hands and steps back. "If I see you with him again, you'll both pay," he says before turning to walk away. "And take a fucking shower once in a while. You smell."

She Smells

She smells like the ocean
Battering the New England coastline
Like hurricane season
Where every storm is named Harper.

She smells like the memory
That comes to your mind
When you hold a seashell to your ear
And close your eyes.
You're there again—
Sand sticking to salt on skin
The heat of sun and burn on your shoulders
And the laughter of your sister echoing
...echoing...
Before you open your eyes
And remember the rush of the water
Was only the blood in your ears.

She smells wild like wind over icy waves
That pound the shore until you can't hear
Memories or echoes
Or screams.

She smells like she belongs
Anywhere but here.

Or maybe it's just me.

seventeen

Harper Apple

"Can I ask you a huge favor?"

I finish shoving the garbage bag into the faded bin before turning. Blue stands there, an extension cord in her hand and her gaze on the corner of the roof instead of mine. I fight the urge to protect the precious stash under the carpet in my closet. I could say no, could tell her the truth: Mom hasn't paid the electric this month.

But then I think of her eating dinner in the dark, of little Olive taking a cold bath, and I know I can't.

"Yeah, sure," I say, gesturing to the outlet on the side of our house. "Go ahead."

Maybe I'll stick around for a third fight on Friday. At this rate, Mr. D's going to rescind my scholarship, anyway. I've been reporting back to him for three weeks now, and I can't imagine he's found a single word of it helpful. Since Royal's warning, I've stayed away from Colt, but if I thought I was going to get some kind of reward for that, I should have known better. The Dolces have proceeded to ignore my existence all week.

I know that's a good thing, and that I should be glad. Dixie and her friends even invited me back to their table, probably because they felt sorry for me when I sat alone. Now that I'm not a target, apparently I'm safe enough to have around.

The problem is, I can't just disappear off the Dolce's radar. I need information about them, something real, not just gossip and rumors.

Or maybe…

My eyes fall on Blue's mom's car, the one that almost never leaves the driveway. Her mom doesn't work, but she also doesn't sell the car to pay for blow every few months. What if I don't need to get in with the Dolces? What if I stay out of their way, stay on the outside, and just look in?

Suddenly I remember something Colt said after we got out of the dumpster. Something about how he doesn't follow them around watching what they do.

"Hey," I say to Blue when she straightens from plugging in the extension cord. "That'll cost you."

She swallows, but then she shrugs, her voice coming out flat as usual. "Sure, what do you need?"

"How much gas does that thing got?" I ask, jerking my chin toward the Cutlass.

"I don't know," she says. "Maybe half a tank."

"You think I could borrow it sometime?"

"I don't see why not."

I wait for her to ask, *will* her to. This itch to talk to someone builds inside me, but I can't just dump this on her. I need her to care, to want to know. I fight the disappointment inside me when she walks away, saying I can come by and get the keys whenever I need them.

Fucking Colt. If he hadn't reminded me what it was like to have a friend, someone to just shoot the shit with, I might not need one now. But I can't talk to him without putting him in danger, and the other girls will just turn this into the latest story on Dixie's gossip blog.

I consider calling Jolene, but that would be too weird. The trailer park is its own little world. There's this odd sense of community among the kids who live there. I didn't really notice it until I wasn't part of it, but thinking back, that's the last time I had real friends. There was this attitude of, *Everyone thinks we're trash, so we have no chance out there on our own, but if we stick together, at least we'll have each other.*

Freshman year, I still hung with Jolene at school, when I showed up, but it wasn't the same. No one accused me of thinking I was better than them, but I'd achieved what they all dreamed of, so I no longer had the same dream. I wasn't one of them. Calling her up to bitch about my rich new school would be rude, like I was rubbing it in her face.

After dinner and homework, I go knock on Blue's door. I figure it's dark, so if I cruise the Dolces' neighborhood, they won't really see the car too close, and even if they do, they won't know it's me. I'm in full stalker mode as I pull out of our narrow street and head north. Fifteen minutes later, I'm on the outskirts of town, driving on a winding road between open fields with horse barns in the distance, endless white picket fences surrounding their lush meadows. It looks like something out of a calendar. I had no idea there was anything this pretty just a few minutes from the gritty, grey side of Faulkner.

Little yellow leaves race across the beams of my headlights, the wind whipping them from the trees at the end of the pastures. I almost miss the turn onto another blacktop road, this one even narrower and winding through the trees that toss wildly in the gusting wind. The sky is dark with storm clouds, and a few fat drops of rain splatter the windshield. My GPS tells me to turn, but when I reach the neighborhood, a gate stands across it.

Of course they live in a gated community. They don't want riffraff like me driving by gawking at their mansions.

I park the car along the edge of the road and get out. Glancing up and down the road, I make sure I'm alone before starting toward the gate. I scale it easily and hop down to the other side. Another covert glance around to make sure I haven't been seen, and I start along the narrow road that winds through the neighborhood. Giant plantation-style houses stand back from the road on each sprawling lot. Some have giant oaks or magnolia trees or willows out front, and all have massive lawns and landscaped yards.

Thunder rumbles overhead, and the trees toss and twist in the wind. Even though it's dark out, the white houses stand out well enough for me to spot the one from the online photo, the lights blazing in all the downstairs windows and half the ones upstairs. These people obviously don't worry about their electric bill, that's for damn sure.

The lack of cover makes me nervous, and I edge toward the house before theirs, since it has a row of trees lining each side of a pathway. Fat, cold raindrops begin to spatter down, and I duck my head and dart behind one of the trees before I notice that the house is only halfway intact. Half of it is a blackened, crumbling shell. Lucky for me, that makes this part of the neighborhood nice and dark. I creep along the white gravel walkway between the trees, staying in the shadows. When I'm at the last one before an exposed stretch, I stop and peer around it, trying to see into the Dolce house next door.

Restless and frustrated, I dart out of the cover of the trees and run along the stretch of gravel to the burned house. My footsteps are like gunshots in my ears, but I don't stop until I reach the house. There, I hunker down behind the pillars on the front porch. After about ten minutes, I decide I suck at this. Apparently determination is not all it takes to be a good spy. From all the action I've seen, you'd think no one was home at all.

There's no sign of movement at the Dolce house. A wide lawn separates the houses, along with a row of bushes in the process of losing their leaves. On the other side of the burned house is a section of trees, so I don't have to worry about neighbors in that direction. At least I have something to do while I wait for the Dolces to show themselves.

I step past a no trespassing sign and into the burnt rubble inside. The people who lived here were obviously rich enough to just leave and start over, because it doesn't look like anyone tried to salvage anything. There are perfectly good appliances rusting away under the layer of soot. I run a finger along the top of the stove, which looks unharmed. Guess the fire didn't start in the kitchen.

I make my way toward the less burned side, wondering if I can scavenge any good finds. The staircase is halfway burned, but I try to use it anyway. A few steps up, my foot goes through the charred boards, and I retreat. The good side of the house faces the Dolce house, and after circling the outside,

I can't find a way up. Judging by the rotted leaves and empty acorn shells collected in corners of the wraparound porch, I'd say the house has stood empty for at least a year, since last fall. I wonder why the neighborhood hasn't demolished it and built a new monstrosity in its place. They probably consider it an eyesore, but I can see the tragic beauty in it, like Miss Havisham sitting in her ancient wedding dress.

I scale a support on the good side and scramble up onto the second-floor balcony. From here, I can see into all the top-floor rooms on this side of the Dolce house, including the one I remember Royal pointing out as his. The light is on in that room, but there's no one inside. However, my eyes are drawn to one of the other rooms, and for a second, I freeze, unable to look away. It's too far to make out faces, but it's easy to see what's happening.

A naked blonde is on a big bed, on all fours giving a blowjob to a dark-haired guy. I stand there watching for a minute without really thinking about it. I came over to spy, but I didn't really think about what might be happening inside the Dolce house. It catches me off guard, though it shouldn't, considering their reputations. I know I should look away, that

I should go back to my car before I'm completely drenched by the increasing rain. But I'm drawn in, and I can't stop staring at the guy, trying to figure out if it's Royal or one of the twins.

Not that it matters. It shouldn't matter. I tell myself it doesn't, but I keep looking.

He's naked, too, his body every bit as toned and sculpted as I would expect. I can see the muscles in his thick arms as he holds her hair in a messy clump behind her head, guiding her. He holds his phone in his other hand, and he's thumbing through it. The casualness of his attention makes it clear he's not filming her but scrolling on his phone while she services him. It's so demeaning I want to stop watching, to save her whatever dignity she possesses, though she obviously doesn't know I'm witness to it.

I turn away, and a shadow moves further down the balcony that makes me nearly jump out of my skin. I stumble back against the railing, and a soft chuckle meets my ears, winding a chill around my body, coiling like a snake. There's a hiss, and a flash of flame, and then his hand cups it as he lights up. I can make out the shadows of Royal's angular face, and relief washes through me, quickly replaced by the correct reaction—fear.

He inhales and then strides toward me, his footsteps heavy and fast.

Fuck. Why didn't I run the second he made his presence known? I grab the railing, ready to vault over and scramble back down or even jump. I'm halfway over the railing when his thickly muscled arm clamps around my middle and drags me back.

"Guess I'm not the only one who likes to watch," Royal purrs in my ear, grabbing my hair with his other hand, his fingers tightening on the back of my head in the exact same way his brother is holding that girl. They can call me trash, but it's clear they don't have much more regard for any other girl.

"Let me go," I warn. "I may be small, but I can end your football career with one well-placed blow."

"Oh, come on now," Royal says. "I'm not going to hurt you. I just thought it might be a little more fun to watch with someone else this time."

He pushes me against the railing, releasing my waist to take a drag on the joint he's holding.

"What do you want?" I ask, my heart racing in my chest.

"I told you," he says. "I just want a little company."

I know he's teasing, but I roll the words over in my mind. He has two brothers, three more friends in his posse, and a squadron of girls ready to fight for their spot in his inner circle. Could a boy like that really want company? Could a boy like that ever feel lonely, like he wishes he had someone to call when he goes out driving, like I did tonight?

His fingers brush over my cheek, and he touches the end of the joint to my lips. It's damp from his mouth, and a little wire of heat curls inside me. I could take the joint, but something stops me. He has this effect on me, so when we're together, it's like this charge surrounds us, and the rest of the world disappears. It's just us, doing this dangerous, seductive dance toward each other, a dance that can only end in devastation.

Royal's fingers tighten on my hair, and his hips nudge mine as he skims the damp end of the joint against my lower lip, his face angled around mine so he can watch my mouth. "Open your lips," he says, his voice low and husky. "Let me put it in."

This time, I can't help the tremor that shivers through me, strong enough for him to feel it. He doesn't taunt me, though. His eyes are deep and filled with hunger that makes my breath quicken with my pulse. Everything between us is backwards—he pulled up my skirt and put his fingers in my underwear at school, and it wasn't sexy, but when he slides the end of the joint between my lips, the erotic charge between us makes me dizzy.

"Give it a little suck," he murmurs, his breath hot against my ear as he bends close.

I let my eyes fall closed before I obey, closing my lips and taking a drag.

Still holding my hair, Royal turns my face toward his. Cold rain stripes my cheeks, but I barely feel it. His hot mouth angles to meet mine, stealing my breath, sucking the smoke from my lungs like its oxygen. I'm glad his hips hold me pinned to the railing, because I'm afraid I might buckle at the power of the sensations roaring through my body. I open my mouth for him, and he gives me back the smoke, filling my lungs until I'm lightheaded.

Royal buries his hand deeper in my hair, cradling my head in his huge palm and dragging my mouth up to his. When our lips meet, white hot electricity crackles through my body like the lightning forking through the sky. I gasp, and he plunges his tongue into my mouth, thrusting roughly against mine. The kiss is instantly deep and intense, his tongue taking full control of mine, stoking the heat inside me like a flame.

His scent fills me up, makes me wet. He smells masculine and strong, like he is. His hips grinding into mine, the thick ridge of his erection making my core quiver and my knees give way. He grips me hard, devouring my mouth like he could suck out my soul through one kiss. His kiss is commanding, demanding, dominating. It's a kiss that gives nothing, only takes.

When he pulls away, it's too soon.

He breaks the kiss and pulls back, holding my head as he blows the smoke into my face in a heady cloud. I've made out with guys, but this was something more than a kiss. It was a communication, silent but filled with hunger and longing, charged with erotic desperation.

"Now watch," he says, his hand falling on top of mine, closing my fingers around the slick railing.

I'd forgotten where we were, what was happening. In the house across the lawn, the light illuminates the room. Another figure appears in the doorway, which is standing wide open. Baron strolls in, a beer in one hand and his sucker in the other. He comes up behind the girl, pops the sucker in his mouth, and pulls down the front of his sweats just enough to free his cock. I can tell even from here it's big, thick, and dark. He rocks his hips forward to put it in with zero warning.

The girl bucks and tries to pull away, but Duke is holding her head by the hair, and he keeps her in position. Baron reaches up to high five his brother before pulling back and thrusting hard into her. I suddenly remember the girls at lunch telling me that if they called, you had to go and let them do whatever they wanted to you. I feel sick and shamefully aroused at once. Royal's hand is holding mine, firm but gentle, nothing like the rough treatment the guys are giving the blonde.

He moves his hand to my jeans, and I tense, but he doesn't try to unbutton them. He slides his hand between my thighs, on top of my jeans. He doesn't feel me up, just leaves his warm hand there, cupping my mound, the tips of his fingers between my thighs. The heat of his hand seeps through my jeans, and it's impossible to ignore as it joins the heat pulsing between my legs as I watch his brothers fuck the blonde hard from both ends. It's all I can do not to squirm against him, get the friction my body wants.

My breath comes fast as I watch the scene unfold next door. Duke finally releases the girl's hair and slides down the bed onto his back. She climbs onto him, sinking down onto his cock and riding him while Baron stands there finishing his beer. When he's done, he sets the bottle down and comes over to the bed again, climbing on and pushing the girl forward. She rests on her hands while he puts it in her ass this time.

Royal's chest brushes my back with each breath. We're both soaked, and I'm shivering but hot at the same time. He takes my wet hair in one hand, moving it aside and rubbing his nose against the back of my neck, sending a chill racing down my spine. "Want me to do that to you?" he asks, sliding his hand from between my legs to the front of my pelvis, pressing gently against my lower belly and hooking his thumb into the top of my jeans.

I jerk back to the present, to reality. We shouldn't be watching this. It's not just naughty or dirty or kinky. It's wrong for us to watch it without them knowing.

"No," I say, twisting in Royal's arms. I'm suddenly facing his chest, with my back to the railing, and I'm not sure that was such a smart move.

His shirt sticks to his skin, and I can see every chiseled line of his body, the ridges of his abs, his pecs sculpted like marble, the hard points of his nipples. I want to touch him so bad it hurts, but I grip the railing on either side of my hips instead.

"You sure about that, Cherry Pie?" he asks, bracing his hands on the railing beside mine, caging me in. "It could be our dirty little secret. I wouldn't tell anyone and ruin your lone wolf reputation."

"My what?" I ask, letting out a shaky laugh. I'm a lone wolf because I have no friends, not because I don't want them. I spent so much time telling myself otherwise and acting like it, that maybe I convinced everyone. Everyone but myself, that is.

I'm okay with him not knowing that, though.

"Your reputation," he says, rocking back and forward on his heels. "You're the badass little chick who came in and didn't want anything to do with the status quo, aren't you? The rebel girl who'd rather go hang out and smoke under the bleachers than buy into our games."

"What about your reputation?" I ask.

"That's why I said it would be our dirty little secret."

"I'll pass," I say. "I'm not into being the king's mistress."

He searches my face for a long moment, then reaches up to cup my cheek. I want to nestle into his touch, to revel in the way my face fits into his huge hand. Instead, I force myself to be still, to watch him. I'd give all the money in my stash to know what he's thinking right now, but his face gives nothing away. Rain trickles down his skin, wetting his dark hair and making it curl, but his eyes are unreadable in the dark.

His gaze flickers to the scene behind me, then back to my face. "Then I guess this will have to be our dirty little secret," he says. "Now let's get you out of here before anyone sees you."

He vaults over the railing, dropping down to the first level and landing on his feet. It's about a ten-foot drop, and I'm not sure I want to jump, but I also don't want to look like a pussy, so I jump, too. When I land on my feet, knees bent, a burst of adrenaline shoots through me. I pop up to my full height like I do that shit every day. I can't help but grin up at Royal, though. I fucking nailed it.

He looks pretty damn impressed, too, and a swell of pride unfurls in my chest like a new seed sprouting. Damn it. I shouldn't care if he's the one fucking a girl next door, and I definitely shouldn't care if he thinks I'm cool.

Too late, a little voice inside me whispers.

A pair of headlights passes the house and swings into the white gravel drive of the Dolce house, and Royal grabs me and presses me back into the shadows until the car disappears behind the house. Then he steps away from me, his shoulders squared.

"I'll walk you to your car," he says, starting that way without waiting for an answer. I catch up to him, scolding myself for the stupid thoughts cluttering my brain. I remind myself that he's an alien, a being from a different world than the one I live in. We have nothing in common, and he's made his feelings about me perfectly clear. I don't even know what to say to him now. Thanking him feels ridiculous.

But he caught me spying on him, and he could have called the cops, or hurt me, and he didn't.

We don't speak again until we reach the car. Royal stops and leans against the driver's side door, his arms crossed over his chest, glaring at me.

So, whatever ceasefire that was back there, I guess it's over.

"Next time you want to trespass, look for cameras," he says. "I knew you were here the minute you climbed the fence."

"Thanks for the tip," I say lightly. Now that we're out here, away from the houses, fear tickles at my nerves. Not that anyone there would have helped me, but we're alone now, in the dark, and no one knows where I am.

Royal works his jaw back and forth. "If you want us to do that to you, show up here again," he says. "Whenever you want. Except I'll be joining if we're nailing you."

I swallow hard, crossing my arms in a mirror of his pose, but I'm holding myself hard to keep from shaking. "You're threatening to gang rape me if I come back?"

"I'm telling you what your presence in my neighborhood means. I know what car you drive now, and I know you wouldn't be stupid enough to think you could get away with spying on us again. So the only reason you'll show up here is to get a chance to experience what you witnessed tonight for yourself."

I swallow hard before nodding. He's threatening me, but to him, it's not a threat, it's a fact. A rule. He's telling me the consequences if I do this again. It may not be fair, but I did come to a place where I don't belong with the intent of violating his privacy. In doing so, apparently I signed away any future autonomy here. If I come back, I'm consenting to having sex with all three of them. That's what it means.

"Is that clear?" he asks, watching me expectantly.

"Crystal," I grit out.

He stares at me a long moment, something funny flickering across his face, and then he turns and walks away. I remember, too late, that his dead sister was named Crystal.

Crystal (#391)

She said my sister's name.
No one has dared
Speak her name to me
For over a year.
A year of silent penance
For a crime they won't admit
That I could commit
Though I did.

She said my sister's name,
Dropped it so casually
You wouldn't know she was
A casualty.
I told her she was dead to me
And then she was.
Where do you draw the line
Between a murder and a prophecy?

She said my sister's name
Clear as day,
—As diamond—
As if it weren't precious
But ordinary.
As if she believed I could bear
The pain of hearing it
As if she didn't see me
As a fragile thing
Who might shatter
Or shatter the world
If she spoke one word.

eighteen

Harper Apple

MrD: I hope you have more for me this week.

BadApple: Working on it…

MrD: So, what did you do this week?

BadApple: I went 2 their house 2 spy on them

MrD: Really?

MrD: What did you see?

I quickly fill him in on the house next door, since that's something anyone could see. Well, anyone who got into their neighborhood. I tell him about the burned out shell, and how I hid there to look through their windows.

MrD: Again, what did you see?

I chew at my lip, feeling dirty and gross for telling an old man about what I saw, but knowing I have to tell him something. The whole reason I went there was to get something for him, after all. And it's not like I owe them loyalty. They're not my friends.

BadApple: I saw them having sex.

MrD: Who?

BadApple: The twins

MrD: With each other?

He adds a winking face, which makes me gag a little.

BadApple: No

BadApple: W/ a girl

MrD: The same girl?

I swallow hard, resistance building inside me. This is very personal information. But then, if he wanted to know their position on the football field, he'd just look it up online. He wants me to tell him things no one else can. Things no one else knows about.

MrD: At the same time, or were they taking turns?

BadApple: Is that really relevant?

MrD: I ask questions. You answer.

BadApple: I just dont c how this has anything 2 do with your Swans club

MrD: Are you having second thoughts about this arrangement?

BadApple: no

MrD: I'm certain there are other girls at FHS who would make my generous gift worthwhile.

MrD: Double-team or tag team?

BadApple: double

MrD: Describe in detail, please.

Gross.

Maybe that expired ravioli wasn't such a good idea. My stomach churns as I slowly start typing out what he wants to know, wondering if this makes me some kind of prostitute after all. It's like working for one of those phone sex hotlines, except I'm texting it instead of saying it aloud.

When I finish, he doesn't answer for about five minutes. I try not to picture a gross old guy masturbating while he reads it, but I keep seeing Mr. Behr in my mind, the way he'd stop what we were doing to jerk himself off for a minute every time he started going limp.

I get up and throw a handful of antacids in my mouth, chewing them as I return to the computer.

MrD: And then what?

BadApple: Thats all I saw.

MrD: That's a tease.

BadApple: Wut

MrD: You stopped before they came.

BadApple: I didnt c that part. U asked what I saw, not for me to write u a jerkoff fantasy.

MrD: Were you aroused?

BadApple: No and again not relevant

MrD: Watching 2 attractive men fucking a young girl in every hole didn't get you wet?

BadApple: This isnt the arrangement

MrD: Just wondered if you were masturbating and that's why you didn't watch them come.

I think about lying to him. What would it matter? He won't know any different.

But again, why even do this shit if I'm not going to fill him in? I might as well make it all up. Eventually, he'll catch on, and there goes my scholarship.

BadApple: I was interrupted

MrD: By what?

BadApple: Royal

MrD: What happened?

BadApple: He kicked me out of the neighborhood and threatened to rape me if I came back.

MrD: lol

I stare at the screen, the little blinking cursor. It's not like I've never heard a rape joke before. But damn. That's cold.

I have to remember that this is a real person. There's a guy on the other end of this communication, a guy who might be a pervert or a rapist or who the hell knows what.

MrD: How'd he seem?

BadApple: ???

MrD: Did he seem like he was high? On drugs? Angry?

Weird questions, but okay. I remember Royal pulling my chin around, the smoke in my mouth, the way he kissed me…

My toes curl and I have to adjust myself in the chair just thinking about it.

BadApple: IDK him that well. He seemed normal

MrD: Did he catch you in the act?

BadApple: ???

MrD: How did he react to the fact that you were trespassing to watch his brothers engage in a sexual act in the privacy of their own home?

BadApple: he was pissed I guess

MrD: You said he was acting normal.

BadApple: he's always pissed.

MrD: Are you going to go back?

BadApple: I prefer not to get raped.

MrD: So, you will watch them at school and try to get in with them there again.

BadApple: ok

MrD: Good. Report back next Friday.

I have a week until I have to report to Mr. D, but I'm not waiting until the last minute this time. I'll just have to figure out a way to follow them without using Blue's car, since Royal thinks that's what I drive. Since I can't afford to skip another fight, I decide to go do my thing tonight while they're at the football game and then track them down after.

I usually stick around for the rest of the night, watching other fights to learn all I can about technique and the fighters themselves in case our paths cross in the ring. Tonight, though, I duck into the back room and quickly pull on a cropped hoodie over my bloody tank and cut-off jean shorts, pull my hair up, and rinse my face and knees. Then I head out.

I track down Dynamo to ask him to unlock the gate. Once the fights start, there's no entrance—or exit. Yeah, totally a hazard, but it's not like they're doing this legally and are worried about losing their license.

"Where you off to?" Dynamo asks as we cross the asphalt outside the building.

"A party," I say. "You know where it is tonight?"

He cracks a smile. "You're going to a party, but you don't know where it is?"

"Yep," I say. "Any ideas?"

"Are you talking about the postgame party?"

"That's the one."

He's quiet for a few steps, until we reach the gate. "So, that's why you stopped coming to the bleachers to smoke out with me."

It's not a question, but I feel defensive, like I need to justify myself to him. I mean, he's the closest thing to a friend I have at Willow Heights. But even if I could tell him why I'm stalking them, it wouldn't be the whole truth. I'm not just interested in the Dolce boys because it's a job, because I need information. Not anymore. I could lie to him, but I can't lie to myself.

The allure of their power drew me in, the mystery and tragedy surrounding them hooked me, and the elusiveness of their attention has me pushing the button like a fucking gambling monkey. They're pros at what they do. They give just enough to make you think you've got a shot, and then they take it away and make you chase after them until you're ready to give up, and then they give just a little more.

"It's not like that," I mutter, even though maybe it's exactly like that. Maybe that's why I feel so ashamed of myself—I'm just like every other Dolce girl, running after the hot, dangerous, powerful guys that every girl wants and every guy wants to be. Colt didn't sound accusatory or even pissed. He just sounded disappointed. He thought I was different, that I was better than that, but I'm not. I'm no better than any other girl.

The Dolces have created something powerful and—almost—unattainable, like a luxury brand that only celebrities can get their hands on, a product that costs a fortune, goes on sale to the public once a year, and sells out in three seconds flat. Everyone wants it, even those who can't get it, those who have to take out a new mortgage to afford it.

Dynamo sighs and unlocks the gate. "I don't know where the parties are," he says. "I don't go to them. I'm not in that circle anymore. I'm sure someone at school was talking about it, but I don't pay attention to that shit."

"Listen," I say, hooking my thumb through the strap on my bag. "I'm sorry."

"I know," he says. "I'm sure they told you I was bad news and threatened you if you hung out with me. Why do you think I hang out alone?"

My throat tightens at his words, the resigned tone in his voice, only the slightest trace of bitterness left, as if he's given up on even his anger. The Dolces have ensured he has zero friends for so long he doesn't even bother to want them anymore. I've had my experience with friendlessness, but my isolation was my own doing. My heart breaks a little for this boy whose every chance at human connection is severed at the root.

"They didn't threaten me if I hung out with you," I say quietly. "They threatened you."

We stand there in silence for a minute, just looking at each other. I stopped hanging out with him to protect him, but it doesn't change the fact that I did it, probably the same as every other friend he's had since the Dolces decided he was an enemy.

He leans an elbow on the chain-link fence, hooking his fingers into it and surveying me from head to toe. "If you go in one of their parties looking like that, they'll eat you alive."

"I wasn't aware the football parties were a formal event."

"Harper," he says, his voice serious. "Look, you're hot, okay? You know it, I know it, everyone in the whole school knows it. That's why those bitches find you so threatening. You do you, and they hate it, because they don't have the balls. But you look like a fucking hood princess, not a Willow Heights princess. If you're trying to get in with that crowd, you gotta fit in, Teeny."

"Yeah, well, that's never going to happen," I say, my throat tight with frustration. "I don't have a thousand bucks to spend on clothes, let alone a fucking purse. I'm never going to be a Gucci girl."

"Then you're never going to be a Dolce girl," he says. "So stop trying."

"I can't."

Colt shakes his head, closing his eyes like he's praying for patience. "Most of my sister's clothes are still in her closet," he says, his shoulders slumping. "She wasn't curvy like you, but she was about your same height. I'll drop off a couple bags on your porch."

I'm glad it's dark out, that the streetlights in the lot aren't enough to illuminate the heat in my face. I'd rather dumpster dive than take someone's charity.

"Why would you do that?" I ask. "You hate the Dolces."

"I don't hate you."

"I wouldn't blame you if you did."

He shrugs and gives me a grin, but it's the one that never touches his eyes. "Maybe when they're done with you, I'll get their sloppy seconds."

I can't help but laugh. "Thanks, asshole."

"A guy can dream."

"So, I'm your dream girl?" I tease.

"Nah," he says. "My dream girl lives on the other side of the country and has never heard of Faulkner, Arkansas."

"Then I'd say about ninety-five percent of the country could be your dream girl," I say. "But not me."

"Yeah," he says. "I keep waiting for it to be my turn, but I always come in second. As my gramps would say, second place is first loser."

"Weren't you first until the Dolces came along?"

"I gotta get back to the fight," he says, hooking a thumb over his shoulder toward the ring. "Promise you won't go to the party until you've got something better to wear."

"You're just full of compliments tonight."

"Promise?"

I stand on tiptoes and give him a quick kiss on the cheek. "I promise, asshole."

It strikes me as I walk away that maybe the reason I feel so comfortable with Colt, the reason he feels like a kindred soul, is that he's the only person in this town who wants to get out as badly as I do.

Instructions for Destruction

First you take out the heir
(What's a kingdom without an heir?)
Then you take the head
So he can't replace the heir.
All is fair.
You move on to the branches
Shearing away each member one by one
Before you strip away the purpose—
Jobs and passions, love and football.
You want it all.
Now you have time to savor the heart
To drill down deep and draw it out
Sucking the sweet sap from it
Wringing it dry before discarding it.
No regrets.
When the family tree has been cut
You burn the stump
And then you start to trace the roots
So it can never regrow.
Call it weed control.

nineteen

BadApple: Hey, I'm looking for something to do tonight. Anything going on?

WHGossipGrrl: little late to start looking!

BadApple: had something earlier

WHGossipGrrl: DeShaun's party was tonight but Dolces left so it's pretty much over.

BadApple: srsly? Ppl only go to see if they'll show up?

WHGossipGrrl: Um yeah

BadApple: sad

WHGossipGrrl: lol

BadApple: After party?

WHGossipgrrl: mostly ppl just break off into their own groups now

WHGossipgrrl: I'm going to go to Quinn's. We're making cake pops if u wanna join!

BadApple: lol thx. Was thinking something a little more… Clandestine

WHGossipgrrl: Ooh clandestine. Me likes!

BadApple: Know where the D boys go?

WHGossipgrrl: They don't stay 2 long at the parties. No one knows where they go.

BadApple: Thx. Have fun baking!

WHGossipgrrl: Have fun hunting the D

She adds a winky face emoji, and I smile to myself even though that led to a dead end. I have to stop myself from asking if they left alone. She didn't say anything that indicated they left with someone, so I'm going to pretend Royal's not partaking in their orgy tonight.

I should give up, but I'm wired. I scroll through my *OnlyWords* app about ten times, a crazy idea forming in my head. What if I don't rely on someone else to tell me how to find them? I mean, they already think I'm an obsessed stalker. What do I have to lose?

BadApple: sry 2 bother again. Do u know any of their msg handles?

WHGossipgrrl: @ Royal

I stand there staring at my screen for a minute, trying not to analyze what it means that she sent me Royal's contact only. Am I that transparent? Or is that the only one she knows? Why does she know it at all? Does she message him? Has he already slept with her, and that's why he lets her thing with Colt go on?

And am I really going to do this crazy thing?

But what's the worst that can happen? He'll tell me to go fuck myself right in my trash pussy, that's what. Nothing he hasn't said before.

Still, I can't make my heart stop pounding when I hit send.

BadApple: whats up

I stand there for a good five minutes, cursing myself and wishing there was an un-send button. Wishing I hadn't been so fucking stupid. He's going to think I'm a stage five clinger and desperate and pathetic and…

Everything he already thinks about me, I remind myself. It's not like I ever had the upper hand. So what if he doesn't answer? Did I really expect him to?

Royal: Sorry babe. Not home. Can't run a train on u tonite

Before I can answer, another avatar pops up in our chat.

BaronNotTrump: IDK Dad might be home ;)

DukeOfBeavertown: She does love an old wrinkle dick

Guess we're all here. I remember Duke on his phone while the blonde serviced him, and I imagine him going about texting me while his dick is buried in some poor girl. She'd still be less pathetic than me right now.

Then an idea pops into my head. A train…

The first time I met these guys, they were down in the empty railyard. Why would they be there except to do something illegal? Presumably they weren't looking for girls blowing teachers in cars. They just happened upon us.

BadApple: r u there?

Royal: yeah what do u need

BadApple: sweet of u 2 offer but I meant r u at the railyard now?

BaronNotTrump: Why would we b there?

I'm already shoving my feet into my combat boots, though. I know I'm right. I can't believe I didn't think of it sooner.

I mean, yes, they could be anywhere. They could be at home and just don't want me there.

They could also be painting the Walton girls' toenails, I think, rolling my eyes at myself.

I know they're not any of those places. They're out causing trouble, and that's a place people go for that reason.

DukeofBeavertown: if that's where u go to give bjs, we'll be there.

BadApple: b there in 5. BJ not guaranteed.

Royal: no

BadApple: c u soon

Royal: Go 2 bed, cherry pie.

I hop on my bike and ride toward the tracks. I know I'm being stupid, that they might not even be there, and if they are, they could rape me or kill me or whatever they want to do to me. Royal obviously doesn't want me there.

But I'm so close. I can feel it. And some weird, feverish obsession has taken me over. I've fallen under their spell, and I have to know more. I have to get in, and tonight is my chance. Even if they never acknowledge me at school, if we're never friends, I could be their dark side companion. The one who shows up to do whatever mischief they're into and then never acknowledges them in daylight. I'd be fine with that as long as I was in, as long as I was a part of something after midnight on a Friday night.

A bit reminiscent of Royal's offer to be each other's dirty little secret…

I don't know how this is different. Maybe it's not, under the surface. This might be smashing windows instead of sex, but the real thing is beneath either of those actions. Those are just things to do. What's below the surface is what draws me to them, what has my quads burning as I pedal toward the tracks as fast as I can, my heart racing, butterflies in my belly at the thought of missing them. Or seeing them.

Both options make my stomach drop like when I was a kid and I'd jump off the swing just as it reached the highest point of its arc, and for a second, I could fly.

What pulls me to the railyard at midnight, past the gangland neighborhoods and the pawnshops with bars on the windows, isn't the thought of a hookup. It's a human connection. It's the chance to shine a light into the darkness I've seen inside those boys, to see my own darkness reflected back at me and know they accept it. To be with people who are like me in some deep, fundamental, fucked up way I can't explain. It's an admission we're already bound together by glimpsing that truth in each other, even if they're not ready to admit it.

I'm ready.

I skid to a stop in the lot right where Mr. Behr liked to park, dropping my bike beside a sleek, black Tesla with the handles inset in the door. I don't even care what they drive anymore, that they're rich and I'm poor, that they're kings and I'm the scourge of the earth. If I could be part of it, I wouldn't care. Part of their tight little circle, their brotherhood, their commitment to each other that runs deeper than blood, down to the bone.

I hear a prolonged hiss and turn, my eyes falling on some empty spray paint cans. They're painting. Even fucking better.

Concealing my excitement, I stroll over like it's no big deal. The familiar fumes of spray paint greet me, and my pulse quickens. I'm rusty, but damn, I've missed this particular type of mischief.

Baron watches me come, a can of paint in one hand and a beer in the other, his lollypop tucked in his cheek. Duke is shaking a can of paint and swaying against a rusty old barrel, laughing his ass off at something Royal must have said. His laughter curls around me, making goosebumps of loneliness rise on my arms at the same time it nestles into a warm place in my chest, a fuzzy little nest that's been empty for so long I can't remember when it was filled. Royal's turned around, painting a giant arc with white.

When I see what they're doing, my excitement dampens. They're not making art. They're making crude symbols. Disappointment sinks into me, but I push it away. I'm still here. Does it really matter if they're making art or just vandalizing the cars? Some people do graffiti to create, and some to destroy. Both are valid.

"What's up?" I ask, tucking a hand into the back pocket of my cut-offs.

"Thought I told you to stay home," Royal says, not turning to look at me.

Duke turns, though. A big, sloppy grin forms on his face as he tries to focus on me. "Hey, it's the blowjob queen," he says.

"What do you want?" Baron asks. It's not a demand, in the belligerent tone Royal would have used. It's like he really wants to know.

"She wants our dicks in her mouth," Duke says, picking up a beer from the top of the barrel, which they've overturned to use as a table to hold their beer and spray paint. "All three of them at once."

"Shut up, Duke," Royal says. He still hasn't turned from where he's drawing a giant penis across the car.

"I don't think they'd all fit in that little mouth," Baron says, watching me with hooded eyes, a bored expression on his face even as his gaze stays sharp. "I'll take her ass. I like anal better, anyway."

"That leaves Royal with… hole number three!" Duke sings out, like he's a game show announcer.

"Trust me, my pussy is hole number one," I say, grabbing a can of paint and giving it a shake. "And you don't win by process of elimination. You have to earn that shit."

"Oooh, kitty's got her claws out," Duke mocks, stumbling over a backpack that lays on the ground at the base of the barrel.

I shrug. "Truth hurts."

Duke chugs the rest of his beer and smashes the bottle on the ground at my feet, making me jump. He laughs and starts dancing around, singing "Truth Hurts."

I survey their setup. Zephyr used to carry his paint in a backpack, too, but his was threadbare and leftover from elementary school, stuffed with a few colors at a time, whatever he could afford. The one lying at the base of the barrel is new, and there must be a dozen cans of all colors of paint on the barrel. I'm itching to use them. I grab another can and go to the next car, which Zephyr has already tagged, and then the next one, where I start painting. For a minute, only Duke's obnoxious singing and the hiss of the paints fills the night. I breathe deep, not sure if I'm high from the fumes or from the freedom I find in this.

"Not bad."

I turn to see Baron standing behind me, watching me work.

"I had a good teacher," I say.

"Didn't know people taught graffiti," he says, flashing a haughty grin as he takes the other corner of the car.

"People teach art," I answer.

"Hey, let me ask you a question," Duke says, staggering up behind us. "If you're the blowjob queen, why isn't my dick in your mouth right now?"

"Because you're a rude, sloppy drunk."

I hear Royal chuckle from the next car over.

"Tellin' it like it is, I see, I see," Duke says. "In that case, you're a rude, bitchy slut."

"Cut it out," Royal snaps.

"Oh, what, only you can call her that?"

I keep painting, trying not to let him ruin my mood, but his words get under my skin. I don't know why I care, why it hurts to know Royal calls me that behind my back. He calls me a slut to my face all the time. But it still stings.

"Just shut up," Royal says quietly.

Duke ignores him and starts in on me again. "How come you're not giving it up yet? You been at school a month now, and you're not even uggo. We should have fucked you by now. What's up with that?"

"I'm just not that interested in dick," I say. "I've got other stuff going on."

"Maybe you're just one of those who takes a little convincing, if you know what I mean. Some girls give it up easy, and some… You just gotta take it."

"Are you a lesbian?" Baron asks, watching me with curiosity as he pauses to chew the bits of candy off the stem of his sucker.

I shoot him a look. "Just because I'm not clamoring to fuck you, I must be a lesbian?"

"He just wants to see you eat a big juicy pussy," Duke says, laughing. "Dude, if you don't like dick, I will totally plow a bitch while she eats you out."

"Zero interest in that scenario," I say, stepping back to look at Baron's work. He's actually doing art, and it's not bad. He checks out mine, too. Then he holds out his hand and gives me knuckles. The good feeling comes pouring back into my chest.

"Wanna continue it up top?" Baron asks. "I'll boost you up and hand you colors."

"Really?" He's strong enough that I could stand on his shoulders and tall enough to lift me up so I could reach the roof of the car and scramble up. I've never painted upside down before, so the idea is intriguing.

"I'll lift her," Royal says, coming over to join us. "I'm taller."

Baron steps away to text someone, and Royal's hands fall on my hips. "Ready?"

"Yeah," I say, swallowing hard. I try not to notice how his hands are so big they circle my entire waist, how warm they feel through the thin fabric of my undershirt, below the cropped sweatshirt, or how close he's standing, so I can feel his jeans graze against my ass.

He boosts me up, and I scold myself for getting distracted. I get my boots on his shoulders and brace my hands against the car for balance. His hands fall on the backs of my calves, his touch warm against my skin on the cool night. Ignoring the badly timed impulses in my body, I grab the top of the car and pull myself up. It's not hard, but I scrape my knees getting up. That's what I get for not taking the time to change into jeans.

He tosses a few colors up, then goes to the next car and starts defacing Zephyr's art. I bite back the urge to tell him to stop, that you can't just paint over another artist's work, but he's not doing art and obviously doesn't give a fuck. He's just here to deface something, to write "FUCK YOU" in giant black letters over the complex and layered beauty that Zephyr Hertz put on an ugly, rusted train car. He took something ugly and barren, and gave you something to look at while it went by, so you don't even notice the desolate metal.

For some reason, it makes me think of Colt's words again. These guys destroy lives. Do they really care if they're fucking up something beautiful? Of course not. They'd probably rather do that than paint curse words on blank canvas.

But then there's Baron, making something instead of destroying it.

"I want up there, too," he says, returning from behind the cars. Royal boosts him up, and he lies on the side with me, reaching down with his can. For a few minutes, we work in silence.

"So, you don't like sex," he says after a while.

I laugh and shake my head. "I like sex fine," I say.

"Not a word I'd use to describe sex."

I think of him fucking some girl while he drank a beer. Seems like the exact word he'd use to describe it.

"I like sex as much as the next girl," I say.

"With guys?" he presses.

"With anyone," I say. "I just think dick is overrated."

"You hear that?" Duke yells, howling with laughter. "The dyke thinks dick is overrated!"

"I'm not a dyke," I say. "I'm attracted to guys."

"Maybe you just haven't had the right dick," Baron says.

"She's obviously never had Dolce dick," Duke says, smashing a beer bottle against the car we're on. Foam and glass sprays everywhere, splattering my hands as glass shards pelt my skin.

"I think *you're* the Dolce dick," I say, glaring at him.

"Hey," Royal growls. "I told you not to come down here, Cherry Pie. You don't have to be here."

"And he doesn't have to keep harassing me," I say.

We glare at each other.

I'm the one who breaks first. I sigh and sit up. "Look, you want to show me you're nasty boys with no respect for women, I get it. It's not like I've never heard that shit before. It doesn't bother me. But if you're going to come at me, then yeah, I'm going to defend myself."

"He wasn't coming at you," Royal says. "He just said you'd never fucked a Dolce, which is a fact."

"Fine," I say. "But I'm not going to sit here like some meek little lamb while someone talks shit about me. If you dish it out, you should be man enough to take it when someone gives it back."

"Now who's talking shit about someone," Duke says, coming up beside Royal. "Saying I'm not man enough? Did I say you weren't woman enough to take the gang bang we're about to have with your tight little ass?"

"That," I say, glaring at Royal and gesturing to his brother. "Fine, he's not talking shit about me. He's just constantly threatening to rape me. You think I'm going to just sit here and take that shit without a word?"

"He's kidding," Baron says. "Have a sense of humor."

"Fine, let's all have a sense of humor. Speaking of, you know what would be really funny? If I called my gangster friends on my street, and they all showed up and raped *your* rich asses to teach you a lesson about walking onto their turf like you own it just because you own the rest of the town. Here, let me get my phone out and call them right now. It's *so* much funnier if they're here in person, surrounding you and outnumbering you three-to-one, so you know it's actually a very real possibility, while they joke about it."

They're all staring at me when I finish. Okay, so maybe I ranted a little too hard there. I take a deep breath and give Baron my sweetest smile. "Still funny?"

"That's not the same," Duke says. "You have sex with dudes all the time."

I roll my eyes. "Wrong. And I'll tell you how it's not the same. Because if y'all all raped me right now, you'd probably get away with it. I came down here alone, after midnight. My shorts are short. I was obviously trying to get in good with you. I'm trailer trash, and I should be lucky three rich guys like you are even interested, right?"

"We're not interested," Royal growls.

"But that's what a jury would say. Meanwhile, if someone hurt you, it would be front page news. The horror! The outrage! The monsters would go away for life. No one would ask you why you came to your attackers' turf, why you were on the wrong side of town. They wouldn't say, you should know that guys who look like you attract attention, so you must have secretly wanted it. They wouldn't say you were asking for it."

"Oh, look, an angry feminist," Baron says. "How original."

"Too much truth for your little paint party?" I ask. "You're three huge guys, you're rich, you're white, you're straight. You're even attractive and healthy and fit. You literally have every privilege there is. You have *no idea* what it feels like to be vulnerable."

"Harper," Royal says quietly. "Shut up."

I sigh and stand, brushing rust off my hands. My big mouth probably blew any shot of getting in with these guys, but whatever. I have a voice for a reason. "Look, I'm not saying you have no problems or your life is easy," I say. "Obviously I don't know shit about it. And I'm sorry I killed your vibe. So, I'm just going to go now."

A pair of headlights sweeps into the parking lot, washing over me as I stand atop the train car, making me look about as tall as the fucking Statue of Liberty. My stomach drops, and a second later, a whoop sounds and blue lights flash.

As if this night hadn't turned shitty enough already. There's zero point in running, since they have me in their sights, but instinct is hard to deny. So is seventeen years of experience. Cops don't come to my neighborhood to serve and protect. They come to bust our asses.

Royal grabs Duke and runs, dragging him behind the train cars as Duke stumbles along, his arm over Royal's shoulder.

Baron and I vault the back side of the train car and take off, too. It's each man for himself when the cops show up.

Except Duke can barely walk, and Royal's not leaving him behind. Of course not. They're brothers. They might be willing to leave me on the train car to get myself down, but they're not abandoning each other. They're ride or die, all for one and one for all. It makes me hurt inside, the thought of them all being caught because of Duke's drunk ass.

I hear the cops yelling behind us, but we don't slow. I catch up to the guys as they stumble into the ditch, and I know they're not going to make it.

"Get down," I whisper-shout, grabbing Duke's arm and yanking him down. They both stumble to their knees, and Royal shoves Duke flat.

A flashlight scans over us, almost catching me and Royal. The twins have gotten down in the filthy ditch already. Royal shoves me to the ground, his weight crushing me as his hard body presses against mine. If we weren't about to get busted, I'd probably be getting all stupid over him right now. I can feel his heart beating hard and fast against my back as he presses me into the dead grass and dried mud.

"I know you're there," calls the cop's annoyed voice.

Royal shifts his hips against mine, lowering his mouth to my ear. His lips brush my earlobe, and my heart lurches in my chest. "I think I want to fuck you right now," Royal murmurs into my ear.

"You're insane," I say, squirming out from under him. This might be a game to him, but I can't just buy my way out of an arrest.

"What's going on?" Duke slurs.

I shush him as I hear footsteps coming closer. I get into a crouching position, ready to sprint away. But then I glance over at the guys. Duke's eyes are unfocused, and I'm pretty sure he's going to make noise and give us away at any second. Baron's face is alive, none of the usual arrogance in his features. His eyes shine with a manic sort of glee, like he gets off on getting nabbed by the police. Royal doesn't look like he's playing anymore. His jaw is set as he holds his two brothers low, out of the beam of the flashlight.

We'll all go down if we stay here like sitting ducks.

"Here goes fucking nothing," I mutter.

I jump out of the ditch and run back toward the train cars, back the way I came. The cop doesn't stick around to search the ditch. Maybe he thinks I'm running for my bike to escape or to hide in the cars. Or maybe he just sees someone running, and he gives chase. He slams into me, and I hit the ground hard, my bare knees and palms grinding across the pavement. He shoves me flat, his knee pinning my lower back as he snaps cuffs onto me.

His radio goes off, and he yanks it free to answer it, his knee rammed into my kidneys. "I got her," he says before holstering his radio. He yanks me to my feet and hustles me around the cars to where the beer and paint are lit up by the strobing blue lights.

"Apple, is that you again?" asks a familiar, strongly accented voice.

"Hey, Officer Gunn," I say, waving my fingers even though he can't see them behind my back. "How's Maisy?"

Hey, I'm a southerner, I can't just see somebody and not ask after their family, especially since we were in the same class for the past few years at FHS.

"She's fine," he says. "She's applying for art schools for next year."

"Cool," I say. "I meant to go down to the gallery and see her show this summer. I heard it was amazing."

"How's your mom and them?" he asks, sounding weary. He picked me up a few times in my graffiti days, and he was probably thinking I'd reformed.

"Just peachy, thanks for asking," I say, giving him a feral smile.

He sighs. "Who were you down here with?"

"No one," I say. "Just me."

He shines his flashlight on the backpack, a fucking Patagonia. "That's your bag?"

"Yep," I say, cursing the stupid rich guys for having to carry even their spray paint in expensive bags. The cop looks skeptical. Officer Gunn is one of the better cops to get grabbed by, since he knows what it's like down here. Hell, rumor has it he grew up in the same trailer park as me back in the day. But it's not so fortunate when he can call bullshit on my claim. He knows I can't afford all that paint and beer, let alone the bag they were carried in.

"Is that what you've been doing?" he asks, shining his light over the car Royal was defacing. He lands the beam on Zephyr's tag at the bottom.

"Is that you?" asks the other cop. "The blimp?"

"It's not a blimp," I protest, but then clamp my mouth shut. If I say it's a zephyr, they might connect it with the kid. For all I know, he has a rap sheet longer than mine. They could trace him back to a fuckload of graffiti once they know whose tag that is.

"Who was with you?" Officer Gunn asks.

"No one," I say again.

"Where'd you get all that paint?"

"I stole it," I say. "I stole it off some rich kids at school."

"Let's just take her in," says the other cop. "She's admitting to the damages."

"You know I can't just let you go," Officer Gunn says, looking like he kinda regrets that fact. "Unless maybe you can tell me who else was down here…"

I think of the guys back in the ditch. No, the guys who are long gone. Even if I told the cops who I was with, they wouldn't catch them. It would be my word against three guys who buy off cops. I think about the look on Royal's face when he was there with his brothers. He was tense, like he knew it was his responsibility to get his two self-destructive brothers out of there unharmed. His loyalty wouldn't let him walk away even if he should. He was stuck there trying to protect one brother who drank with reckless determination and one who wanted nothing more than the thrill of getting caught. Even if I was a rat, which I'm not, I respect that loyalty too much to turn them in.

"No one else," I say. "I told you, it was just me."

"Did you see anyone else back there?" Officer Gunn asks the other cop.

"It was just her," says the guy. Maybe he's paid off, or maybe he's just tired and wants to get the night over with. They've made their arrest, and now they'll have to file paperwork, and the more kids they grab, the more paperwork they'll have. It's really not worth it for a petty crime like vandalizing a train car that's not even in use.

They put me in the back of the patrol car while Officer Gunn makes a quick sweep around the cars and then comes back. He grabs the backpack and stuffs all the paint cans and beers inside. I can't help but feel bad about all that wasted paint. Zephyr could paint a masterpiece with that.

As we pull away, I press my forehead to the glass and look out at the barren railyard and wonder if I just made a huge mistake. Sure, loyalty's great, but like pride, it's never done anything for me. Loyalty doesn't put food on the table. And those boys, they have only loyalty to each other. They wouldn't hesitate to throw me to the wolves at the first opportunity.

Maybe I really am just like my mother. I thew it all away for a man. I got myself arrested, took the fall, so that they could walk away without a backwards glance.

That's what I wanted them to do, I remind myself. There was no point in all four of us getting arrested, getting another mark on our records. But as I watch the empty lot disappear behind us, I can't help but think about how they all would have banded together if it were one of them in handcuffs. They would have refused to be separated. They would have all turned themselves in to keep any one of them from being alone.

I lay my head back on the seat and close my eyes so I won't have to see the empty lot. Whatever fever gripped me when I biked down here has broken.

I'm not one of them, and no amount of wishing will change that. I rushed down to be with them, to feel like part of something, but I'm not. They didn't want me down there at all. Royal told me to go away. They weren't looking forward to seeing me show up. They weren't sorry to see me hauled off in cuffs. They watched me take the fall so they could cut and run, even though they probably could have talked their way out of an arrest.

I don't need them, I tell myself, willing myself to believe it the way I used to. *I don't need anyone.*

Needing people is more than a weakness, it's a waste of energy. I am the only person I can count on. Whether it's the Dolce boys, or Jolene, or Mr. Behr, or my own mother, when shit goes down, I always turn to find nothing but the wind at my back.

Vulnerable

You think I don't know vulnerability, but
Do you?

What did it feel like to you, little girl?
Did it feel like ropes that rubbed away your skin and down to the bone,
Or like helplessness that made you hate yourself so deep
You had to become someone else
Just to survive
To you?
What did it look like to you, little girl?
Did it look like pitch blackness when you woke in the night,
Gripped tight in terror's teeth,
Or like the stars behind your lids when they kicked out your teeth
To you?
What did it smell like to you, little girl?
Did it smell like blood
and vomit
and dirt
and spit
and piss
and worse
To you?

Little girl, I know vulnerable,
And soon
you will
too.

twenty

Harper Apple

1:13 AM: BadApple: I know it's late and I'm really sorry 2 bother u, but I need help

1:15 AM: BadApple: I know u don't owe me anything. IOU more than I can ever repay and I haven't properly thanked u and I'm sorry 4 that 2.

1:20 AM: BadApple: Ur probably sleeping n u wont get this until morning, and that's fine I don't want 2 wake u but I don't have anyone else to ask. I'm sorry.

1:22 AM BadApple: guess it helps if I tell u I got picked up by the cops. I just need u 2 come get me out in the morning or whenever. They r about 2 take my phone. They said bail is $100 but my mom wont pay it n they wont let me go get it. I have it. I can pay u back.

1:31 AM: BadApple: I'm sorry I haven't given u what u wanted yet and I know I fucked up, so if u need 2 get someone else to do this I understand. Or if u want payment in another way, that's fair n I shouldn't say I wont do it bc IOU whatever u ask n more.

1:33 AM: MrD: Christ, stop blowing up my phone. So you got arrested, big deal. I'll bail you out in the AM. I don't need anyone else bc you're going to give me what I asked for.

1:35 AM: BadApple: thank u. I'm sorry.

2:15 AM: BadApple: Wow ur fast. Just leaving now. U didn't have to get up and take care of it now. Thank u SO MUCH tho. How can I get the cash 4 bail 2 U???

*

I don't know what to expect when I walk into school on Monday. It's a small town, which means news travels fast. While news of my arrest wouldn't be any big deal at Faulkner, where kids were picked up for little shit all the time, Willow Heights is different.

A few people whisper when I walk down the hall, but it's not too bad. I'm barely at my locker two minutes when Dixie comes rushing up. "Oh my god," she says. "When you said you wanted to get into something, I didn't know you meant something *illegal*."

"Um, yeah, Dixie," I say. "I thought that was implied."

"Can I have a quote for the blog?" she asks, waving her phone at me. "I mean, I know you're probably not proud of it, but everyone's going to find out, so you might as well control the narrative, you know? If you put it out there, with your spin, before they hear it from someone else…"

"What kind of quote do you want?"

"I don't know," she says. "Something badass. What'd you do?"

"I got arrested for graffiti down at the railyard," I say. "That's not very badass. It's not like I killed someone."

"Oh my god, that's perfect," she squeals. "*So* badass."

I can't help but smile as I close my locker. It doesn't take much to impress the girls here. One fight in the hall with their queen bee and a little arrest—which turned into nothing after Mr. D talked to them and had them drop the charges—and suddenly I'm a badass? By the end of the day, people are actually shying away from me like I might cut a bitch just for looking at me wrong.

I mean, I'll take it over the comments about my sluttiness. I decide to just roll with it. In fact, on Wednesday I realize that no one has even called me trash, put anything weird in my locker, or "accidentally" dropped their garbage on my plate at lunch. And the Dolce boys don't talk to me a single time, not even in the class where I sit with Royal. He even does his part of our assignment, seemingly content to pretend he doesn't know me.

After the first couple days, the fuss about my arrest dies down, too. My new girl status seems to be wearing off, like the girls told me would happen. It probably has more to do with it being Willow Heights' Homecoming week than anything else, but I appreciate the lack of attention however it came to pass.

Homecoming is apparently an even bigger deal here than at Faulkner. Student council decorates the whole school, there are pep rallies, dress up days for spirit week, all that shit. There's a Mummers Day parade with mums to the floor, girls campaigning to be queen, and more assemblies to pep us up. And even though I'm not into the whole crowning thing—I skipped the dance last year and walked to the gas station to steal sodas and candy with Blue and Mav—I actually pay attention to the nominees this year.

All three Walton girls are nominated, as well as a handful of cheerleader Dolce girls, and Dixie. If it weren't for her, I probably wouldn't care. She tries to explain it away, blushing and saying it's just so there will be a candidate who everyone can relate to, but she's obviously happy about it.

"You have to come to the dance," she tells me on Friday.

I assure her that I don't, but I wish her luck as I head out. I've made it an entire week without being singled out by the Dolce boys. Maybe my arrest accomplished something after all.

Frustrating as it is, though, I know I can't just avoid the drama and go on with my life. I owe it to Mr. D now more than ever. Sad, but my confidante and closest friend is apparently a pervy old dude. Because when push came to shove, when I had no one else, he was the one I turned to. He's the one I tell about the bullying at school, at least when it comes from the Dolces.

I make it to the bike rack before I have to eat my words. Duke is standing there, leaning on the rack with his feet crossed in front of him, his hands resting by his hips, looking so fucking sexy it's no wonder the girls all drop their panties for him.

I'm not sure who grabbed my bike and brought it home, but I'm assuming it had to be Mr. D or one of the guys, though I'm sure they wouldn't put a bike rack on that ridiculously fancy car of theirs.

"Thought you had a car," I say, pulling at the tangle of bikes to find the one without proper pedals.

"I do," Duke says.

A guy shoves in front of me to get his bike, but Duke grabs him and drags him back. "Dude," he says. "Show some fucking respect. Harper's getting her bike."

I narrow my eyes at Duke, then pull my bike out and step aside for the other guy to get his. "That wasn't necessary," I say. "I'm not in a hurry."

"He was being a dick," he says.

I raise a brow at him.

"Right," he says. "I heard I was a colossal dick to you the other night, so… I'm sorry."

"Wow," I say. "I wouldn't think you Dolces were capable of apologizing, seeing as how that implies admitting you were wrong."

He flashes me a grin. "I don't remember anything, so I can't admit I was wrong," he says. "But if my brothers tell me I owe someone an apology, I figure I got pretty out of hand."

"It's okay," I say, throwing my leg over my bike. "Not my first rodeo with a drunken clown."

He smiles and shakes his head. "Are you really that poor, or is that bike some kind of statement?"

"Hey, look, the colossal dick is back."

"Right," he says, pushing off the rack and holding up both hands. "None of my business. So, am I forgiven?"

I shake my head at his audacity, but I really wasn't mad at him to begin with. Yeah, he was being a belligerent asshat, but it wasn't the kind of thing you hold a grudge over. Some people are mean when they're drunk, like Zephyr's dad. Some people are giggly and clumsy and horny, like my mom. And some people are just plain obnoxious.

"You're off the hook," I say when Duke stands there expectantly.

"Cool," he says. "I'd offer to seal it with a fuck, but I don't think Royal would like that."

I narrow my eyes at him. "Why would Royal care? He doesn't like high school girls, and he didn't want me around in the first place."

"Riiight," Duke says, nodding. "Well, I hope that hunk of twisted metal gets you home before it disintegrates in moving traffic. I've got a game to play. See you around, Jailbird."

"See ya, colossal dick," I shoot back. "I hope you break all the other guys' necks before they break yours."

*

The weekend passes uneventfully. I win a couple fights and a couple hands of poker and bring home some money for my stash. I still haven't paid Mr. D back, but he says not to worry about it. I give him every scant bit of info I have on the Dolces, including that Royal smokes pot, though I have to fabricate the circumstances in which I found that out, since I didn't tell him after the spying incident. I also tell him about the incident leading to my arrest. Guilt nibbles inside me when

I tell him anything. I hate feeling like a snitch. But I owe him way more than I'm giving.

When I step outside on Monday morning, my bike is gone. In its place is something that looks like it could roll into the Tour de France in style. It's all sleek lines, with padded handlebars in the "hook 'em horns" position, super skinny tires, and paint gleaming a dark, subtle teal sheen on top of gunmetal undertones. I glance around for the clothes that Colt promised, but there's nothing else. I barely dare touch the bike. It's so pretty I'm afraid to leave fingerprints on it. And then I wonder if the cops are going to show up and say I stole it, since it looks like the kind of bike that costs as much as a car.

There's a little bow on the seat, though, and a bell on the handlebars that's shaped like a red apple. I pluck the bow off and look under it. There's a combination for the lock that holds it to the support beam on our porch and two words. *Bye Week.*

I don't know what that means—should it say *buy week*? And if so, I'm never going to be able to buy this—but I don't have another way to school, so I unlock it and take off.

I've never thought much about biking. A bike is a mode of transportation, and though it's nice to have brakes and full pedals, I can get around pretty well without.

But this bike…

It's like flying. Like gliding through the air. I feel weightless as I speed along without having to pedal hardly at all. I'm at school so fast I'm a little disappointed. I want to keep riding, to fly through Faulkner like a kite, swooping around curves and diving over curbs. The heat of summer has finally broken, and the weather is that perfect, gorgeous temperature we get for a couple weeks between the sweltering sauna of summer and the grey rain of winter.

I could ride all day, through town from the giant oaks with their rust colored leaves blowing across the parking lot of Willow Heights, past the stores and restaurants, all the way to the north side where the Dolces live, where there's actual scenery. I could ride my bike along the winding roads, pretending I was in some other place, some other town. I'm not even out of breath as I hop off and lock my bike up next to the other Canyons, Orbeas, and Diamondbacks.

I pass my seat in first period and head to the back table, where Duke Dolce sits with Cotton Montgomery, DeShaun Rose, and Everleigh Walton.

He lounges in his chair watching me approach, all haughty arrogance and expectation. I shove the sticker from under the bow at him, the only clue I have. "Was this you?" I ask.

"I don't know what you're talking about, Cherry Pie," he says with a slow grin.

"I can't buy this," I say, glancing at his friends, my face heating. They know I'm poor, but that doesn't mean I want to go around saying it in front of people who already look down their noses at me.

"What is it?" Everleigh asks, leaning over to see what's written on the little sticky square.

"Bye Week, baby," DeShaun says, stretching his long arms over his head before laying one along the back of Everleigh's chair.

"What's Bye Week?" I ask, looking back and forth between them.

They all stare at me like I asked if puppies were cute.

"Is she serious?" Everleigh asks.

Cotton shakes his head and gets out his laptop, like I'm too hopeless to even bother with.

"Baron?" I ask Duke, holding his gaze.

"Could be," he says.

"Royal?" I press.

"It's Bye Week, Cherry Pie," he says with a wink. "Anything's possible."

"Bye—*Week!*" Cotton and DeShaun chant in unison, deep in their throats, and they all high-five.

Maybe it wasn't any of them. Maybe it was Colt. He said he'd bring me clothes. He could have brought me his sister's bike. Sure, it looked brand new, but I can't think of a reason Royal would get me a bike. Duke's the one who said mine was trash, the one who might have owed me a little for what I did. And I already told him he was forgiven.

Royal hasn't spoken a word to me since the arrest.

I go to my seat and try not to think about it. I wish he'd make up his mind. Every time I start to put him out of my mind, he reels me back in. And once I'm in, he pushes me away again. I'm getting whiplash trying to keep up with his game of red light-green light.

But if it was him… Does that mean I have a shot after all?

Dixie rushes into class at the last minute and slides into her seat at our table, out of breath. Her cheeks are pink from the nip in the air outside, her eyes sparkling.

"How was homecoming?" I ask, glancing between her and Quinn, feeling like I'm missing something.

"Oh, it was fine," Dixie says. "Lo won, but everyone knew she would."

"Maybe next year," I offer.

"Everleigh will win next year," she says, not sounding at all concerned by this.

"What's this Bye Week thing?" I ask. "I take it everyone's not fired up to support bisexuals. Is it a sportsball thing?"

The teacher glares at us, so I don't get an answer. A few minutes later, though, an email comes through from Dixie with a link to her blog.

Willow Heights Gossip Grrl

Bye Week!

If you're a WHPA lifer, you know what Bye Week means. It's the time of year when everyone goes a little crazy, battle lines are forgotten, and inhibitions fly out the window... And a few surprises emerge!

If you're new to the halls of WHPA, Bye Week is more than a week off for the football team. It's a week of fun and community, where we're all just a little bit more relaxed, and, if you ask me, a little bit better. The social ladder is put in storage and boundaries between cliques melt away.

This year, it's also Halloween, which means things will get even crazier than usual! The regular rules don't apply this week. It's the perfect excuse to do that crazy thing you've been too afraid to do. Take the next step and wear a couples costume with that cutie you've been vibing with. Get into a little trouble this weekend. Confess your feelings to a secret crush you thought was out of your league! Anything goes!

The Scoop:
All eyes will be on the Dolce boys this wild weekend. Will they finally make things official with one of their Dolce girls? Rumor has it the Waltons are vying for permanent positions on their arms and in their... Hearts. 😉 One thing's for sure: There's bound to be a few new couples by this time next week!

Must have item of the week: An invite to Cotton Montgomery's annual Bye-Week Bash. Anyone who's anyone will be there!

I resist the urge to scroll down Dixie's blog and read more. I don't want to know what's been said about me in her other posts. Still, I decide to check in on the blog more often. It was hugely informative, and for once, I'm not in the dark. I leave a comment thanking Dixie for her explanation and shoot her a smile as we work.

Dreams

I dream
Of her tight little body under mine
Helpless and loving it
Begging for more
As I pound her senseless
Until she comes
Undone.
I dream
Of sinking into her slick pink cunt
Licking the wetness from her lips
Until she quivers like a rose petal
Coated in shimmering droplets
Translucently bruised
Magnificently broken.
I dream
Of fucking her into submission
But when I wake
It's me who is fucked.

twenty-one

Harper Apple

I want to talk to Royal about the bike, but I know better than to ask at lunch when his friends are around. He's a complete asshole when he has an audience. It's only when we're alone, or in science, where the tables are set up for partners instead of groups, that I can talk to him. When I get to class, he's already there, leaning back in his chair with his long legs spilling from under the table. His flawless face is serious as always, and even though he's looking at his phone and I can't see his eyes, my breath catches stupidly in my chest at just the sight of him.

God, I'm so fucking ridiculous.

I drop into the seat beside him, frustrated with myself for being so fucking affected by him. I want to be cool like he is, but better. I don't want to just pretend I don't feel it. I want to stop feeling it, to become immune to Dolce fever entirely.

"Thanks for the bike," I say. "That was very thoughtful of you."

He looks up from his phone, and I see the shadows of a bruise on his jaw. I'm sure I'm right about him fighting. But you can't just go up to someone and ask, the way you could ask if you saw them at the football game last weekend.

The corner of his mouth twitches into a smirk. "No, Stalker Girl. It wasn't thoughtful. It was settling up."

I give him some side-eye.

"I know I don't owe you shit," he says. "I told you not to come down there, and you did, and you got arrested. That's on you."

"Fair enough," I say, determined to be as cool as he is. Our attraction is palpable, crackling like electricity in the space between us. I know he feels it, too, but aside from one time, he's never acknowledged it or reacted to it. If he can put it aside and force himself to be unaffected by it, then I can, too.

"That was to make it clear we're more than even, in case *you* thought we owed you more."

"Got it," I say, reminding myself this is all business. It doesn't matter if there's an attraction between us. He's obviously not interested in acting on it, and I have no interest in fucking a guy who already calls me a slut when I haven't even given it up.

"Good," he says, opening his textbook. "So leave me the hell alone and stop talking to me."

"Gladly."

Okay, then. Guess that's it. Royal made it clear his gesture wasn't out of kindness or even generosity. It was a bribe to get me to leave him alone. Apparently the Bye Week peace between social groups has limits.

"I mean it," Royal says quietly, his hand covering mine. He leans close, his dark eyes burning with intensity. His long fingers wrap around the back of my hand, squeezing until I have to clench my teeth to keep from protesting. "Leave us the fuck alone, Harper. You don't know what you're doing. You don't want to get involved with us. Trust me on that."

I nod, remembering that he said the same thing about Colt. Is he doing the same thing to me, isolating me and making sure I don't have a single friend for the rest of high school?

Fine. I can make it fine on my own. I've been doing it for years.

"Got it?" Royal asks, crushing the bones in my hand together until I have to wince.

"Got it." I gasp, panic racing in my mind when I think of what will happen if he injures one of my hands and I can't fight. I'm afraid to even struggle, afraid it will snap one of my fingers. Something inside me breaks in that moment, even though my bones don't.

This is a game to him. He'll never understand the fear I feel right now. He'll never know what it's like to have everything in your world resting on something as fragile as a fist. If he couldn't play football, he'd still have the money and status and the big name. Without my hands, I'm ruined. Done.

"Let go," I whisper, my eyes blurring with tears of pain. "Please."

He takes his sweet time loosening his grip and releasing me. "Good," he says, flicking to the next page in his book. "Let's hope you have the brains to obey."

I suck in a breath, cradling my hand in my lap. I may have cried uncle, but I sit there fuming through the rest of class, vowing to find something good on them, something dirty enough that Mr. D will be able to take them down. Hell, I'll do it myself if he doesn't. I don't give a shit about the Darlings getting back their place in this town, but I wouldn't mind watching the Dolces fall from grace—preferably in spectacular fashion.

I don't want to take their place like the Darlings. I'll be out of here in two years. I have zero interest in being a Dolce girl or even picking up the crown when it rolls from their heads and crowning myself queen. I don't need to rule. I just want to watch them fall. Hell, I'll throw the party to celebrate their end and dance on the ruins of their kingdom as it burns.

This isn't just about getting information anymore. This shit just got personal. No one lays hands on me and gets away with it. Yeah, it'll be twice the work to get information for Mr. D and revenge for me, but they're going to learn not to fuck with the wrong girl. They can try to get rid of me, but I'll be there haunting them like a vengeful ghost at every turn. I'll figure out their every move, and wherever they are, I'll put myself in their way and wreck their plans.

For all I know they set me up to get arrested the other night. Baron went to make that phone call, after all. He might have been telling the cops to come get me, and they planned to ditch me to take the fall, not realizing Duke was so drunk he'd slow them down. From now on, they won't be able to make a move like that without me knowing about it. If they cut me down and call me a stalker, fine. If they make my life hell, I'm strong enough to endure it.

Getting into their inner circle is obviously out of the question. I got myself arrested to save their asses, and they still don't trust me.

So, I spend the week getting in their way. I sit at their table at lunch, even when Duke takes my food and reminds me that he declared I couldn't eat until I sucked his dick. I borrow Blue's car and drive by their neighborhood when I know they'll be coming home soon and might see my car. I comb through all of Dixie's blog posts from this year to see what's been said about them, who they've dated, anything that could give me an edge.

It all hinges on this weekend. That's when it all goes down. There's an air of anticipation, of celebration, but the school is also on hold—and on edge. Everyone seems restless without the game to look forward to, and there's a hushed current of excitement about having a whole weekend free for anything that comes along.

I keep my ears and eyes open for whispers about what's being planned. There's the party, of course. The Waltons and Dolces of the world wouldn't have it any other way. But I'm looking for something more clandestine that the boys might get into after the party. I may not know them well, but I think I'm starting to figure them out. They'll show up to the party, probably get drunk and fuck some poor girl senseless, and then they'll need a fix for their darker urges.

Maybe not the twins, but Royal will.

I don't know how I know this, but I do. Maybe because it's what I'd do, and because I know there's something deep down in the darkest part of him that is like me. He'd never admit it, since I'm trash and all that bullshit, but he knows. Maybe that's why he hates me so much, why he insists that I'm trash. He doesn't want to admit, even to himself, that we're the same in our darkest hearts.

He'd destroy me if I said it, but I think I've got him figured out. He's bored by parties, hookups, adoration. He needs something more, something money can't buy. Dixie said he needed someone to tell him no, but I don't think it's that, either. He needs someone to be real with him. Someone who doesn't worship his golden arm on the field, who doesn't bat her eyes and spread her legs when he smiles at her. This isn't about a girl at all. He needs more. He needs the crack of knuckles on bone, the ache of a good bruise, the splatter of blood on his face. It's hard to be fake in a dirt ring with the stink of blood in your nose.

All week, I ignore the chatter about the party. I don't have an invite, anyway. I want in on something else, the quieter whispers, the nods and secret handshakes where money passes. If Colt is involved in the fights, someone else must be. When I play poker, the high rollers are mostly older, but there are some younger kids, too, and they don't go to Faulkner. I study the faces in the hall, looking for someone familiar, for someone who could get me in on whatever's brewing.

By Thursday, I'm about out of options. I don't know who to ask, so I go to the girl with her finger on the pulse of the school.

"Anything going on this weekend?" I ask Dixie, sliding into a seat at lunch.

"Yeah," she says, looking at me like I'm missing a few braincells. "The Montgomery party. It's the biggest party of the year since the Darlings quit having theirs."

"I was thinking more along the lines of an afterparty."

"You need a party after the party?" Quinn asks.

"Or maybe a different kind of fun," I say. "For people more like me."

"Ohhh," Susanna says. "You think there won't be drugs?"

"No," I say, shaking my head. "I mean, something for people who aren't really into the party scene."

"I'm not going," Quinn says. "You can come over and bake with me and Susanna."

I can't help but laugh, even though I'm frustrated. "Even further from what I'm looking for."

"I think I know what you mean," Dixie says. "You're going to want to talk to Colt for something like that."

Of course. I'm so fucking stupid. Colt's the king of the underbelly of Willow Heights. One little problem with that—I'm forbidden from talking to him.

But it's not like Royal has hidden cameras around the school. If I talk to him in class…

Baron's in the only class I have with Colt, though.

"Any chance you have his number?" I ask Dixie.

"Why would she have Colt Darling's number?" Susanna asks, peering around her friend.

"It's in the school directory," Dixie says to her food, her cheeks going pink. Apparently not all of her friends know about her little Friday trysts with the school's bad boy. "Or I can ask him later. I have a class with him this afternoon."

She gives me a meaningful look and I drop it. But later, she catches up with me at my locker. "I know what you're after," she whispers like she really is a connection for buying drugs. She glances up and down the hall and then pulls me behind my locker door. "I couldn't say anything in front of Quinn. She's not really into that kind of thing, and our family would shit a brick if they knew I was going, but there's a race on Saturday night. You can put money down if you have it, but most people just go to watch and hang out. Whatever happens that night, you can never talk about it at school. Never."

"First rule of fight club," I say with a grin, feeling a buzz of energy just from knowing. This is what I've sensed in the halls all week. The big event, the culmination of Bye Week. "Thanks, Dixie."

I'm about to close my locker when a hand grabs it and pulls it back. Gloria Walton stands there looking from me to Dixie like she caught us talking about her.

"Hey, Lo," Dixie says.

"I need to talk to Harper," Gloria says.

Dixie waves and tromps off like she's not leaving me with a pit viper.

"Come to un-invite me from your party?" I ask. "Don't worry. I'm not crashing."

"I heard you were going after Royal Dolce," she says. "I just wanted to say—don't."

"I think you have to be friends to invoke the 'I saw him first' clause."

"I don't like Royal."

"Then why are you so worried about it? Afraid you'll be tossed from the throne if he breaks his no-high-school rule for someone else when he wouldn't do it for you?"

"He told you he didn't like high school girls?"

"Yes, and so did everyone else."

"Good," she says. "Then you already know. And in case you hadn't figured it out, they're all bad news, and he's the most…"

"Emotionally unavailable?" I say, quirking a brow. "You don't have to tell me that."

"I was going to say fucked up, but yours works, too."

For a second, our eyes meet, and I think she's being real with me. A little smile passes between us. But she's a more dangerous type than Royal. Boys can make everyone else believe you're trash. Girls can make you believe it yourself.

"Wow," I say. "I didn't think Waltons cussed. But again, why are you telling me this?"

"Call it… An act of charity," she says. "I'll tell you the same thing I told my sister. He may look like the prettiest package under the tree, but once you peel off that shiny paper, there's nothing but black coal inside."

"A little early for Christmas analogies, don't you think?"

She sighs. "Make your snarky comments if you have to, but just know, he has secrets you'd rather not know. Trust me. If you're smart, you'll run far and fast in the opposite direction when you see him coming. Whatever you think he'll do for your reputation, it's not worth what he'll do to your heart."

"You know, in a weird way, I think you're actually trying to look out for me right now," I say. "What I can't figure out is why you care."

"Maybe because it's Bye Week," she says with a shrug. "Or maybe it's because we have more in common than you think, but neither of our reputations would hold up to us being friends."

"Why does everyone keep saying I have a reputation?"

She rolls her eyes. "Everyone has a reputation. And yes, I admit, being Royal Dolce's girlfriend would put the cherry on top of mine. I don't know what it would do for your bad girl rep. Probably make you lose street cred."

I snort at that. "I have zero street cred."

"Just don't say I didn't warn you."

"I honesty appreciate it, Gloria. But I can look out for myself."

"If you say so," she says, and she tosses her hair and struts off, making me wonder if I just imagined she was trying to do me a solid. Maybe she really was just warning me off because she wants Royal for herself. Not that it matters.

If I can get in with the Dolces, I will. But it's not for the reasons she thinks.

Lo(w)

She cheers for us
On the field
As if we're worthy
Of her best.
How can something I did
In my darkest hour
Shine so much light
On my finest?
She sits next to me
In class, at lunch, in the lounge
But we never speak directly
It's against hotel policy—
Don't ask, don't tell.
It's just as well.
She gets me
ice from the first-floor machine
"Busted up again,
my friend."
"You know I'm sorry."
That's as close as I come
To spilling these truths
I guard jealously
Like treasure
Not poison.
She looks the other way
As we carefully weigh our secrets
And unspoken lies
On stretches of silence
In which we decide
It's better not to know.

twenty-two

Harper Apple

Gunfire echoes through the dark streets as I approach the "industrial" sector of town, which consists of a factory that makes maxi pads, the railyard, and a few warehouses, including the one that houses the Slaughter Pen. I nearly jump out of my skin when the loud pops sound again. Not that I've never heard gunshots, but I live in the bad part of Faulkner, Arkansas, not Los Angeles.

Still, I wonder what I'm getting myself into as I jog toward the huge lot behind the factory where Dixie told me to go. Suddenly, I regret telling her I'll see her there. I should have asked her for a ride. I was expecting a party, not a shootout.

As I get closer, the sound of squealing tires and the smell of burning rubber fills the air. I can see smoke drifting over the lot as I lope across an empty street and edge into the crowd.

Dorothy, we're not in the Heights anymore, I think to myself as I look around, taking stock of the situation. There are more people than I expected, but it's not just a bunch of rich kids out to wreck their cars and make their daddies buy them new ones. This is a town event.

There's a girl I remember dropping out of Faulkner last year, in a Winnie the Pooh costume pushing a stroller with a baby dressed as a jar of honey. A group of buff, twentyish guys speaking Spanish and drinking Tecate, their faces painted in Day of the Dead makeup, and a group of black girls in sexy nurse, devil, fairy, and bunny costumes, whispering and eyeing them from a few feet off. A middle-aged man in a Superman suit wraps his jacket around the shoulders of a woman who looks old enough to be his grandmother while she leans heavily on a cane. Two kids dressed as ninjas and clutching cans of Jumex dart through the crowd.

I start to relax as I wade in deeper. This is the Faulkner I know, the one I've always known. I feel my phone buzz and take it out to see a message from Dixie telling me where she is.

I make my way in that direction, toward the center of the lot, only to be interrupted by the squeal of tires as a car does a doughnut across the lot, leaving long, dark skid marks behind. A girl hangs out the window, her blonde hair streaming in the smoke that billows up from the tires. She shrieks, and the crowd cheers.

As I pass a group, I hear a scrap of conversation—"Gloria Walton and Royal Dolce"—and I turn that way. I don't see anyone familiar, though, and I don't know who spoke. I turn back toward the lot, my chest tightening. Is that who was in that car? Royal and Gloria?

I push my way a little closer, but this time, I hear my own name. I turn to see a tall, buff guy wearing a sleeveless shirt despite the chill in the air. His tats make up the sleeves, I guess.

"Harper Fucking Apple," Maverick drawls. Of course he's too cool to have dressed up. I don't blame him. I'm not dressed up, either. "I thought that was you. Where you been, baby?"

"What's up?" I ask, jerking my chin at him.

"What the fuck happened to you?" he asks, hooking a finger through my belt loop and pulling me closer as the crowd jostles us. "You look like shit."

"Same," I say. "Your beard is dumb."

It really is. He just has a little patch on his chin.

He grins and tugs at my belt loop. "I haven't seen you at school lately. You ditching the whole year again? Or shacked up with some asshole who needs a visit from me about that eye."

I shrug and touch my black eye. "I transferred. And this is from a fight. If you ever came on Friday nights, you'd know that."

"How's your ink holding up?" he asks, releasing my belt loop and lifting the hem of my shirt. He gets down in a crouch to examine the tattoo that runs over my hip and onto my torso. I hook my thumb in the top of my low-rise jeans and pull them lower still, holding my breath when he leans close so I can feel his warm breath on my skin.

He traces his fingers lightly over the design, and a shiver goes through me. Yep, still the same old Mav. If I was the same old Harper, I'd go home with him tonight, even knowing that it would never go anywhere. I always knew he wasn't the kind of guy I could hold onto, and it never bothered me. Maverick gets girls, but he never keeps them.

I'm about to pull away when a towering figure appears out of nowhere, grabs Maverick, and hurls him to the pavement.

"Why the fuck are your hands all over this girl?" Royal demands, looming over my friend.

Mav's on his feet in a second flat, his fists already swinging. Royal dodges aside and slams a fist into Maverick's jaw. Mav stumbles back, then dives forward. Before he can close the distance between them, I jump in and slam a palm against each of their chests, shoving them back.

"What the fuck, Royal?" I ask.

"Yeah, that's right," he says. "What the fuck is about accurate. Why were you showing this guy your pussy?"

"I'm outta here," Mav says. "I don't need to fight over a girl. See you around, babe."

He turns and disappears into the crowd. Royal yanks me around to face him, his grip biting into my shoulders, his dark eyes boring into mine. "Answer me."

"I wasn't showing him my pussy," I say. "I was showing him my tattoo, which he was only interested in because he's a tattoo artist."

"I know what Maverick is," he snaps.

"You do?"

"Everyone knows Maverick," he says, giving me a long, calculating look. "Did he give you that tattoo?"

"Yeah, so?"

"Did he also give you that black eye?" he asks, his voice steely.

I scowl up at him. "No."

"What happened?"

"Where'd you get that bruise on your jaw last week?"

We stare at each other a long minute. My heart thuds in my chest, and I think for a second he might admit it, that he fights.

"Football," he mutters.

"Really?" I ask. "Because I was thinking you got it at the Slaughter Pen. What I don't understand is why. You've got all the money in the fucking world."

His eyes harden. "What about you? Where'd you get the money for a tattoo that big?"

"We're friends," I say. "He did it for free."

I try to step around him, but he steps in front of me to block my way. "You fucked him, didn't you?"

"How is that your business?" I ask. "I don't go around demanding a list of all those golden pussies you've wet your dick in."

"You did," he says, glaring at me. "I know how that asshole operates. If you don't have money, you pay with pussy."

I try not to let his words sting. It's true that Mav fucks a lot of girls he works on, but that's because he's an artist, and he's inspired by his muses.

Isn't it?

Or am I really such a sucker that I fell for that line? Maybe he kept coming back on occasion because I was easy, because I never asked questions or demanded commitment. Sex with him was fun and uncomplicated, with no expectations from either of us. But the truth is, I didn't want more. I accepted him for who he was. He didn't use me any more than I used him to get some cool ink.

"Well, you always said I was a whore," I say to Royal, shoving past him, my throat tight. "Don't act so shocked that you were right."

"Harper," he calls, but I don't turn. I'm smaller than him, and I can slip through the crowd toward the center, where a handful of cars have stopped doing doughnuts to line up. A strong hand clamps around my upper arm, turning me around again. I notice some WHPA kids watching, whispering, thirsting for gossip. All eyes are always on the Dolces.

"What are you doing here?" Royal asks. "Did you just come looking for a hookup?"

I shrug. "Maybe. What's it to you?"

"You're racing," he accuses. "You're just a little badass trifecta, aren't you?"

I snort. "Trust me, if I could afford a car, even if it was a heap of junk held together by duct tape, I'd never risk it doing something like this."

"Then you came to watch me," he says, a triumphant smirk finding his lips. He lays a hand on my waist, pulling me closer.

His thumb moves back and forth just above the top of my jeans, the warmth sinking through my tee shirt and making stupid things happen in my low belly.

I step back from him, so frustrated I could scream. "What do you want from me?" I demand, forcing my words past the ache in my throat. "You treat me like shit, and then you kiss me, and then you tell me to leave you alone. You act like I don't exist, even this week, when 'anything goes.' But as soon as some other guy shows interest in me, suddenly you give a shit?"

"Maybe I do," he says quietly. He reaches for me again, then drops his hand to his side. His unfathomable eyes search mine, begging me to understand something that I can't. How can I understand anything about him when he won't let me?

"That's fucked up, Royal."

"I know."

Someone in a *Scream* mask yells for him, and his gaze flicks behind me to the row of cars.

Suddenly, I'm so fucking tired. Tired of the games, tired of his school, tired of this town. I sigh, my voice coming out defeated. "Go hang out with your friends, and let me have mine. You know that's how this ends."

"What if I can't do that?" he asks. "What if I can't watch some guy feeling you up?"

"So, what is it?" I ask. "Now you like me?"

"No," he says, glaring at me.

I sigh. "Fine, I'll be the first to admit it. I might have started to like you at one point. I fell under your spell, got the Dolce fever, wanted to be in your little Dolce girl fan club. But you made sure to crush every bit of that feeling before it could go too far. I get it, I do. I don't want to be your dirty little secret, and you'd never risk your reputation to be with me. So, that leaves us… Where?"

"Here," he says, ignoring his brother, who is yelling for him. "Here we are."

"What do you want?" I ask again. "You want to go on looking down your nose at me and calling me a trashy whore, or you want to get all up in any guy's face if he touches me, like I belong to you? You can't have it both ways."

"Why not?"

We stare at each other another long moment, and then Duke comes bounding over and grabs Royal. "Come on, dude, you're going to lose me a shitload of money. Get in the car."

Royal lets Duke pull him away, but he turns back to look at me one more time, like he's making sure I'm still there, still watching. Some people whoop when Royal climbs into a white Cobra with shimmering dark blue stripes. To my surprise, I see Gloria Walton sitting on the door of a sleek, sparkling green Mustang convertible. She waves and blows kisses, but she doesn't look like a Southern Belle in a parade, the way she did just last week on the Homecoming float. Then, all the cheerleaders wore those old-fashioned pastel gowns that looked like confections from Quinn's baking channel and had their hair shellacked into place.

Today, Gloria's blonde hair streams down to her waist, blowing out like ribbons in the chill Halloween night. She's wearing simple, skin-tight jeans and a white tank top that shows off her toned, tan shoulders. But her crowning beauty is her face—the freckles scattered across her cute little nose, the huge smile that is the exact opposite of the plastic grin she wore in the parade, her eyes lit up like sparklers with so much excitement. There's something so pure about her joy that I can't help but smile back, even though it puts an ache deep in my chest.

I can't remember the last time I felt joy like that.

I take in the other cars. Unlike the ones that fill the lot at Willow Heights, most of these aren't new, luxury cars. They're a mix of classics, regular cars, Camaros, Chargers, and the like. I spot a few Faulkner High kids behind the wheels, as well as some older racers.

Colt steps out of the crowd, Dixie clinging to his hip. Instead of her usual goth getup, she's wearing a Cinderella costume complete with puffy blue dress, crown, and wand. In her other hand, she holds a checkered flag like we're at Nascar. She giggles and ducks her head at something Colt says. He wraps an arm around her middle and raises his arm. He's holding a gun, but it doesn't look like the kind I heard on the way here. He fires a shot, and Dixie drops the flag.

The cars shoot forward, spinning their tires and revving their engines. They spew smoke and exhaust, the clamor deafening. They're all roaring so loud it's clear they've been stripped of mufflers, and one of them has jacked up the exhaust pipe to make it sound like gunshots. That's what I heard earlier. Not a gang shooting, not Colt's little pistol, but a tailpipe.

Cheers break out down the street as they pass another crowd gathered somewhere further on. I wave to Dixie, and she comes scurrying over, her face flushed.

"Did you see me? I got to hold the flag!"

"I saw," I say, smiling at her. I raise a brow and nod behind her. "I also saw you and Colt. Is that a thing now?"

"Oh, you know," she says, waving a dismissive hand. "Bye Week!"

"If you say so," I concede as Colt comes up behind her.

"Hey, Appleteeny," he says, flashing me a smile and sliding a possessive arm around Dixie's waist. He looks around like he's trying to find someone. "I could have sworn I saw Royal following you like a lovesick puppy, but I must have been mistaken."

"You were," I assure him. "He was just making sure I knew once again that he thinks I belong in the gutter."

"Sure he was." He shakes his head. "Never thought I'd see Royal Dolce chasing a girl. Guess he finally found one worth chasing."

"And I never thought I'd see you with a popular girl," I say. "Good for you. She's a good one."

"Oh, I'm not—" Dixie stammers, turning pink and busying herself fixing her tiara. "I wouldn't say I'm *popular*. I just like to be part of things. Everything." She giggles, glancing up at Colt. He grins down at her, looking genuinely happy for once.

As if to prove my point about her status, a handful of girls in Harry Potter attire rush over to hug Dixie, squealing her name and jumping up and down with her in excitement about her flag-holding. Apparently it's a big deal.

Colt hovers back, letting her relive her moment and bask in the glory. But I notice he's looking at her with something different, like he's just seeing her for the first time.

"I should have known you'd be here," says Eleanor Walton, stepping up beside me in a Sookie Stackhouse costume. Everleigh, dressed as Taylor Swift, tags along behind her, a starry-eyed grin on her face, obviously high as hell. Eleanor doesn't seem to have bought into the whole Bye

Week truce, as she gives me a dirty look that says she doesn't appreciate my attendance.

"Your sister street races," I say, trying to take the high road. "I'm impressed."

"You think you're the only tough chick at Willow Heights?"

"No," I say. "I just didn't expect her to be one."

"Why?" she asks, her tone way too confrontational, as if she's intentionally trying to start shit. "You think just because we're cheerleaders who carry Gucci bags and date the best guys that we can't be cool?"

"Well, yeah," I say. "Kinda. But she proved me wrong. I don't mind saying she's cool as hell."

"Duh," Everleigh says, then giggles and sways on her feet.

Eleanor huffs like I insulted her. "We don't need your approval," she says. "And stay away from Royal. I saw you pulling your whole drama queen act, making him chase you. It's not going to work, you know."

"It might," Everleigh says, giggling and swishing her purple dress.

Her sister shoots her a dirty look before turning back to me. "He might throw you a pity fuck, but trust me, that's all it will be."

"You obviously don't care," I say. "So, it must be worth it."

"Don't even go there," she says. "That's not how he sees me. I'm girlfriend material. Who do you think he'd introduce to his mother? A Walton, or a girl with thigh tattoos showing under her slut skirt?"

"I'm not interested in his mom," I say, raising my chin and leveling her with a stare. This girl is pissing me off. The more she tells me I'm not worthy of Royal Dolce, the more I want to land him just so she can't.

She rolls her eyes. "Yeah, he's a guy. You wave fresh ass under his nose, he'll go sniffing after it. But he'll never see you as more than a girl he slummed it with on Bye Week. I'm the real deal."

I cock a brow. "Then why are you so threatened?"

Two cars come roaring up the street toward the lot, their speed making them a blur as they streak toward us.

A buzz goes through the crowd, and I hear the same names repeated from earlier. *Gloria Walton and Royal Dolce.*

I spot a few people holding slips of paper, and the pieces fall into place. They're betting on the race.

Eleanor grabs my arm, her nails digging in. "I gave you fair warning," she hisses. "Stay away or learn the hard way. But whatever you do, I'll be the one doing a victory lap in the Shelby GT."

I know zero about cars, but I know a thing or two about being underestimated. So I shut my mouth and watch the two cars fly past Dixie, who brings the flag down. The two cars careen around the lot, skidding their tires and sending up plumes of white, acrid smoke. People scream and scatter when Gloria's Mustang slides too close, sending them stumbling away choking on the fumes. Royal's white car blurs by just as she turns, and I suck in a breath, sure they're going to smash into each other. He whips by her, though, missing her by inches. Instead of freaking out that she was nearly sideswiped, she laughs and pumps her fist, her hair flying crazily as she does another doughnut.

Royal's car skids to a stop in front of us, his tailpipes belching exhaust, the engine roaring so loud I cringe. The window is down, his arm draped along the sill as he leans out, a bright white smile lighting up his gorgeously tan face. "If you know how to handle a stick, hop in and let's ride, baby."

The line is so cheesy and Duke-like that I can't help but laugh. Beside me, Eleanor lets out a little squeal, shoving her tray of True Blood into Everleigh's hands and skipping forward to claim her victory lap.

Fuck that.

I take a giant stride, catching up to her and grabbing her ponytail and jerking her backwards. As she flails to keep balance, I casually move my foot into the path of her backpedaling legs, adding a little more strength to my grip on her hair. She goes down with a shriek of fury, but I don't stick around. I slide across Royal's sleek hood, open the passenger door, and drop into the seat with a triumphant grin.

twenty-three

Harper Apple

The car shoots forward so fast my stomach drops out like I'm on a roller coaster as I'm flattened against the seat. My heart stops, and a scream escapes before I can stop it. Royal laughs, expertly turning into the skid as his car slides around, spitting up smoke and noise in its wake as he careens past Gloria, missing her by a hair as she waves for someone to get in her car.

After a minute, I catch my breath and look over at Royal, about to tell him he's insane. But he's smiling so big, and for once, his eyes aren't deep with pain. He's just in the moment—daring, reckless, happy. It breaks my fucking heart.

On impulse, I lean across the console and kiss him hard on the cheek.

"You're fucking crazy, Stalker Girl," he says.

"Ditto," I say, smiling back.

"Be my rail meat, baby," he says. "Get in the window. I'll give you the ride of your life."

I don't think about it. I don't think about the future, or what I'm going to tell Mr. D, or if I'm going to keep my scholarship, or how I'm going to get out of this town. I give myself to the moment, like he is. I give my brain permission to shut off, to think only of this moment, not whether I'm going to make it out of tonight alive.

I slide up onto the windowsill of the passenger side, sitting on the door with only one arm and my legs still inside the vehicle, holding on. Royal's car skids, and the crowd rushes by in a blur of painted faces and colorful costumes. I wave and whoop as we zoom past another car that's arrived, weaving in and out in an intricate death-defying dance.

And then we're out of the lot, skidding onto the road. Instead of screaming in fear, a whoop of exhilaration leaves me, the wind snatching it from my mouth and whipping my hair out. As we rocket through the empty streets of Faulkner, I open my mouth again, and I scream. I scream louder, longer, refusing to let my voice be stolen from me. All the fear and frustration and joy of the moment come pouring out of me. I stay out as long as I can, screaming through Faulkner with the roaring power of the engine accompanying me.

At last, Royal pulls off next to a bridge. I don't even know where we are, just that we're on his side of town. It's dark, but the half-moon is bright, illuminating the bridge and the small river below. He cuts the lights, and we're alone, with only the moon to witness. He turns to me, a haughty grin on his face. "You like that, huh?"

"Who wouldn't?" I say, laughing and shaking back my wind-blown hair. My heart is suddenly stammering in my chest.

He looks me up and down, biting back a grin as he shuts off the engine. "You know I get to fuck you now, right?"

"What?" I ask, still breathless with laughter and exhilaration.

"You got in my car when I won a race," he says. "You're my prize."

"Royal," I say, leaning across the seat. I wrap my arms around his neck and kiss him softly on the lips. "You don't have to win a race to get me to fuck you. Just be a man I'd want to fuck."

He stares at me a long moment, then slides a hand behind my head and brings my mouth to his. Like the first time, the moment our lips meet, white-hot energy electrifies me. I tremble with the power of it, and he sighs and draws me closer, slipping his tongue between my lips. He caresses my tongue with his, working into a rhythm that makes my body pulse with pure lust. I bury my hands in his hair and arch my back to get closer. He holds me gently even as his mouth skillfully and forcefully commands mine to submit.

I do. I let myself go to this moment, too, letting him cradle me and slowly fuck my mouth with his tongue. His kiss is deep and filled with a yearning that makes my teeth ache, like he can't get what he needs no matter how long and hard and deep he kisses me. Our mouths move together until my body is tingling with heat, every inch of me answering the longing in his kiss, wanting to be the thing that quenches the insatiable thirst inside him. His hands stay buried in my hair, his thumb caressing my cheek, my ear, my jaw; his tongue owning mine with every stroke.

We kiss, and kiss, and kiss. Leaves skitter across the roof, and the wind whips through the car, a chill in the air that sucks the fevered heat from our bodies. Clouds move over the moon and then off again. I run my hands over his huge arms, the muscles bulging and knotting under my palms, my fingers not even fitting halfway around his bicep.

I remember thinking he was a black hole that would never be filled no matter how much he took, and I know I was right. I could kiss him for the rest of my life, could fuck him forever, and it would never touch the void he's trying to fill with me, or other girls, or fighting, or football, or racing.

But I don't care. I want to try. I want to be the thing that makes him laugh like winning, the person who makes him feel better for even a moment, if only on the surface. It feels good to be so wanted, so needed. And god, my body is more live than it's ever been, every cell in my being vibrating with the need he puts inside me. My swollen lips ache from how long we've kissed, and my core clenches with need, throbbing with hunger to be filled with him, even if only for a moment, for a night, when no one else knows.

I'm the one who gives in first, who moves my hands from his shoulders to his sculpted chest, down his washboard abs, onto his muscular thighs. I slide my palms up, my heart racing before I even touch his cock. I reach the top of his thighs and run my thumb along the iron ridge that strains against his jeans.

"Harper." He breaks the kiss, pressing his forehead to mine. His voice is choked, and his eyes are closed. His long, thick lashes make shadows on his cheeks in the moonlight. "Harper," he whispers, his breath ragged against my hot lips.

"Royal," I say, sliding a hand behind his head, lacing my fingers through his thick, dark hair. I run my other hand over his cock, circling my flattened palm against the thick head of it. "I want to. I want to fuck you."

His cock throbs against my palm, and he sucks in a breath. He pulls me in, pressing his forehead to mine hard enough to hurt. Then he releases me, pushing me back to my seat. "No."

"Royal," I say, sliding a hand over his thigh but not moving to touch him more intimately. "It's okay. I want to. You *are* a man I want to fuck. The only man."

He turns the key, lighting up the bridge in front of us. "Now who's all up in someone else's face, acting like she owns me?" he asks, a smile tugging at the corner of his lips.

"What?" I ask, stung. "I'm all up in your face?"

"I was making a joke," he says, leaning over to grab my seatbelt. He snaps it into place and tucks my hair behind my ear. "About what you did back there to Eleanor. That was pretty hot."

I cross my arms over my chest, holding back the hurt, keeping it from turning into something snarky like, "Apparently not hot enough."

Royal sighs and turns to face forward, shifting into gear and pulling onto the road. I have no idea what just happened. I'm not super experienced, but I know that guys don't usually turn a girl down at that point in the game. He got me all keyed up and then shut it down with zero warning. I just wish I knew why.

No means no, though, and I respect that. He doesn't want to fuck, and yeah, the rejection stings, but I'm not going to be a little bitch about it. Guys can withdraw consent, too. He doesn't owe me an explanation.

I tell myself it's better this way. I was caught up in the moment, in my attraction to him. I don't actually want to have sex with a guy who doesn't—or can't—feel about me the way I want him to. Being rejected still hurt my pride, though.

We pull back into town in silence, moving along the quiet streets the way we came. The air in the car is different, though, depleted of the charge that filled it on the way here. At last, Royal pulls up into the lot, driving to the very back, behind the factory. There are only a handful of cars left. On a little stretch of dead grass, someone has made a fire from pallets, and a few dozen people stand or sit around it on canvas chairs.

"You going to tell me what happened back there?" I ask, hating myself for needing to know, for not being cool enough to let it go and ask no questions, the way I could with Maverick. But Royal is not Mav. The way I feel about him is already deeper than anything I felt for Maverick, more explosive, more desperate. It scares me to feel this way, to want so much from someone.

"No," Royal says, getting out of the car and slamming the door.

"Okay then," I mutter, unbuckling my seatbelt. I take a deep breath and try to harden my heart, to remind myself I don't need anyone, that I already know I can't count on anyone, Royal least of all.

My door opens, and he takes my hand and pulls me up. He smooths my hair behind my ears with both hands, his fingers lingering on my cheeks until I look up at him.

"Don't ask me questions I can't answer, Harper," he says.

"Can't, or don't want to?" I whisper.

"Ones *you* don't want me to," he says. "It's the last night of Bye Week. You can accept that and spend it with me, or you can go home."

"Does it matter?" I ask. "If I go or stay, nothing will be any different tomorrow, will it?"

He swallows, his dark eyes searching mine for a long moment.

"No," he admits. "It doesn't change anything."

Now it's my turn to swallow hard, suddenly sure I'm going to cry, and that will change everything. "I should go," I say, tearing my gaze from his and sidestepping him.

He closes the door, his hand catching my elbow. His grip is gentle this time, and he doesn't turn me to face him, doesn't force me to look into his eyes. "Stay," he says quietly.

We stand there a long moment, neither of us moving, neither speaking. I imagine going to the fire to join our friends, sitting on his lap like we're a couple as mismatched as Cinderella with her tattooed prince charming, staying up until morning lights up the sky, holding onto this night until every minute is gone. I imagine drinking a few beers, joining the quiet murmur of voices like nothing is wrong, like there's only tonight, a night when boundaries disappear. Tomorrow, it will be like it never happened, so none of it matters.

"Give me a reason," I say at last, my back still to him. I try not to sound like I need it, but I can hear the edge of desperation beneath the hopelessness in my own voice. Tears press inside me like lava threatening to erupt, to rip me open from the inside out.

He's silent a minute, and then he drops his hand from my arm. "I can't."

His own voice is quiet and flat, empty of the emotion that choked mine.

I take a slow breath, then square my shoulders and walk away. There's no use in staying, in prolonging the inevitable. I let myself live in the moment tonight, and I'm already paying. Yes, there were beautiful moments. I went after what I wanted. I didn't just have a good time. I had *fun* for the first time in too long. After that, when we were together by the bridge, I got swept away, and that's something I don't do.

And this is the price of that.

This moment is ugly and painful like the shards of broken glass digging into the mud in the ditch as I step over it and head for reality.

I tell myself I'm not making a mistake. I force myself not to look back.

I feel things for Royal that I've never felt before, complicated, terrifying things. But if he can't give me a reason to stay, I can't stay. There's a gulf between us, a chasm of blackness that fills us both, and if one of us tried to step across, we'd be swallowed whole. We're too much alike, with no light to balance out the darkness inside us.

I step into my silent house and pull the door closed behind me. For once, I'm not relieved to find Mom gone, probably passed out drunk on a friend's couch or up all night smoking crack with a new boyfriend. The house is too quiet without the intoxicated snores of her and her skeezy men. I turn on every light in the house, but it still feels too dark, too empty. I turn off the lights again and lie in bed, pressing my fist to my chest, trying to crush out the ache of loneliness that grows inside me like a cancer.

"I don't need him," I whisper, closing my eyes. "I don't need anyone."

A tear creeps out the corner of my eye. I don't even believe my own lies anymore.

He said nothing will change, but he's wrong.

It's already changed.

The Way It Is

She makes me want to hurt
Everyone who's ever touched her soft skin.
She makes me want to fall
Apart into all the ugly-broken-bad pieces left.
She makes me want to leave
My throne for a life in the gutter with her.
She makes me want to lose
Control and smash into her like a wrecking ball.
She makes me want to break
The rules that hold my precarious life together.
But I can't
Hurt fall leave lose break,
So she will have to.

twenty-four

Harper Apple

The atmosphere on Monday is subdued, as if everyone is stumbling around trying to shake off the Bye Week stupor. Maybe they're just hungover from the weekend, but more likely, they're waiting for the Dolces to give them a clue, to point them in a direction. These boys are gods here—revered, feared, and worshipped in equal measure. The Dolces haven't said jump, so everyone is waiting to ask how high.

It creates a restless, irritable tension in the air.

And even though Dixie said what happens in Bye Week stays in Bye Week, she also said new couples emerge. Everyone seems to be waiting to see who paired up. I'm not immune. I wonder if Dixie's posted her blog yet, if she's finally ready to claim her bad boy. I'm also not immune from being the subject of gossip and speculation. I hear my name more than once, see people whispering and casting curious glances in my direction.

Guess that happens when you hop in the king's chariot and disappear with him for a few hours.

I run into Colt coming out of breakfast, but he just gives me his usual nod and keeps going. Bye Week is over, after all, and we're not in the same circles. Actually, we're both outliers, circle-less loners. And I'm tired of living by the Dolce rules, ones that change every day, with no warning. I can walk past Colt every day without saying a word to him, but he's still my friend. They can't change that.

I eye the pancakes with longing but grab a ham and cheese pocket instead, taking off after Colt with breakfast still clutched in one hand.

"Hey," I say, catching up with him in the hall.

"I thought your boyfriend didn't allow you to talk to me," he says.

"Don't have a boyfriend," I say with a shrug, biting into my breakfast. "And don't take it personally. Royal doesn't want me talking to any guys, not just you."

"Do you even hear the words coming out of your mouth right now?"

"I know," I say. "It's fucked up. But he's not my boyfriend. He made that very clear the other night."

"Really?" Colt says. "Because I seem to recall *you* leaving *his* ass in the dust at the end of the night."

"It wasn't like that."

"What's it like, then?" he asks, his eyes skating over the clusters in the hallway, on alert. Shit. I'm putting him in danger. I only wish I knew how to fix it.

"What's the point in hanging out for one night, pretending reality doesn't exist, if you just have to go back to reality the rest of the year? It's not worth it."

"Maybe it is."

"Shit," I say. "I'm sorry. I didn't mean it like that. No judgment of you or Dixie. If you're okay being her dirty little secret, that's your business. I don't think any different of either of you. It's just not something I could handle."

"*I'm* not the dirty little secret," he says, staring at me.

"Then… She's yours?" I ask skeptically, cocking my head. "How? She's pretty and popular and everyone loves her."

"This isn't about us," he mutters. "It's about you and Royal. You turned your back on a Dolce. There will be consequences."

"I didn't turn my back on him," I say. "I offered to be with him, and he didn't want that."

I look up and see the three Dolce boys approaching, their posse of football dudes and Dolce girls trailing behind. I glance over to warn Colt, but he's already gone, melted into the crowd.

"I thought I told you not to talk to that guy," Royal says, stopping in front of me.

"Oh, I thought it was Maverick I wasn't allowed to talk to," I say. "There are so many people I'm not supposed to talk to, I forget them all. Maybe you should just tell me to stay away from all guys."

"Fine," Royal grits out. "Stay away from all guys."

"Got it," I say, sidestepping him.

Duke reaches out an arm in front of me, resting a hand on the locker and blocking my way. "And I thought I told you that the next thing you put in your mouth at this school would be my dick."

"I'm awfully hungry," I say, biting viciously into the dough. "I don't know if I'd risk putting something in my mouth that you don't want me to bite off."

Duke leans closer to me, his pose threatening. "I can make you swallow all your teeth to keep that belly full while I fuck that pretty little mouth. Don't worry, Cherry Pie. I'll top them off with gravy."

"Fucking try it."

Baron crosses his arms and looks down at me, the stem of his sucker pulling the corner of his mouth down in a deeper scowl. "This one's getting awfully mouthy," he says. "I think she needs a reminder of her place."

"Trust me, I know my place," I say. "And I know yours. I'm happy to leave you alone. And yet, you're the ones always getting up in my space."

Royal scoffs quietly. "That's what you were doing outside my house? Leaving us alone?"

I swallow hard, glancing from him to his brothers. I can't tell by their faces if he's already filled them in about that little incident.

"Take her in the basement," Royal says, nodding to a door a bit down the hall. "We'll give her a little reminder."

My heart stammers in my chest, but I suddenly realize they must be talking about the very place I need to go most—the Midnight Swans' lair.

But fuck if I want to go down there like this.

An excited murmur ripples out from us, starting with their football buddies and traveling down the hall in both directions. I take in my surroundings. There's a classroom before the door he indicated, but even if I called for help, there's no guaranteed that the teacher is in already. Classes haven't started, and lots of people are still eating breakfast and going to lockers. The nearest door to the outside is at the end of the hall past the café. I'm fast, but their legs are longer, and I've seen them on the football field. They would catch me in two steps.

Fighting seems like a better option. I've incapacitated lots of people in fights.

Baron reaches for me, and I swing. My fist lands squarely between his eyes, sending his glasses flying. His sucker tumbles from his lips and rolls across the hall. He stumbles back, cursing and covering his nose. Duke grabs me around the middle and hustles me down the hall. I throw an elbow, hitting him in the ribs. He curses, but he keeps going. I kick him in the shins, my heel searching for a good blow to his kneecap.

Royal opens the door and shoves me into the library. For a second, I think he's going to knock me out or threaten me to make me stop fighting. Instead, he goes to a corner and pulls away a whole section of the old-fashioned bookshelf. It swings open to reveal a darkened doorway. Fucking cool, if I weren't about to be trapped in there.

Duke shoves me toward the door, dropping me back on my feet. I grab the sides of the doorframe, but Royal pushes me inside.

I stumble and pitch forward in the darkness, but Royal grabs me, keeping me from tumbling down a set of stone steps. As my eyes adjust, I can see them and the wall beside them, but I can't make out a single thing at the bottom. Before I can turn to fight, Royal shoves me forward. I stumble down the steps, barely keeping my feet under me.

When I reach the bottom of the stairs, he releases me and shoves me forward again just as the door above closes, plunging us into darkness. My shins collide with something hard, and I trip and topple forward. My hand meets the floor, a cold, smooth stone. I scramble to my feet and spin around, raising my fists to throw a punch if anyone dares touch me. I heard the scuff of footsteps and take a slow step back, my heart racing in my chest.

The only sound in the room is the echo of our breathing. I ease my way back, searching for a weapon with one hand while keeping the other raised.

Suddenly, a bare bulb blinks on overhead. The room looks like something out of a nightmare, not a fancy school like Willow Heights. Two leather chairs with stainless steel arms sit to my right, including the one I tripped on. There's a door behind me, along with several more bookshelves. Across the low, poorly lit room, another cluster of leather chairs sit empty.

I scan the room, searching for a weapon.

"We warned you what happens if you disobey," Baron says. His glasses are bent, and his sucker is gone, and his eyes sparkle with that malicious gleam I saw when we were running from the cops. "But it seems you're just determined to keep testing us. You leave us no choice but to make good on our promises."

"What promises?" I ask, edging toward the bookshelf. Maybe I can throw one at them, catch them off guard just enough to dash past them and up the stairs.

Duke stalks toward me. "You gotta choke on my dick for every time you've eaten since I told you I wanted that mouth around me before it was around anything else here. And you owe our boy here some action in that sweet pussy of yours for the stunt you pulled the other night. You tossed aside some guaranteed action, so you gotta step up and take her place."

"I don't owe you shit," I say. "And yeah, you can all three rape me in here, but I will never bow to you again. *Never.* I'll go to the cops, and you'll probably get out of it, but I'll still be standing. You can take everything from me, but you'll never get the one thing you want so badly—my respect."

"You think your respect is worth something to us?" Royal says, his eyes hard.

"That's cute," Baron says. "She's so innocent."

Without looking away from me, Royal gives an order to his brothers. "Put her on her knees."

I run for the bookshelf, but I don't make it there before they grab me, dragging me back to Royal and bearing down on my shoulders while they each hold an arm. I struggle, but Baron kicks my feet out from under me, and a second later, my knees hit the hard stone floor. I throw my hair out of my eyes, out of breath with fear and fury. "Forcing me to my knees doesn't make me want to kneel for you willingly," I snarl up at Royal.

He steps forward, gently stroking my hair back. "Oh, sweetheart. Do you think I care if you kneel willingly? You said you'd never kneel, and yet, here you are on your knees before me. Do your words taste good when you eat them?" He smiles down at me almost tenderly, tucking a lock behind my other ear. "And what a pretty sight it is. I don't care how you got there. The end result is the same."

When he strokes my face, I turn and snap my teeth at him, clamping them shut on his finger. He jerks back, wrenching his bleeding finger free. "See what happens to your cock if you put it near me," I growl, spitting blood at his feet.

"Take her clothes," he orders, his voice flat. "I can break her. You'll see."

"Now you've gone and pissed him off," Duke taunts. He jerks down my skirt, and I writhe in their hold, terror sinking its teeth into me. I kick out, but Duke drags my arms behind me while Baron wrestles my skirt off, my underwear with it. I scream, but it's choked with fear as they rip my shirt off my body.

When I'm naked, they force me back to my knees, Duke's iron grip still around my wrists like cuffs. I'm hyperventilating so hard I can't scream, can't think.

Baron unbuttons his pants and slides a hand inside, stroking himself. "She's feisty," he says. "I bet it'll take a train in that big juicy ass to break her."

"No." Royal's voice is quiet, but it commands all attention.

His brothers both turn to him. I do, too. When I raise my face to his, I see that his eyes are as empty as his voice. There's no hope for me there.

"This one is mine," he says in that same quiet, hollow tone that raises goosebumps all over my body. His eyes rake over me, making me feel even more horribly, terrifyingly helpless.

"Really?" Duke asks, an edge of whining in his voice. "But the sluts are always the freakiest."

"Shut up," Baron says. "He never wants them for himself."

He's watching Royal with cautious fascination, like he's watching a rattlesnake approach.

Royal steps forward and grabs a handful of hair at the crown of my head, pulling my face up. He reaches down and gives one of my nipples a hard pinch. I panic, thrashing and struggling to free my hands from Duke's hold. But even if I broke away from him, there are two more guys over twice my size between me and the stairs. Panic strikes through me over and over, and it's all I can do not to go ballistic.

"Look at you," Royal says flatly. "On your knees, where a whore belongs. What's the matter, Cherry Pie? You've been chasing us like a thirsty bitch since the day you set foot in Willow Heights. Following us to our house, sitting at our table, putting yourself in our way every chance you get. Now you have our full attention. All three of us to yourself. Tell me this isn't what you wanted."

"It's not," I grit out, pressing my trembling knees together on the cold, unforgiving stones. I wanted in, but not like this, stripped of all my clothes and dignity, completely vulnerable and powerless before these three huge, powerful savages. Not like this, forced to my knees against my will, with no choice in any of it.

"You wanted the Royal treatment the other day," Duke says. "Now you're going to get it. Wreck her, man. I'll hold her still."

"No," I blurt out, adrenaline charging through me so hard my whole body shakes uncontrollably. "Please. You said—you said maybe you cared. Royal, you don't have to do this. This isn't who you are."

"I know who I am," Royal grinding the words out slowly, his eyes still glazed like he's in a trance. "I'm a Dolce. And you… Are a whore. You came from a whore, and you'll never be anything but a whore. And now, I'm going to make you pay. I'll ruin you so deep you can't even beg me to stop."

He reaches for his pants, his fist tightening in my hair, holding my head in place.

"You're right," I say in a rush, any idea coming. "I'm a whore. Which means *you* have to pay."

"Fine," he says, his voice laced with disgust, his cruel mouth turned down in a scowl. He reaches for his wallet, pulling it out and flipping it open with one hand.

"I don't want money," I say.

"I don't think you're really in a position to bargain," Duke says. "You're naked on the floor in the janitor's closet. We can do whatever we want to you." As if to prove his point, he reaches down and pinches my ass hard enough to make me choke back a sob. But there's no time to cry.

"You could," I agree, blinking back the tears in my eyes. "But does it really prove I'm a whore if you take something from me? Or does it say something about what *you* are?"

"What do you want?" Baron asks.

"I want you to erase the picture," I say.

"There's no picture," Royal says.

"I saw you take it."

Duke leans forward, his breath warm on my ear. "It's a video, Cherry Pie."

I close my eyes, not wanting to think about that right now. "Erase it," I say. "And I won't fight. I'll suck your dick in exchange for that payment, just like the whore you say I am. I won't bite you, or fight back, or anything. I'll give you the best head you've ever gotten in your life."

The twins both look to Royal. His jaw is tight, but he nods as he pulls down the front of his pants, just far enough to free his cock. "Afterwards."

I swallow hard, trying not to gape. He's every bit as huge as I thought, thick and long and straight, his skin smooth with thick veins running up his shaft. My mouth goes dry, and I press my knees together with more than fear. I shouldn't be able to feel anything remotely close to arousal right now, but a cock is a sexual thing, and my body responds. My pulse flutters in my throat, and my heart slams hard against my sternum. I wet my lips, and Royal pushes his cock down to my lips.

I run my tongue over the tip, and I feel Royal shudder above me. A surge of heat courses through me, and I strain forward against Duke's hold, angling my head to run my tongue over every inch of Royal's soft skin, lapping him up like the thirsty bitch he said I was. I kneel up as far as I can and sink my mouth over his glorious girth, stroking my tongue back and forth over the vein on the underside of his cock.

"Look at her go," Duke says, laughing as he leans around to watch. "Give it to her like a slut."

Royal's fingers tighten in my hair, and he draws my head back. His eyes are terrifyingly blank, like looking into a pool of ink.

"I don't fucking trust you," he says, gripping my jaw with his other hand. He hooks his thumb over my teeth, pulling my mouth open. "Don't move. Just sit there and take it."

He pushes back into my mouth, one hand gripping my hair so hard tears blur my vision, the other hand holding my lower jaw in place. He starts thrusting into my mouth, his cock slicking over my tongue and into my throat until I gag. He slams in harder, driving into the back of my throat with bruising force while I choke and try not to puke.

It's just a blowjob, I tell myself. I've given dozens of them. I've given them to a gross old guy I never liked to begin with. And this isn't a gross old guy. It's a beautiful, damaged boy who I would've done this willingly for, with no payment, just two days ago. And if it's not an ideal situation, at least I'm getting something out of it.

It's worth it to have that video erased, even if I'm not blowing him anymore. I'm immobilized while he fucks my mouth hard and fast, for what feels like hours. Tears pour down my cheeks, and I feel spit trickling out the corners of my mouth as I try to swallow the salty tastes of his precum in my throat.

At last, I start choking so hard he has to pull out. I lean forward, doubling over while I spit and cough uncontrollably.

"Ah, man, such a waste of a good cough," Duke says. "I could be getting off inside that sweet pussy right now."

"No," Royal says in that same hollow tone. I swallow the last of the spasms in my aching, bruised throat and straighten slowly, my face hot from the coughing fit. He's already put himself away, even though he didn't cum, and I sink back on my heels, trembling with relief that it's over. He busies himself pulling strands of my hair from between his fingers and dropping them onto the floor. "Let her up."

Duke releases me while Baron stands back, watching me like he's afraid I'm going to attack. But all the fight has drained out of me. I feel numb as I pick up my skirt and pull it back on.

I keep telling myself it could have been worse. It could have been so much worse.

Nothing that bad happened. One blowjob. That's it. One more guy whose dick has been in my mouth. They barely touched me. I'm fine. I'm lucky.

When I'm dressed, I stand and smooth my hands over my skirt. I face dead-eyed Royal squarely, not letting that creepy stare unnerve me. "Erase the video."

He takes his phone out of his pocket, scrolls through, and then hands it to me. There's the thumbnail of the video, a little arrow in the middle. I swallow hard and click play. I don't watch the whole thing, only about ten seconds. That's enough. The person on the floor could be anyone—anyone with hair exactly like mine. It's not a dead giveaway, but it's easily identifiable if someone suggested it was me. The worst part is Mr. Behr. A gross, hairy white belly bobs against my head with every heavy breath he takes.

I stop the video, my hands shaking, my face burning with shame and humiliation. It's okay. It'll be gone forever, and no one else will ever have to see it. It'll only be burned into my brain for the rest of my life, the shame of it hitting me in a fresh wave every time I look at these boys and remember it's burned into their memories, too.

But there's nothing I can do about that. I hit delete, grateful that Royal gave me the satisfaction of erasing the evidence of my worst moment myself. I check the photo on either side of the video to make sure he doesn't have more. Then I hand the phone back.

"Transaction complete?" he says with a haughty smirk.

I nod, suddenly desperate to get past him, out of this creepy room. What if they won't let me leave? What if they're only toying with me, pretending it's over?

"Can I go now?" I ask, my voice as wooden as my legs feel when he moves aside and sweeps his arm toward the stairs.

My heart is thudding, my knees trembling with every step. I'm sure they're going to stop me. I glance around, but there's nothing in the room to bring back for Mr. D. It's completely ordinary.

When I reach the top of the stairs, I glance back. Royal is standing at the bottom, watching me go.

I turn and slam my shoulder into the door as hard as I can, not daring to hope it will be open. It swings wide, and I rush out, nearly sobbing with relief. Instead, I hurry across the library, knowing I'm not in the clear until I'm out of this room. I burst into the hall and balk, blinking at the sight of the small crowd outside. They step back, melting against the walls as I step forward, my knees threatening to buckle with each step.

When I'm in the hall, I force my gaze to stay straight, not to dart to the people on either side of me or drop to the floor. I've only taken a dozen steps when DeShaun, Dawson, and Cotton step away from the wall, into my path. DeShaun starts rolling his hips, one hand in the air like he's riding a mechanical bull—or fucking someone from behind.

Cotton and Dawson pump their fists in the air, too. "Choo-choo," Cotton calls, his voice echoing down the hall like a train. The next time, Dawson joins him.

"Choo-choo," DeShaun echoes, still mimicking sex moves.

I swallow past the ache in my crushed throat, my hands going to my skirt automatically, gripping the edges as my step falters. Everyone in the hall picks up the chant until it echoes down the hall, through the school. I don't know how I make it to the front doors of the school, but the next thing I know,

I'm standing at the bike rack, trying to get my breathing under control.

I stare at my bike—their bike. They gave me that bike. It's tainted now. I don't want to touch it. But I don't want to leave it, either.

I'm still there five minutes later, caught in indecision, when I hear footsteps. I know I'd better go before someone decides for me. But how can I get on this expensive bike that settled a score? I don't want anything from them.

But how can I leave it? It's barely used. I could sell it for a few months of rent money somewhere far from here. Haven't I earned it?

"I didn't take you for a runner," says a voice behind me. I turn to see Gloria Walton approaching, her kitten heels clicking on the sidewalk. "I thought you were stronger than that."

"It takes a lot of strength to run when you've been beaten into the ground." I'm surprised at how normal I sound, even a little snarky.

Gloria plants a hand on her hip and shakes back her perfect, Barbie hair. "I fucking told you so."

"Congratulations," I say, bending to unlock my bike. "You've got everyone all figured out. Give yourself a gold star and a degree in psychology."

I need to get away from here, from her, and this is faster than on foot. Guess my decision is made.

"Where are you going?" she asks.

"Does it really matter?"

She sighs and hooks her thumb through her purse strap. "Are you on birth control?"

I scowl at her. "No."

"Then you're freaking out that you're pregnant right now, and you're wondering how you're going to afford a morning-after pill. So, come on. Let me take you to the clinic."

"I didn't fuck them," I say, drawing back.

She blinks at me without comprehension a few times. "Oh," she says at last. "Okay, then. I've got everything you need right here."

She starts digging in her purse and produces a pocket-sized packet of wipes. "This is for Duke," she says. "I hear he loves a facial, and who wants to walk around all day knowing that's on your face, am I right?"

Without waiting for an answer, she hands me one and goes back to her purse, pulling out a pack of gum and passing me a stick. "This is for Baron. I'm no prude, but I am a lady, and who wants to swallow all that nasty stuff?"

She shudders and makes a face before rooting through her bag again. "And Royal, well, I hear he never cums, but I bet your throat is killing you right now. These will get you through the day, but you might get your own for tomorrow."

She deposits a handful of throat lozenges in my palm and smiles.

"You just carry all that stuff around with you in case they force you to blow them in the basement?"

"Oh, no," she says. "Like I said, I'm a lady. I don't do that stuff. But, you know. It took me a while to get there. If you really want something bad enough, you'll put up with just about anything, won't you? And if you're strong enough, you'll outlast everyone else, and you'll find yourself at the top."

"If that's what it takes to get to the top, I'm happy on the bottom."

She shrugs. "I'll believe that when I see it."

I narrow my eyes, staring at her. I've underestimated her every step of the way, but she's smarter and tougher than I gave her credit for. "Why are you being nice to me?" I ask at last.

Everybody wants something.

"Don't be so suspicious," she says. "I'm a nice person. Plus, women should stick together, don't you think?"

"Is that why you filled my locker with trash?"

"No," she says, looking away. "But maybe that's why I'm being nice. I'm sorry I did that. I got caught up in trying to impress someone who doesn't deserve it."

"Now you're telling me you don't care about being a Dolce girl?" I ask. "I don't believe it."

"Oh, no," she says. "I care about that. I have a reputation to uphold, and having a Dolce boy on my arm at prom will be a crowning achievement—more so than the crown. But when I graduate, we won't keep in touch."

"So… What?" I ask. "It's all for show?"

"It's a balancing act," she says. "Good thing I have cheer to help me with my balance."

I give her a halfhearted smile. "Sure."

"I care about being a Dolce girl," she says. "I just don't care about the Dolce boys. Not in the way you think I do. I mean, I feel for them. I hear their mom left them without a word. Everleigh heard that they don't even talk to her anymore. I thought that's why they hated women so much, but I don't know. I think it goes deeper than that."

"Lots of guys grow up without moms and aren't psychos," I say, picturing Zephyr's dark house that always stank like a bar, the one he didn't like us to go inside because his dad might be home. Still, he managed to be a regular kind of fucked up.

Gloria shrugs and shifts her weight to one foot. "Today you have to do what's best for tomorrow," she says. "Sometimes, you forget tomorrow, and you do what benefits you most today, and you realize it's a betrayal of the person who matters most."

I stare at her as she echoes back words I think to myself every fucking day. The words that sum up today better than any I could find. I did it. I got rid of the video. I should be relieved. But I'm not sure it was worth it.

"You matter most," I say, halfway to myself.

"The person in the mirror always does," she says, smoothing her silky blonde hair over her shoulder. "That's why I trashed your locker, though. I'd forgotten that. And yes, I did other stuff, and I probably should apologize. I really was trying to help you out, but without damaging my rep."

I roll my eyes. "So all those times you told me I looked like a skank, it was for my own good?"

"Well, yeah," she says, widening her eyes at me like it's obvious. "I was trying to help you fit in."

"Bullshit."

She gives me a little smile. "Do you hate me?"

"We're cool," I say, wiping my eyes with the wet wipe in case there's salt around them. She's complicated, but I don't hate her.

"Yes, we are," she says, snapping her purse and standing up straight. "So, now you're going to pop that piece of gum in your mouth, tighten up your pony, and walk your ass back into school."

"You're right." I could use a day off—I need one. But we don't always get what we need. I can't afford to take that time.

If I do, they've won. It'll make them think they've broken me. They need to know I don't break. Ever.

"Of course I am," Gloria says. "And if you really want to repay me, you can give me the name of that hot guy you were talking to at the race."

I start to laugh, to tell her she's not Maverick's type. But then I remember a different Gloria, the one who threw down with me in the hall because I tossed a roach in her face, the one who races cars and looks like every guy's wet dream while she does it, and I give her his number. And then I walk into school beside this girl who is everything I didn't know I needed until this moment. She's right. I'm too strong to run. Running won't show them anything except that I'm a coward. Walking back into school is the only way to prove them wrong.

The best revenge is to show them that they don't get to decide what I am. I decide if I'm my mother or not. I decide if I'm a whore. I decide whether or not I belong at Willow Heights.

And my decision is to stay. I won't run. I'll fight.

I will show them just how much I matter.

The Baron

The baron hacked his way through the town
Leaving destruction in his wake
Until every house was reduced to rubble
And the streets ran with the blood of the conquered,
But he was never satisfied
Until he hacked into his mother's chest
And saw that it had always been empty.

twenty-five

Harper Apple

BadApple: I know it's not Friday but I have good news

BadApple: I got what u wanted. Got down to the basement u were talking about, where ur Swans club meets

MrD: It's the Midnight Swans.

BadApple: Got a look at it. So can deliver wut u asked. Wut do u want 2 no?

MrD: What were you doing down there?

I knew this was coming, that he'd want to know. I've already decided to tell him. After all, this pays my debts, and I'm ready to be done with these little chats. I got into the basement, and I got something on the Dolces, something bad enough for him to use it as blackmail or whatever he needs. Because some of the things they said, and Gloria said, let me know I'm far from the first girl they've forced onto her knees for them.

And yeah, maybe I found a way to take control of it in some small way, at least. Maybe I made it consensual by asking for and accepting payment. But not every girl has.

I start typing, my fingers slow and numb on the keys as I fill in every gory detail.

When I finish, my heart is pounding, and I have to jump up and pace the room so I don't get sick. But I did it. I told him. I paid my debt to him, and I got the video erased. I'm free. Free of those psychos, free to leave them alone and stay the hell away like they want.

The app chimes, and I sink back into the chair.

MrD: Good work.

I stare at the words, at the little green cursor blinking. A shiver goes through me, and I wrap my arms around myself and rub them to keep myself warm. He's not my friend, I remind myself. He's a creepy old guy, and I already know how cold he can be. Still, I just shared a humiliating, traumatizing experience with him, and all he can say is that I did a good job.

BadApple: Nice knowing u. Thx 4 scholarship n everything.

MrD: You're welcome.

MrD: But don't act like this is over.

BadApple: I got u what u wanted. I got down in the basement, I got u info on wut the guys who run the school are doing down there. My debt is paid.

MrD: Lol

MrD: Your debt is paid when I say it is.

A shiver races up my arms again, and I curse the colder weather, the damp chill in the house that never quite leaves until April, when Faulkner turns back into a sauna.

BadApple: That wasn't the deal.

MrD: Are you still at WHPA?

BadApple: … My debt is never paid until I leave the school?

MrD: I say when your assignment is over. I want you to keep watching, keep reporting back.

BadApple: This has nothing 2 do w ur secret society

MrD: I'll worry about that. You keep doing what you're doing, and you keep your scholarship.

MrD: Understood?

BadApple: yes

MrD: Good. Report back on Friday.

BadApple: k

MrD: Oh, and Harper?

MrD: Make every report as good as this one.

*

It's worse the next day. As I walk into school in the morning, girls snicker and hide behind their phones, looks of disgust flickering over their faces. Guys do that stupid miming gesture with their hands moving toward their mouths and their tongues poking into their cheeks, denoting the blowjob. I guess it's better than them thinking I fucked them all.

I try to ignore them, but blood rushes in my ears and my brain feels stunned and empty. I open my locker, and a cascade of condoms, lube, and little novelty sex stuff cascades out. To my surprise, I find myself thinking about what Gloria would do. She must have gone through this on her way to the top. Somehow, that makes me feel better. She started here, and now she's homecoming queen. People will forget. The Dolces fuck everyone.

I pull out my books, dropping a cardboard backing with little nipple clamps hanging from it like earrings. I close my locker and turn to see Dixie hurrying toward me, her brow furrowed with concern.

"Are you okay?" she asks as we start down the hall, past a group of guys looking at their phones.

"Peachy," I say.

"Really?"

"Sure," I say. "Guess I'm a real Dolce girl now."

"Oh," she says, her expression falling. "You didn't see the blog this morning, did you?"

I narrow my eyes, studying her closer. There's something else in her expression. Guilt.

"No," I say slowly. "What did you post?"

"It wasn't me, I swear," she says in a rush. "The blog was hacked. It happened once before. I deleted it as soon as I saw it, but… It already had a lot of hits."

My blood runs cold as I notice all the people looking at their phones, groups of them crowding together, others laughing hysterically, and all of them staring at me when I walk by. Because of course some of them saved that shit, and now they're sending it around school.

"Oh, Harper," Gloria says, giving me a pitying look and shaking her head as she walks by with her friends. She may have been nice to me, but some things even she can't overlook.

For a second, I let my guard down. I thought *maybe…*

I thought if I gave up my pride and bowed to the will of the tyrants that run this school, they'd take the target off my back. I thought I could rise above, if I was just willing to stay strong, like Gloria said. I thought I had a chance to claw my way up from the bottom of the heap, that if I just worked hard enough, maybe the world wouldn't stomp me back into the ground this time.

I should have known better. I should have listened to what my mom said when I told her I was going to Willow Heights so I could leave this town.

Girls like you, they don't get out…

"What was it?" I ask Dixie, my teeth clenched so hard my jaw aches. I already know. But some masochistic part of me has to hear her say it.

"It's a video," Dixie whispers, her eyes full of sympathy, like she thinks I'm going to break down and cry.

But I'm not sad.

I'm pissed.

I storm down the hall, ignoring the snickers, the stares, the rude gestures. I don't stop until I see Royal. He's leaning casually against his locker, his buddies all around him. I'm too mad to care, to think, to consider repercussions or that I'm just giving them something more to laugh about, more fodder for the gossip mill. I don't care anymore. I don't even see their mocking faces. All I see is red.

I fly at Royal, shoving past his buddies and slamming my hands into his chest as hard as I can, trying to shove him down. He barely budges. An indulgent smirk plays over his lips as he grabs my hand when I try to push him again. "What's the matter, Cherry Pie?" he asks, a taunt in his voice.

"How could you?" I snarl at him, shoving him again. Because what am I supposed to say? What can you say to something like this? There are no words for the shame, the hurt, the betrayal. I'm shaking with rage, because there's not one fucking thing I can do about what he did. It's already out there.

He chuckles in response. "Oh, was I supposed to keep your whore status a secret? Don't worry, babe. Everyone already knew. I just confirmed it."

I can't think straight, can't think of a response. All I want to do is make him hurt, make him feel a fraction of what I'm feeling. But he can't hurt because he can't feel anything. He's a monster, and monster's don't have hearts.

"This isn't a game," I growl at him at last. "You're ruining people's lives, Royal."

I try to pull my hand away, but his grip tightens. Fury explodes inside me, just like it did in class that day. He doesn't care if he breaks my hand, if I can't fight, if I can't get money to get out of this town. He doesn't care that he released a video that colleges will see when they search my name, that will keep me from getting into a good school, from ever leaving this town. But I care. I reach back with my other hand, and I slap him across the face.

The crack sounds all the way down the hall, and there's a shocked intake of breath from the crowd gathered to watch the drama. Royal's head jerks to one side with the force of the blow. My palm stings, but I don't feel the pain. My fists ball up, still trembling with fury.

In one motion, Royal grabs my throat and spins around, slamming me up against the locker. His fingers tighten, cutting off the blood to my brain, making me lightheaded as his palm presses in on my windpipe until I can't breathe. I struggle, but he's too strong, too big. He leans close, watching me the way he did at the tracks the first time I met him, when he told me he could kill me. I remember that even as my brain starts to shut down, deprived of oxygen.

Royal leans close, his nose caressing mine with taunting gentleness as he watches me struggle for breath. "Think about this the next time you think you can hit me," he murmurs. "And then know that my dick will be inside you while I choke you out if it happens again."

I fight to stay conscious, to hold his gaze and reach something deeper inside him, beneath the cold, steely surface of his eyes. I try to speak, to beg, but his hand chokes off my voice. So, I struggle in silence, trying to communicate with my eyes, to reach the scared little boy hiding in a darkness so deep he's forgotten the necessity of light.

I'm the only one who can crawl through that darkness, as familiar as my own soul, to reach him. But I need time, I need oxygen, I need strength to keep going. As I strain for breath, my nails biting into his skin until he bleeds, I think maybe it's too late. Too late to find something alive inside those cold, dead eyes that watch his own blood trickle down my fingers without so much as blinking. I know he's trapped inside there, behind the monster. That he sees that I'm suffering, that I'm dying. That he cares. I'm sure he does.

But he's too far gone.

His eyes lock on mine, and he clenches his fingers tighter, pushing me down into the darkness, the emptiness. The blackness begins to swallow me, sucking me into the hollow pit of his soul. "Life's a game, darling," he whispers. "You just got played."

*

Get book 2 here: http://books2read.com/brutalboy.

Want more of Royal's side? Sign up for my Newsletter to get an exclusive chapter retold from Royal's point of view! https://landing.mailerlite.com/webforms/landing/q5z4y6

You'll also be the first to hear when the release date changes, see the cover, get sneak peaks, and more.

Also Available from Selena

Willow Heights Prep Academy: The Elite (complete trilogy)

1. Bully Me
2. Betray Me
3. Bury Me

Willow Heights Prep Academy: The Exile (complete series)

1. Bad Apple
2. Brutal Boy
3. Boys Club
4. Broken Doll
5. Blood Empire

Willow Heights Prep Academy: The Endgame

1. Dangerous Defiance
2. Darling Doll
3. Deviant Deception

Willow Heights Prep Academy: The Envy

1. Dirty Demise
2. Evil Deeds
3. Filthy Elite
4. G.F.

Willow Heights Prep Academy: The Enemy (2025)

Made in United States
Troutdale, OR
03/13/2024

18443163R00275